Blast from the Past

A Mac Faraday Mystery

By
Lauren Carr

Blast from the Past

Designed by Acorn Book Services

Publication Managed by Acorn Book Services
www.acornbookservices.com
acorn.book.services@comcast.net
304-285-8205

Cover designed by Todd Aune
Cover Image: gunskill 2 © morrbyte/fotoli.com
Spokane, Washington
www.projetoonline.com

ISBN-13: 978-0985726775
ISBN-10: 0985726776

Published in the United States of America

To Our Men and Woman of Law Enforcement

On the Front Lines—You've Always Got Our Backs

Blast from the Past

A Mac Faraday Mystery

Blast from the Past

Cast of Characters
(in order of appearance)

Tommy Cruze: Head of a major East Coast crime syndicate. Spent over ten years in prison for murder.

Archie Monday: Personal assistant, editor, research assistant to world-famous mystery author Robin Spencer, who passed away two years ago. Lives in the guest cottage at Spencer Manor.

Mac Faraday: Retired homicide detective. His wife had left him and took everything. On the day his divorce became final, he inherited $270 million and an estate on Deep Creek Lake from his birth mother, Robin Spencer.

Gnarly: Mac Faraday's German shepherd. Another part of his inheritance from Robin Spencer. Gnarly used to belong to the United States Army, who refuses to talk about him.

David O'Callaghan: Spencer police chief. Son of the late police chief, Patrick O'Callaghan. Mac Faraday's best friend and half-brother.

Deputy Chief Arthur Bogart (Bogie): Spencer's Deputy Police Chief. David's godfather. Don't let his gray hair and weathered face fool you.

Robin Spencer: Mac Faraday's late birth mother and world famous mystery author. She gave birth to Mac as an unwed teenager and gave him up for adoption. After becoming America's queen of mystery, she found him and made him her heir. Ancestors founded Spencer, Maryland, located on the shore of Deep Creek Lake, a resort area on Western Maryland.

Police Chief Patrick O'Callaghan: David's late father. Spencer's legendary police chief. The love of Robin Spencer's life and Mac Faraday's birth father.

Randi Finnegan: United States Marshal assigned to protect Archie Monday.

Violet O'Callaghan: David's elderly mother. She suffers from dementia.

Wilson Terrance: Chief of the United States Marshal's field office in Cumberland, Maryland. He had been friends with J. Edgar Hoover.

Ginger Altman: Administrative Assistant, United States Marshal's field office in Cumberland, Maryland.

Hector Langford: Spencer Inn's chief of security. The lean, gray-haired Australian has been with the Spencer Inn for twenty-five years.

Leah Juliano: Italian immigrant. Owner of Dockside Cafe, a gourmet coffee shop located on Deep Creek Lake.

Sari: Leah's six-year-old daughter. She doesn't talk.

Special Agent Sid Delaney: Special agent with the FBI's organized crime bureau.

Special Agent Tony Bennett: Special agent with the FBI's organized crime bureau. No relation to the singer by the same name.

Alan Richardson: Tommy Cruze's high-priced lawyer.

Ariel Richardson: Alan Richardson's wife and law partner.

Tonya: Spencer Police Department's desk sergeant.

Dr. Dora Washington: Garrett County Medical Examiner.

Russell Skeltner: Half-owner of the Skeltner Cove Bed and Breakfast, surviving spouse of Mary Catherine Skeltner.

Mary Catherine Skeltner: Half-owner of the Skeltner Cove Bed and Breakfast, located on the shore of Deep Creek Lake. Dies from a fall down the stairs. Or was she pushed?

Nora Crump: Tourist from Lancaster, Pennsylvania. Wife of Gordon Crump. Witness, suspect, or supposed victim to what happened in the Dockside Cafe.

Gordon Crump: Tourist from Lancaster, Pennsylvania. Husband of Nora Crump. Witness, suspect, or supposed victim to what happened in the Dockside Cafe.

Every saint has a past and every sinner has a future.
Oscar Wilde

Prologue

Campus Library, University of Maryland, College Park, Maryland—Twelve Years Ago

Kendra Douglas could have sworn that she heard someone walking up in the library stacks. While her head told her that the footsteps she had heard were only her imagination, the pounding in her heart insisted that someone was hiding up there, and that he likely had a knife—a big, sharp knife.

She blew her blonde bangs out of her emerald green eyes, did a toss of her head to flip her hair back over her shoulder, and squinted up at the bookshelves in the loft above the librarian's desk.

If I stare hard enough, I can see him.

No one materialized. With a perfect combination of fear, imagination, and bravado; she stood up from her chair, squared her shoulders, and stuck out her small bosom.

Guess I need to go up and check—the same way I have to every night when I close up the library. She slumped. *And, just like always, I'll find no one up there.*

Kendra sucked up every nerve she had and ascended the stairs to the loft.

What's that?

She whirled around to search the shadows down on the main floor.

She listened.

Silence.

Will you stop scaring yourself, Kendra? You've got to stop reading all those Robin Spencer books late at night. It's gotten worse since you took her class.

At the top of the stairs, she forced herself to stride bravely across the length of the floor while checking every aisle for stragglers—or, better yet, for killers to confirm that her sense of danger was not always her active imagination.

No one. See? Now grow some guts, lock up, and go home to bed. Maybe you should skip Mickey Forsythe tonight … but maybe not.

Excited about the prospect of finishing Robin Spencer's latest book, a signed advance review copy that the author had given her as a gift, Kendra hurried to check every corner of the library without fear. She was in too big of a rush to be scared.

You are one weird girl, Kendra. How many graduate students fall in love with a fictional character? You do know Mickey Forsythe isn't real, don't you? At this rate, as long as you're looking for a man like Mickey Forsythe, you can give up on ever getting married. He ain't real.

After tossing her book bag over her shoulder, she stopped at the front door, turned to do one last visual sweep of the main floor, switched on the security system, and stepped outside into the cold night air.

Kendra pulled up the hood on her winter coat to block out the bitter February wind. A jog to her car in the student parking lot would pump her blood and stop the chill that made her teeth chatter. For further protection against the cold, she ducked behind the hedges that lined the sidewalk to block out the wind.

"No! Please!" a man's pleading voice wailed from the parking lot. The cry was followed by a scream of terror.

Kendra stopped. She held her breath. She could hear men's voices in the parking lot only a few yards away.

"You're making a mistake!" A man was sobbing.

"No, you've made the mistake." The other man's voice was as cold as the wind biting her cheeks.

"Aahhh!" the other man cried out.

This is like something out of a Mickey Forsythe book. No, Kendra! This isn't a Mickey Forsythe mystery. This is real. That man is really being hurt. What would Mickey do? Hide!

Ducking back into the shadows of the hedges, she made her way to the end of the sidewalk.

The man screamed in agony. He sounded weaker, as if he didn't have much strength left.

Kneeling down to keep low, she clutched her bag and reached inside for her pepper spray. Slowly, holding her breath, she peered around the edge of the hedge. She swallowed to keep down the shock that shot up from her gut and through her chest in an attempt to escape in the form of a shriek at the sight she saw.

They were under a lamp that illuminated the parking lot. Across the parking lot, a white sedan was parked in one of the professor's parking spaces. A long silver limousine had the sedan blocked in its space. A black van was parked on the other side of the professor's sedan.

Kendra realized that the sedan belonged to Dr. Bert Reynolds. She couldn't miss him. He had a reputation with the ladies. Two men held the professor by the arms while a third man beat him again and again about his head and body with a ball bat.

No longer was his handsome face so attractive.

"Listen, all you have to do is confess," the man holding the bloody ball bat said. "If you would admit to bonking my wife, then we'd all have more respect for you."

The parking lot light bathed his bald head so it shone like a white ball on a billiard table. He had the squat, muscular build of a gorilla. With his long camel-hair coat he looked like a dressed up ape.

Two other men dressed in black clothes stood off to the side watching the beating like a couple of spectators. Occasionally, one would make a comment to the other and they would both laugh.

Seeing that he was unable to fight anymore, the two men dropped Dr. Reynolds to the ground.

"Are you going to admit it?" Gorilla Man asked.

Kendra heard something, but she could not understand what the professor said. Whatever it was, it displeased Gorilla Man because he slammed the bat against the knocked downed man two more times.

"Confess!"

Professor Reynolds rolled over and covered his face with his arm. Sobbing, he cried out indecipherable mumbled words.

"Excuse me, what did you say?" Gorilla Man bent over him.

Professor Reynolds gestured as he spoke again.

A smile stretched across Gorilla Man's round face. "That's what I wanted to hear. The truth." He stood up. "Now, we can all respect you." He went over to one of the goons. "You know what else, Dr. Reynolds? They say confession is good for the soul."

The goon handed Gorilla Man a long silver pistol. It shone under the street lamp.

Seeing the gun, Dr. Reynolds wailed, "Please! I did what you asked! I have a wife and two kids."

"Right now, your soul needs all the help it can get." Gorilla Man emptied the gun into Professor Reynolds. He shot until it clicked to signal that there were no more bullets. After handing the gun back to the man who had given it to him, he turned to the two men who had been watching from the side. "Clean this up."

One of the men who had held Dr. Reynolds opened the rear door of the limousine. As Gorilla Man climbed in, the man, who appeared to be a driver, asked where they were going next.

"Next stop is to have a word with my wife."

The driver closed the door. He and his companion climbed into the front of the luxury car, and it disappeared into the night.

Clutching her mouth with both hands, Kendra Douglas shivered in the hedges while wishing that she was more like Mickey Forsythe.

Chapter One

Spencer, Maryland – Deep Creek Lake – Present Day

"Gnarly, it's time to go for your appointment."

Lovely in her soft grey Chanel suit, rose-colored blouse, and stylish pumps, Archie Monday, assistant to the late Robin Spencer, hurried up the stairs to the second floor of Spencer Manor and down the hallway to the master suite. The rose leather clutch bag under her arm was a perfect match for the fedora she wore over her pixie-styled blonde hair.

"Gnarly, are you in here?" She threw open the double doors to find the German shepherd sitting in the suite's bathroom doorway. "There you are. It's time to go." She gestured for the dog to come to her.

Instead of obeying his favorite human, Gnarly whined and turned his attention back to the happenings inside the other room.

"Go where?" Mac Faraday called out to her from the bathroom.

She crossed the width of the suite to peer in at him. The sight that greeted her wasn't what she had expected from the son of Robin Spencer, whose roots were as blue-blood as they come.

The clichéd appearance of a wealthy man calls for him to be tall, dark, and handsome—maybe ruggedly handsome—and at the very least, well-groomed. A man of wealth is best able to achieve this requirement by hiring others—like plumbers—to do the dirty work.

Two years after his inheritance allowed him to retire from his career as a homicide detective, Mac Faraday had chosen to ignore that rule.

His middle-class upbringing had a different rule: If you can do it yourself—no matter how dirty the job—it's a waste of money to hire someone else to do it for you.

Determination had drawn Mac's handsome face into a scowl. His blue eyes were narrowed into slits focused on the toilet in which he was plunging away. Water splashed upwards to spill over the sides and drenched the lower half of his sweatpants down to his bare feet.

Even in this less than glamorous setting, Archie did find his arm and chest muscles, bulging from the workout, appealing. When Mac yanked the plunger up from out of the toilet, in the process splattering the water across his firm stomach and down the front of his pants, she reconsidered that assessment. *Maybe not that appealing after all.* She asked, "What are you doing?"

"What does it look like?"

"Why?"

"It's stopped up." He shook the dripping plunger in Gnarly's direction. "And I have a feeling I know who did it."

Uttering a whine, Gnarly moved to hide behind Archie's legs.

She jumped to the shepherd's defense. "Why are you blaming Gnarly? He doesn't use the toilet. You're the only one who uses this toilet."

"You've used it." Mac reminded her of her frequent nights spent with him in the master suite. "Maybe I should blame you."

She folded her arms across her bosom. "I wouldn't go there if I were you."

"That's why I'm blaming Gnarly." He again pointed the plunger at the dog. "Look at him. Do you see that guilty expression on his face? He's done something, and I suspect it has to do with this toilet."

"Even if he did drop something into it, how did he flush it?" She giggled. "Mac, he's a *dog*."

The phone on the bed stand rang before Mac could come up with a response. "Answer that, will you?" He returned to his plunging.

"I need to take Gnarly to the groomer," she called in to him while trotting to the king-sized bed that they had been sharing.

Mac Faraday had inherited the mansion from Robin Spencer, who, as an unwed teenager, had given him up at birth. However, his late mother had stipulated that her research assistant and editor, Archie Monday, was permitted to live in the stone guest cottage tucked away in the rose garden for as long as she wanted.

The beautiful green-eyed blonde had come with the house, and Mac Faraday was in no hurry for her to move out … nor was she in any hurry to leave.

Spencer's police chief David O'Callaghan didn't sound his usual jovial self when Archie answered the phone. After a quick hello, he asked for Mac.

"David, you sound terrible," she observed.

"My weekend's been shot," he replied. "One of my cruisers was stolen last night."

"Are you serious?"

Mac came into the bathroom doorway. "What's wrong?"

She told him, "One of David's police cruisers got stolen."

David told her the reason for his call. "Tell Mac that I'm going to miss the game this afternoon. I need to fill out a ton of reports and find out how someone was able to break into our garage to steal a police cruiser." He added, "Our guys are going to be the laughing stock of the state for this."

In Archie's other ear, Mac was asking, "Does he need any help finding the scum who stole it?"

"It was probably some bored teenagers pulling a prank," she told them both.

"Committing a felony doesn't make for a very good prank," they told her in unison.

Seeing the time on the alarm clock on the bed stand, she announced, "Gnarly and I are late." She handed the phone to Mac.

"Where are you taking Gnarly?" he asked her.

"To the groomer," she said. "It's the first Saturday of the month."

"What does that have to do with it?"

"Mac?" David called to him from the phone.

"Gnarly has a standing appointment for the first Saturday of the month," she said with her hands on her hips. "Ten-thirty with Misty. He gets the works."

"What's 'the works'?"

"Mac, are you there?" David asked him.

Archie ticked off each item on her fingers. "Shampoo, deep conditioner, teeth cleaning, toenails clipped, aromatherapy—they're having a special today on strawberries and champagne—and—and this is Gnarly's favorite—a deep body massage."

Gnarly pawed at her hand.

"For a dog?" Mac's voice went up in pitch.

"Dogs need pampering, too."

"How much is all this going to cost?" Mac asked.

"Only two-hundred and twenty-five dollars."

"Only two hundred and twenty-five dollars?" Mac objected. "I don't spend that much a year on my own hair, and I'm a human."

"And you look like it." She kissed him. "I have to go. Misty is very popular. She will only hold Gnarly's appointment for ten minutes. Once I was late, and she gave his appointment to a chow. Gnarly was in a snit the whole next week until Misty was able to fit him in."

Gnarly uttered a whine mixed with a bark before charging down the stairs. Archie tucked her handbag under her arm and hurried after him.

With a shake of his head, Mac sat down onto the bed and brought the phone to his ear. "Dave …" All he heard from the other end of the line was a dial tone.

❋   ❋   ❋

Gnarly loved riding in Archie's royal blue Escalade. Mac would always order him to the back seat, which the German shepherd would ignore. Not so with Archie. When riding with his favorite lady, he was invited to ride shotgun in the front passenger seat and stick his head up through the sun roof when the feeling struck him to do so.

After climbing into the SUV, Archie noticed that the bangs of her shortly cropped blonde hair were curling funnily. That would not look good at the book club luncheon at the Spencer Inn, for which she was already running late. While the automatic garage door went up, she licked her fingertips and finger combed it.

Gnarly pawed at her arm to urge her to get moving.

"Sorry, Gnarl, I can fix them later at the Inn." She put the car into gear and backed out of the garage, which housed Mac's black SUV and red Dodge Viper. The last stall was still home to Robin Spencer's yellow classic 1934 Bentley Park

Ward convertible, which the late author had rarely driven. Mac had yet to drive it. He was afraid of wrecking it.

In the heart of Maryland, the cedar and stone home, known as Spencer Manor, rested at the end of the most expensive piece of real estate in the resort area of Deep Creek Lake. The peninsula housed a half-dozen lake houses that grew in size and grandeur along the stretch of Spencer Court. The road ended at the stone pillars marking the multi-million dollar estate that had been the birthplace and home of the late Robin Spencer, one of the world's most famous authors.

Along the stretch of Spencer Point, Archie waved to the Schweitzers, who lived in the last house before crossing over the bridge, and then turned right onto Spencer Lane, which took her around the lakeshore. She noticed the Spencer police cruiser fall in behind her after she made the turn.

With her eye on the speedometer, she eased her foot on the gas to stay under forty-five miles per hour. With the other eye, she glanced at the black and gold SUV through the rear-view mirror. She squinted in an effort to see who was driving.

It wasn't Deputy Chief Art Bogart. He had his own cruiser. David was still at the station. Any of the dozen officers on the police force would have waved to her when she drove past.

I have a bad feeling about this… who's that in the passenger seat?

The alarm inside her head kicked up the tempo a notch. The Spencer police department did not operate in teams. The force was too small. Each officer had his own cruiser and patrolled alone. If backup was needed in the small resort town, another officer would be only a few minutes away.

Something's not right—not right at all.

The blue lights flashed on in the cruiser behind her.

"We have company, Gnarly." She eased her SUV over to the side of the road. Through the trees on the right, she could see that the lake was tranquil. Most of the residents of Spencer were still waking up and starting their day. Across the road, the woods and trails led up the mountain on which rested the Spencer Inn, another part of Mac Faraday's inheritance.

In her side and rearview mirror, Archie watched the two men with silver police shields pinned to their uniforms, dark glasses, and hats, get out of the cruiser. She could see by the fit of their shirts that they were wearing amour vests.

Gnarly looked over his shoulder and growled.

"Easy, Gnarly."

While the driver approached Archie's side, his partner came up along the rear passenger side. They were both wearing utility belts with guns, batons, and radios.

With her right hand, Archie reached into her clutch bag that she always kept tucked in between her seat and the hand break.

The driver reached around behind his back.

"Down, Gnarly."

Gnarly lay down in the seat.

When she saw the butt of the gun come out from behind his back, Archie, her eyes on the target in her side rearview mirror, fired three shots from her pink handgun, engraved with *The Pink Lady* across the muzzle, over her left shoulder. The first shot took out the rear driver's side window before ripping through the gun man's neck. The other two went through his head before he hit the ground.

In one movement, Archie threw her right arm around to fire out the rear window at the partner who only managed to get one shot before she hit him in the lower neck. Her second shot went through his head.

The world seemed to stop.

Breathing hard, she clutched the gun and stared in the rear view mirror for any sign that they were still alive and would try again.

The next thing she was aware of was Gnarly clawing at her. When she didn't respond, he licked her face. She had no idea of how long she had been sitting there.

"Oh, my!" She heard someone yell.

Archie opened up the car door and stepped out.

A car filled with tourists had driven up to the scene. Seeing the woman in a Chanel suit holding a pink handgun and standing over two dead police officers next to a cruiser that still had its blue lights on, they immediately became hysterical. The tires burned leather on the road when the car sped away.

After checking out the two men, Gnarly, assured that they were dead, came back to sit in front of Archie. His big brown eyes were questioning. *What just happened here?*

Archie knelt down and took the paw he offered her. "Well, Gnarly, it's a long story."

Chapter Two

"Lucky thing I know every officer in the Spencer police department," Archie told David as he knelt to examine the two dead men lying in the road. "When I saw two of them riding together, especially since I didn't recognize them, I knew that they were in your stolen cruiser and something was up."

"Or rather going down." The police chief wiped the sweat dripping from his blond hair down the back of his neck.

Most of Spencer's small police force was on the scene. After getting the call from Archie, and after being visited by the car filled with hysterical tourists, David ordered Spencer Lane blocked off until he and his officers could investigate.

As inconvenient as it was, motorists were sent either back and around to the other side of the lake or up over Spencer Mountain.

After taking Archie's pink handgun into evidence, Deputy Chief Art Bogart scanned the dead men's fingerprints onto his computer pad to send into the AFIS. If their prints were in the national database, they would be able to identify them.

That would get them a step closer to finding out what had happened.

Like every devoted companion, Gnarly refused to leave Archie's side until he knew she was completely safe.

David got the warning from his men at the end of Spencer Lane seconds before Mac Faraday roared up in his Viper. "Archie!" he called out before leaping out of the convertible to run to her. He was so anxious to get to her that he hadn't stopped to put on a shirt or shoes. He gathered her up into his arms and hugged her so tight that he threatened to break her petite frame in half. After letting go, he clutched her face in both of his hands and kissed her. "Are you okay?"

Breathless from his kiss, she could only nod her head.

"What happened?" Mac observed the two dead bodies lying in front of the stolen police cruiser.

"A couple of car thieves messed with the wrong lady," David said. "I'll never make fun of her pink handgun again."

"Who are they?" Mac asked him.

Deputy Chief Art Bogart threw open the door of his cruiser before stepping out to make his announcement. "A couple of high-priced assassins—just got a match from their prints in the AFIS." He pointed his computer tablet to the dead driver. "Benny Hillerman—suspected killer in thirteen hits." He then pointed at the dead partner. "Frank McCrumb—suspected of seven murders. Those are only the deaths the feds believe they know about."

"The mob." Mac clutched Archie's hand in both of his. "They must have thought you were me." He could feel her hand tremble.

She gazed up at him. Her mouth opened, but then shut again. She glanced over at David.

"You need to tell him," the police chief said with his hands on his hips.

Mac looked from him to Archie and then back again. "Tell me what?"

Archie pulled Mac to the path going down to the lake. "Let's take a walk."

"No," David said firmly. "I don't want you out of my sight."

Bogie agreed. "David and I will go over here." He pointed to his cruiser. "We need to call the sheriff and state police about this."

Mac was further concerned when David didn't step away before asking him, "Do you have your gun?"

"Always." Mac pulled his Beretta out from where he had it tucked into the waistband behind his back.

"Good."

Mac noticed both David and Bogie scanning the trees and landscape around them while stepping over to the deputy chief's cruiser. "Archie, what do you need to tell me? What happened here?"

Clinging onto both of his hands, she gazed down at the ground.

Gnarly pressed his body against her leg while staring up at Mac.

She sighed before saying, "I never told you how I met your mother."

"Yes, you did," Mac said. "She was teaching a special graduate course in mystery at a university. You were one of her students and got a job as her teaching assistant. You two hit it off, and after you graduated, she hired you as her editor and research assistant."

Archie smiled softly. "That's not exactly the truth. Not all of it."

"What isn't true?"

"One, I never graduated."

"So you dropped out." Mac gestured at the two dead men. "What does that have to do with this?"

"There was something else I left out," she confessed. "Why I never got to graduate."

"What?" Mac sucked in a deep breath and held it.

"Something that happened between when I was Robin's TA and when I came to work for her—my last semester of school."

"Archie, you're scaring me."

Gnarly whined and hung his head.

"Did you ever hear of Tommy Cruze?" she asked.

Mac nodded his head quickly. "Big syndicate boss. The feds worked for years trying to bust him for drugs, prostitution, white slavery, and murder."

"A dozen years ago he was put in jail—"

"For murder," Mac said. "He killed his wife's lover. They think he killed his wife. Her body was never found."

"But the reason they put him away was because there was a witness," Archie said. "Not only did she witness the murder, but when his men took the body to dump it, she followed them and then went to the police."

Mac was nodding his head. "Oh, yeah, I know all about that. When I was working homicide in DC, we all followed that trial. This one citizen, this woman went up against Tommy Cruze, the biggest, baddest mobster on the East Coast, and put him away."

Archie said, "It wasn't easy for her. His people managed to kill one of the witnesses before the trial, and later two people who had testified against him—even though they were in the witness protection program. This witness had to give up everything—even quit school—to go into the federal witness protection program—but it was what she had to do to stop Tommy Cruze."

Mac stared down at her. Her eyes were emerald pools of tears. "That was you."

Wordlessly, she nodded her head.

"I don't believe it."

"Believe it."

In silence, he cocked his head at her. "But—" He scratched his ear. "My mother was world famous. How could you work as an assistant for someone who—"

"*She* was famous, not me," Archie said. "I was never anywhere around the cameras or PR people. When she made public appearances, I was elsewhere."

"But Robin knew so many people," Mac said. "She would interview criminals or people who were connected to underworld types for book research."

"*Her*," she said, "not me." She sighed. "Listen, even the US Marshal's office wasn't keen on the idea, but before they placed me with Robin, Cruze's people had gotten to two witnesses who had testified against him. Robin had figured out how it could all work. Her friends in high places told my handler and her boss to let me decide. I figured …" She shrugged. "What did I have to lose? Robin was offering to let me hide in the world I dreamed of living in: books, literature, travel—all from behind the scenes. I did my research online or in libraries. As for when we were meeting her sources who were connected to the underworld—I had a totally different background and identity."

She held her hands up to her face. "I lightened my hair and cut it short—that's why I wear it like this. Robin paid for me to get cosmetic surgery on my face—" She smiled. "Did you really think all this beauty happened naturally?" She waited in silence to see if her attempt to lighten the mood had succeeded.

Mac backed up a step and looked her up and down. Finally, he asked, "Why didn't you tell me?"

Tears came to her eyes. "I wanted to."

"Robin knew and protected you." He turned to the police cruisers. The police chief and deputy chief were watching them. "David and Bogie knew. Everyone knew but me."

"When the US Marshal's office places a witness in the area, they contact the local police to let them know. Pat O'Callaghan was chief of police then. He told none of the officers working under him until he was dying. Then, he told David and Bogie." She cried, "I wanted to tell you, but I didn't know how. I'm sorry, Mac."

He shook his head. Fearing she would collapse from her grief, he took her into his arms. Gnarly pressed up against them as if to participate in a group hug. "Don't be sorry. You have nothing to be sorry for. You did nothing wrong."

"But I should have told you," she sobbed into his ear.

"I understand…" He kissed her cheek. Then, he pushed her away and kissed her mouth, which was salty with tears. "I think you're the bravest woman I ever met, Archie Monday, or whatever your name is."

"I love you, Mac." She collapsed back into his arms.

The three of them, Mac, Archie, and Gnarly, stood together as a group while she sobbed against his bare chest. Mac sensed that the fear or reality of the attempt on her life had finally hit her.

David came over to join them. "Is everything okay?"

Stroking Archie's hair while she clung onto him, Mac nodded. "We're as okay as we can be …"

"If you're not mad at her, I guess you're not mad at me either."

Mac shook his head. "I don't care about who knew what when. I'm more concerned with finding out how Cruze uncovered where she is."

As if to answer his question, a black sedan pulled up and around Mac's car.

"Oh, no!" Archie pushed Mac away and hurried toward the car.

A woman with dark hair shortly cropped to her head, and dressed in a black pantsuit, jumped out of the driver's seat. "O'Callaghan!" She advanced on David.

The police chief lunged in her direction. "Finnegan!"

Archie jumped between them. "Randi, you be nice to David."

"Oh, I'll be nice to him," she yelled. "All I want to do is help him—help him find my fist at the end of his nose!" She threw a fist in David's direction while Archie pushed her back.

"You want a piece of me, Finnegan! Come on!" David was ready to take her on, only to find Bogie blocking him with the deputy chief's massive hand against his chest.

The silver-haired deputy chief, possessing the solid build of a wrestler, stood up with his arms straight out to his sides to hold the battling man and woman apart. Neither David nor Randi could get beyond the enormous officer between them.

Bogie's gray hair and weathered face fooled many rookies. The officer had been with the Spencer police department longer than some of the younger officers had been alive. More than once, Bogie had been forced to adjust a cocky young rookie's attitude by using his years of experience and massive muscles to pin him to the mat.

"I take it from her attitude that she's a fed," Mac asked Bogie.

"Randi Finnegan. US Marshal," Bogie replied. "Archie occasionally checks in with her in Cumberland. A few times, she's come into the station to see David, usually to give him grief about security in Spencer." His salt-and-pepper eyebrows went up toward his gray hair. "Those meetings are never pretty."

Her dark eyes boring on David's blue eyes, Randi approached him like a gun slinger ready to do battle. "You just leave your police cars sitting around so assassins can use them to commit murder?" With both hands, she wrestled against Bogie's hand, which was blocking her access to the chief.

"Now you listen here, Finnegan," David argued, "my department's procedures are none of your business."

"They are when my charges are put in danger. Why didn't you call me when you let your cruiser get stolen?"

"I only discovered it was missing minutes before this went down."

"And you didn't warn her?"

"He did warn me," Archie said. "David called me about the missing cruiser, but I didn't think—"

"You didn't think?" With a sarcastic laugh, Randi redirected her attention. "Archie, that's how killers get close to you—It's the oldest ploy in the book! They pretend to be police officers." She gestured at the cruiser. "They steal police cars."

"Archie did think," Mac said. "In case you haven't noticed, she's still standing, and they're not."

Finnegan looked the bare-chested man in the damp sweatpants and bare-feet up and down. "No thanks to your police chief."

"Now you take that back!" Mac charged at her to find Archie holding him back.

The group of law enforcement officers turned into an angry mob with the police chief and Mac trying to get at the US Marshal. Squeezed in the middle, Archie and Bogie tried to keep the peace by holding them all back.

"David O'Callaghan is the best police chief in these parts," Mac told her. "He's taken very good care of Archie— better than you—considering that I haven't laid eyes on you until today and, frankly, with that attitude, I don't care to see anymore of you."

Grasping his arm, Archie tried to lead him away. "Mac, calm down."

"I don't want to calm down." Mac shook her hand off and pointed at the marshal. "I have a question for you, Finnegan. How did Cruze's men find Archie? How did they know she was here?"

All eyes were on US Marshal Randi Finnegan. Her attitude drained from her body. Her face turned white.

Bogie repeated the question. "How did they know?"

"Tommy Cruze got out of jail eighteen days ago," she said. "A judge let him out when it turned out that one of the feds who investigated his case was found to be dirty."

Archie shrieked.

Mac gasped, "Are you kidding me?"

David stuck his finger into Randi's face. "How is it that you, me, and more importantly *she*," he pointed at Archie, "weren't informed about this? If I knew, I would have been prepared to protect her. Instead, she had to take care of it herself."

"I had no idea," Randi said. "I only found out when I contacted the home office after Archie called me about this." She whipped out her cell phone. "Get in the car, Archie."

"What?" Archie asked while Mac clasped her arm as if to hold her there.

"I said to get in the car. We're relocating you. Now!"

"No."

The federal marshal lowered her cell phone from her ear. "We don't have time to talk about this. Cruze is out. He knows where you are. You're in danger. We don't even have time to pack—"

"I'm not going." Archie turned around and clung to Mac.

"I'm not letting her go," Mac said.

When Randi stepped toward Archie as if to forcibly take her, Gnarly stepped in between them and barked. Archie clasped his collar to hold him back.

David and Bogie took positions on either side of Archie.

"We'll take care of her," Bogie said. "We've been taking care of her for this long, and we're not stopping now."

David said, "As you can see, she does pretty good at taking care of herself."

"She got lucky this time," Randi said.

"I'm not letting you take her away from me," Mac said.

"If you want to be with her, fine. You can go into the program, too." Randi waved her arm in a gesture for them both to get into the car.

"I'm not going into the program," Mac said. "I have friends and family. I'm not going to leave them all behind to hide from a killer."

"That's your decision." Randi said, "Archie, I understand how you feel. You're in love. But don't be a fool. Cruze and his people are ruthless. They'll stop at nothing, including killing the people you care about."

"I did nothing wrong," Archie said. "Why am I the one hiding? Cruze is the one who did something wrong. He killed innocent people, and now he's tried to kill me." She folded her arms across her chest. "If anyone should be running scared, it's him."

Chapter Three

"I can't believe I let you talk me into this." Cursing, Randi Finnegan punched the button on her radio to turn off the station David had turned on without her permission. "I should be back at Spencer Manor with Archie, trying to talk some sense into that pretty little head of hers."

"Mac, Bogie, and my officers will protect her, and Gnarly won't let her out of his sight." David pressed the button to tune in to the sports station to catch the score for the ball game that he was missing. That was another thing he needed to get Tommy Cruze for.

"You really don't know Cruze's people." She shook her head before punching the button off again. When David reached for it, she slapped his wrist. "My car. My radio. My station. I hate baseball."

"I sensed from the first time we met that there was something seriously wrong with you. Now I know."

She grumbled, "I am so fired for letting your people take Archie without me going with her."

"I need you with me to see your boss," David said. "You admitted it. Without you, he won't talk to me about who the possible leak is. For all we know, it's him."

"Wilson is the most straight up guy there is," she said with a shake of her head. "He knew J. Edgar Hoover."

"Just because he's old doesn't mean he's not crooked."

"It's not Wilson."

"Then maybe it's you," he said. "You know everything about Archie's whereabouts, habits, and cover."

"How do I know it's not you?" She shot back. "It was your cruiser that got stolen. Who gave them the key to the garage? How many people on your force know about Archie?"

"Bogie and I are the only ones who knew about her. No one else." From the passenger seat, he shot a glare in her direction. "They didn't use any key to break into the garage. They took out the security camera before breaking the lock with bolt cutters."

When he turned back to look out through the windshield, David noticed that she had turned down a two-lane country road to cut over the mountains heading east. "Where are you going?"

"To the field office I work out of in Cumberland."

"Why aren't you taking the freeway?"

"This way is faster," Randi said. "It's more direct."

"It's not faster," he said. "It's longer. It'll take us through every mountain ghost town in Maryland." He pointed across her to the side window. "Take the next left and go up to the freeway."

She gritted her teeth. "My car—"

"I know!" He mocked her. "My car, my radio, my driving—grrr! Next time I'm driving!"

"Hopefully, there won't be a next time."

They continued to ride along in silence, both worried about where Archie was, and if she was safe. They would have preferred to be back at Spencer Manor standing guard over her, but this was something they had to do now. They needed to find the leak who had betrayed their friend and find out what other information he or she had divulged to Tommy Cruze.

"How's your mother?" Randi jolted David out of his thoughts.

He sat up in his seat in time to notice a goat and her baby on the porch of a dilapidated farmhouse located only a couple of feet from the road. With a slight swerve of the car, they could have been driving across the front porch to run down the critters. "She's in a nursing home."

"Really?" Randi's tone went up an octave. "I'm sorry. When did that happen?"

"A couple of months ago," he said while staring out the passenger window. "I had to put her there after she stabbed me with a fork."

"What did you do? Change her radio station?" It was a hollow attempt to lighten his mood that failed.

"She thought I was Dad," he said. "I tried to ignore it or handle it or whatever. Her nurse kept saying that she was becoming more difficult. Every time Mom would see me, she'd be more hateful…"

"Because she thought you were your father?" Randi asked, "What did your dad ever do—"

"Dad didn't *do* anything. She had imagined it all in her mind. She was convinced Dad was having an affair with Robin Spencer. It got worse after Mac moved to Spencer. Dad was already dead, but her dementia got the best of her and she took it out on me. One day, she stabbed me in the chest with a fork." He rubbed the left side of his chest. "I ended up in the ER. Luckily, it wasn't too deep. The next day, I sent her to the nursing home."

"Why did her dementia get worse when Mac Faraday moved to Spencer? What does one have to do with the other?"

David turned to look at her profile. "You don't see it?"

She glanced over at him.

David's eyes narrowed. He cocked his head at her. "If you look, you can see that the only difference between me and Mac is that my hair is blond and his is brown. He gets that from Robin. I got my hair from my mother. We both have Dad's eyes."

"Mac…Robin Spencer's illegitimate son… you mean your father—" She had to fight to keep her car on the winding country road while looking over at David to see the family resemblance that she had missed.

"It was before he had met Mom. He wanted to marry Robin, but she was only seventeen years old and her parents would have none of it. They sent her away to college. By the time Robin came back, Dad had married my mom. But Dad swore to me, and so did Robin, that he never broke his marriage vows." He sighed. "But Mom let herself get so consumed with jealousy that she lost her mind." He said in a low voice, "When I go to see her, she either won't talk to me, or tries to attack me. Last time, the doctor told me that I shouldn't see her alone anymore. Me, big, old police chief, needs a body guard when he visits his own mother."

"I'm sorry."

David responded with a shrug. "How's Butch?"

"Butch?"

"Your husband."

"We're divorced."

"Really?" David turned to her. "When did that happen?"

"It was final six weeks ago."

"Archie never mentioned it."

"She never mentioned your mother."

"What happened?" David asked. "If you don't mind my asking…"

"Butch was offered a transfer to another part of the country. He wanted to go. I didn't. I told him to stay. He said he'd rather go. I said if he went, I'd want a divorce because I never heard of a cross-country marriage that worked, especially in our profession. He said fine. That was that."

"Let me get this straight," David said, "You gave him a choice of staying and being married to you or leaving, and he left?"

"Yes."

"Where was the transfer?"

"Alaska."

David laughed.

"It's not funny," she insisted.

"Depends on how you look at it."

"Which is?"

"Your husband moved to Alaska to get away from you." He continued to laugh.

"He did not."

David shrugged. "If I was your husband, I'd move to Alaska to get away from you."

"If you were my husband," she sputtered in anger, "I'd slip pesticide into your coffee."

"If I was your husband, I'd drink it."

❊   ❊   ❊

"I've imagined you moving your toothbrush in here under much more pleasant circumstances."

The sudden sound of his voice made Archie jump to knock over her cosmetics case and spill the contents all over Mac's bathroom floor. Fighting to keep the nervous tears out of her eyes, she stooped down to pick up the rolling perfume bottles, make-up cases, and loose earrings. "I'm sorry. Look at the mess I've made."

"Will you stop apologizing?"

He was kneeling on the floor with her, his hand on hers, which was clutching a ruby earring. In a flash, she remembered him giving it to her along with the matching necklace that Valentine's Day. *Was that really only last month? Everything seems so long ago since the shooting.*

After Bogie had released her from the scene of the shooting, Archie went to her cottage to change her clothes into slacks and pack some of her belongings to move into the more secure manor. She had returned to the master suite to find that Mac had showered, dressed in jeans and a light sweater, and mopped the bathroom floor from where he had been plunging his clogged toilet.

Mac cupped his hand under her chin. "You've done nothing wrong."

"I made a mess of things."

"No, you haven't," he said. "Cruze did."

She smiled softly at him. "Cruze didn't drop his stuff all over this floor. I did."

He smiled. "Mess or not, I'm glad you're here…in my room…staying with me." He kissed her. "When this is over, I may never let you go back to the guest cottage."

She swallowed. "Mac, it's been over ten years since Cruze put out that contract on me. It's not going to be over until one of us is dead."

"The one who's going to end up dead won't be you."

"How can you be so sure?"

He cupped her face with both his hands. She peered into his blue eyes, so much like his birth father, Patrick O'Callaghan, a man Mac had never met. She had met him, and could see why Robin Spencer had fallen in love with him. Mac had been blessed with the best qualities of both his parents—his father's quick thinking and courage, his mother's imagination and wisdom, and both of their unbending strong-will.

"I won't let anything happen to you," Mac said.

She threw her arms around his shoulders to kiss him. The jewelry she had gathered up was still in her hands. As they parted, they gazed into each other's eyes.

The clearing of a throat made them realize they were not alone.

"I don't mean to interrupt," Bogie's voice came in from the bedroom, where he had stepped away to allow them their privacy, "but there's a phone call for Archie. It's Misty from the Doggie Hut."

"Oh, no!" Archie almost knocked Mac over in her haste to get up and out of the bathroom to grab the phone from Bogie. "Misty! Gnarly's appointment. I completely forgot!"

Feeling her excitement, Gnarly jumped up onto the bed where Archie sat to talk on the phone. He hung his head over her shoulder as if to listen in on the call.

"You missed an appointment with Misty?" Bogie asked. "Do you know how hard it is to get in to see her?" He turned to Mac. "Gnarly will be lucky if he can get back into her scheduled before Christmas."

"Poor Gnarly." Mac's tone dripped with sarcasm.

"Misty is the hottest dog groomer in all of Deep Creek Lake," the deputy police chief said. "I once pulled over a Mercedes with an Irish Setter that had just left from seeing Misty. She smelled of Irish Crème and was wearing a crisp emerald green bandana. Cutest dog you've ever seen."

"What about the driver?"

"Gave her an eighty-five dollar ticket for speeding," Bogie said, "but her dog was really cute." He glanced around behind Mac into the bathroom where the plunger was resting next to the toilet. "You got a clog?" After Mac nodded his head that he did, the deputy chief said, "I was a plumber's apprentice back when I was in school—before getting drafted—before I became a cop. Want me to take a look at it?"

Mac stepped aside and gestured for Bogie to go to work. "Be my guest."

Archie hung up the phone with a whoop. "We did it, Gnarly." She grabbed his head in both hands and kissed the German shepherd on the snout.

"What did we do?" Mac asked.

"Misty can squeeze Gnarly in tomorrow."

"You can't take him in tomorrow," Mac said.

"Why not?"

"What if Cruze's men make another attempt?"

Archie stood up. "I'm not locking myself in this mansion and closing the blinds and never leaving again. If I do, then he wins. We're not going to let them scare us out of living our lives." She pointed at the shepherd on the bed. "I'm taking Gnarly to see Misty tomorrow, and then we're going to lunch at the Spencer Inn."

"And what if Cruze's people make another attempt like they did today?" Mac asked.

She reached around behind her back and took out a blue Ruger thirty-eight caliber pistol. "I have a baby blue Ruger semi-automatic with their names on each bullet."

Admiring the small pistol, Mac folded his arms across his chest and chuckled. "How many guns do you have?"

"Only six." She returned the gun to where she had it tucked into her rear waistband. "Most of them are gifts. The pink one that Bogie took into evidence this morning was from your mother. I hope I get it back. I have a lot of sentimental attachment to it. This blue one is from your father. I also have a pearl-handled handgun that David picked up for me at an antique gun show for my birthday."

"I don't believe it," Mac said, "a girl who prefers guns to diamonds."

"Cruze taught me something when he killed those other witnesses and the marshals guarding them," she told him. "I can't depend on other people to protect me. I need to take care of, and protect, myself. I never even held a gun before I went into the program, but I learned how to handle one, and I'm proud to say I've become a very good sharp shooter."

Mac was digesting the introduction to a side of Archie that he had never known existed when she turned around to where the German shepherd was sitting on the bed. "Come on, Gnarly. We're going for a walk."

It wasn't until she had left the room before Bogie came out of the bathroom to ask, "Did she say she was going for a walk?"

"I guess we're all going for a walk." Mac and Bogie ran after her.

Chapter Four

The US Marshal's field office in Cumberland was small and non-descript. Located on the second floor of a professional building, it consisted of only a few offices in which field agents would come in to get their assignments before leaving to work out in the field. The only ones who kept office hours were Wilson Terrance, the chief of the field office; and his administrative assistant.

When Randi led David off the elevator and down the hallway to the office, he noticed that the reception area and the administrative assistant's desk were empty. Randi waited a moment and looked around before calling out to ask if anyone was in.

"Back here," Wilson called out from his corner office. "Ginger had to go run a quick errand." He stepped into the doorway and waved them in.

As they stepped into the chief's small office, David was struck by how he and Randi, a tall woman, towered over her boss. He thought Randi was joking when she had commented that Wilson Terrance knew J. Edgar Hoover. She wasn't. Her boss had a picture of the two of them hanging up on the wall next to his display of certificates and awards. The elderly man's small build, stooped posture, and slow demeanor reminded David of Yoda from the Star Wars films. The young police chief wondered why the ancient federal agent hadn't retired ages ago.

Wilson may have been old and small, but he made up for it in spunk. "So, you're the police chief who let a couple of mob assassins steal his police cruiser?" He chuckled.

"I didn't let anyone steal anything," David said. "Maybe they wouldn't have been stolen if one of your people didn't leak where you've stashed your witness in my jurisdiction."

"Now don't go jumping to conclusions—"

"Why didn't you notify us that Cruze was out of jail?"

"The minute Ms. Douglas showed up at the police station after witnessing him committing murder, she was a woman with a target on her back," Wilson said. "Douglas was on his hit list the whole time he was in prison."

"Douglas?" David glanced over at Randi.

"Before she went into the program," she explained, "Archie Monday's name was Kendra Douglas. We had to change her complete identity. New name, social security number, and a new background. She went even further to conceal her identity by getting cosmetic surgery to change her appearance. We weren't crazy about her accepting a position working for such a public figure as Robin Spencer; but, considering the additional lengths she went to, we thought she would be safe."

"Archie is the only person I know who doesn't have a Facebook page," David said. "But in spite of all that, Cruze found her, which tells me that someone leaked her new identity to his people. If Archie and my people had known Cruze was out—"

"I guarantee it wouldn't have made any difference," Wilson said, "I didn't know about it until I checked into his status after Finnegan here called me about the attempted hit."

"I disagree," David said. "Being forewarned is the difference between being on alert and getting ambushed like Archie was this morning. She was damn lucky. It could have turned out a whole lot worse."

"It's crucial to Cruze that he make an example of Archie," Randi Finnegan said. "Now that he's out and he's aiming to regain his position as top dog, it doesn't look good to his people for the little girl who put him behind bars to be running around free. It's a matter of saving face. So he had to step up the game. That meant he had to put extra effort into locating her."

"By getting to people on the inside who would tell him where to find her," David said. "Who had access to that information?"

"Only me, Finnegan, and my assistant," Wilson said, "had access to Douglas's new identity and location."

"Where did the news of Cruze's release stop?" David asked.

"What?" Wilson asked.

"Who knew about it and didn't pass it on?" David looked over at Randi, who had turned to glance down the hallway.

"When did Ginger leave?" she asked Wilson.

"A couple of hours ago." He sat up in his chair. "Right after I told her to call Washington to find out why they never notified us about Cruze's release."

David pointed toward the empty desk in the reception area. "If your office works like mine, everything coming in goes through one person—the administrative assistant. If she held onto that information and never passed it on to you, would you be any the wiser?"

Wilson's wrinkled lips set into a tight line.

"Ginger had access to Archie's whereabouts." Randi turned to Wilson. "Do you have Ginger's cell phone number?"

The old man was already leafing through his address book.

David went out to the reception desk. "Do you have the password to get onto her computer? Maybe we can find to whom she gave Archie's information."

Wilson called after him, "Ginger wouldn't be so stupid as to send it in an e-mail that could be traced by security." He slammed down the phone. "She's not answering her cell phone."

"Did she say where she was going when she left?" Randi asked.

"No." Wilson shook her head. "She told me that she had to run a quick errand. She does that…fairly regularly. Now I'm wondering what type of errand."

"If she left after you told her to find out about Cruze getting out, then she had to know the jig is up," David said.

"She's running," Randi said.

"Let's go check her house," David said.

Wilson handed them a slip of paper. "Here's her home address. Call me when you find her."

❋   ❋   ❋

"How long have you known this Ginger?" David asked on their way to Ginger Altman's home, a split-level in an older subdivision outside of Cumberland, Maryland.

"Long enough to know that I never did like her," Randi said. "Big blonde hair and boobs and high heels. She played Wilson from the first time she sashayed into the office. She hated me because I could see her for what she was."

"A traitor?"

"A player," Randi said. "If she's the leak, it isn't because of any loyalty to anyone but herself. I'd bet money on it." Holding out her hand, she rubbed her fingers together. "She did it for cold, hard cash."

When they pulled into the driveway of the suburban home, David noticed the expensive red convertible in the driveway. "'You had her nailed. Does her salary pay enough to buy a forty thousand dollar sports car?"

"Nope."

He also noticed the black van parked on the street in front of the house. "Who does the black van belong to?"

"Maybe her friends."

Keeping their hands on their guns, they got out of the car and crossed onto the walkway leading to the front door.

David saw the muzzle of the gun poke through the curtains of the front window. "Gun!" He tackled Randi Finnegan to the ground.

The shots took out the front window. Keeping low, David picked up Randi with one arm while firing his gun. They scrambled across the lawn and dove behind a thick oak tree.

"Ginger's friends don't want us joining their party," he told her.

"Never did like that bitch." Randi checked for the bullet in the chamber of her gun. "Now I know why."

"If that van belongs to whoever is shooting at us, we're between them and their way out."

"And we're blocking in her car," she said, "So why are we the ones pinned down behind a tree?"

David peered around the tree to the house. Through the bullet-shredded curtains, he could make out the muzzle of the gun and the top of the shooter's head.

"How many are there?" she asked.

"I can only see one." He judged the distance from the tree to the cover around the corner of the house. It was a good twenty feet. "I'll draw his fire. When he gets up to shoot at me, you take him out."

"Why do you get to draw his fire?" Randi asked.

"Because I'm wearing a bullet proof vest under my shirt and you aren't."

"How do you—" Remembering him grabbing her when he tackled her, she stopped. "You draw his fire."

David drew in a deep breath. "Count of three."

"Who's counting?"

"I'm counting."

"Why do you get to count?"

"Are you serious?" David asked. "We're pinned down by a maniac wanting to kill us, and you're going to argue with me about who gets to count to three? If it's that important to you, you count."

"Well," she said, "if you're going to be that way, you count."

"No, you count."

"I can be just as big of a man as you are."

David's chuckle held a naughty tone. "I don't think so."

A shot from inside the window broke off a branch of the tree, and it landed next to them.

"Let's both count," he said.

"Good idea."

"To three."

They counted in unison. On three, David ran for the corner of the house. As he had predicted, the shooter had to rise up to fire at the running officer. From behind the tree, Randi fired off five shots toward the broken-out window. David dove for the corner of the house.

The shooting stopped.

The gun dropped out of the window when the shooter collapsed.

Silence fell over the house.

Randi and David practically tiptoed up to the front door. Inside, they found the living room riddled with bullet holes. Both of them put on evidence gloves while observing the gun man sprawled across the back of the sofa where he had been perched. His brains and blood soaked the top of the sofa and spilled down the front onto the seat cushions.

"I'm assuming this isn't Ginger," David said.

Shaking her head, Randi searched the bottom floors, dining room, and kitchen and looked out to the back porch, which extended out to a small backyard.

When she went upstairs, David followed. The top floor contained three bedrooms and a bathroom. The master bedroom door was open. Two suitcases rested on the floor in front of a walk-in closet. Both lay open with clothes waiting to be folded.

Her clothing ripped open, the missing administrative assistant was stretched sideways across the bed. After the assailant had his fun, he finished the job by gutting her. Her blood was splattered all over the walls and ceiling. It soaked through the mattress and bedding.

"This is what I was talking about when I said you don't know what Cruze's people are capable of,'" Randi said.

David squatted down next to the suitcases. "She was running."

"These people don't believe in leaving loose ends."

Seeing a cell phone on the bed stand, David said, "They wouldn't have known she was a loose end unless someone told them. Like her. If she was stupid enough to be a leak, then she must have been stupid enough to call them for help when she had to go on the lam."

Randi picked up the phone and hit the button to bring up the call log. She took out her phone, turned on the speaker, and dialed the last called number. The phone rang two times before a male voice answered, "Alan Richardson here."

Randi hit the button to disconnect. Her dark eyes narrowed to slits.

"Who's Alan Richardson?" David asked.

"Tommy Cruze's lawyer."

Lauren Carr

Chapter Five

Hector Langford was the chief of security at the Spencer Inn. A lean, gray-haired Australian, Hector had been with the Inn for over twenty-five years and knew the resort town of Spencer inside and out. When Mac had first met him, Hector had taken great delight in informing him that Robin Spencer had often asked for his help in planning her murders for her mystery novels.

He had also known Archie Monday since she had first come to Spencer. When Mac contacted him for help in guarding her, Hector contacted every security officer who wasn't on duty at the Inn. In less than a half an hour, two SUV's with the Spencer Inn sign on the front door panels arrived with six armed guards to keep watch over Archie.

The men who spilled out of the SUVs didn't look like the average hotel security personnel. Clad in ballistic vests and utility belts complete with guns, they looked like a small private army, which they were. Each man wore an ear mike to communicate with the rest of the team, which was led by Hector himself.

After getting directions from Bogie, Hector ordered the men to spread out and work in partnership with the Spencer police officers already guarding Spencer Manor from any attempted hit on its lady.

With such a large force looking out for Archie, it was a sight like none that Spencer had seen before when she headed out to take Gnarly for his walk. It was reminiscent of a teen pop star out and about with her entourage. While the German shepherd led on the leash, Mac was on one side of Archie. In his deputy chief's uniform, Bogie was on the other side. Carrying a semi-automatic sub machine gun poised for an attack, one Spencer police officer was on the lookout for any assault from the front, while a Spencer security guard brought up the rear. He was similarly armed with his own sub machine gun.

"This really isn't necessary," Archie told Mac.

"After what happened this morning," Mac said, "I think it is. This is ridiculous."

A long, black limousine slowly approached from behind them.

"We have company," the rear guard called up to them.

They all clasped their guns. Archie clasped the handgun she had behind her back. As the limousine pulled up ahead of them, the rear window lowered. She gasped and grasped Gnarly's leash when she saw the bald head with an ugly face look out at her.

Mac's arms went around her and he thrust her behind him while Bogie blocked her from the other side. His mouth foaming with fury, Gnarly's barks drowned out the deputy chief's orders for everyone to be ready.

"Well, Ms. Douglas, it's been a long time." Tommy Cruze smirked at her. "I see you've moved uptown since we last saw each other. You must have some powerful friends. Is this your lover, Lieutenant Mac Faraday, formerly of the DC police department?"

"We've never met," Mac said.

"But we have had mutual friends," Cruze oozed. "Pearson. Rick Pearson. I believe he was a drug dealer, at least that was what he told me he was at the time—until I found out differently. Terrible accident he had. Ate his gun."

"You son of a bitch," Mac said. "Pearson's wife was pregnant."

"Pity for her." He nodded in Archie's direction. "You'd better be careful of your man, Ms. Douglas. Hate for him to have the same type of accident his friend had."

Uttering snarling barks, Gnarly was up on his hind legs trying to get at the mobster while Archie held him back.

"Or maybe one of your two children might have an accident, Lieutenant Faraday," Cruze said. "Lovely daughter you have, by the way. Looks just like her grandmother when Robin Spencer was her age. Some of my people would love to take her out for a good time."

In the blink of an eye, Mac's gun was out of its holster with the muzzle in Tommy Cruze's face.

The bodyguard in the front seat was out of the car and aiming his gun at Mac.

The Spencer police officer pressed the muzzle of his gun against the back of the guard's head.

The driver jumped out of the car to point his gun at Mac, only to find Bogie aiming his gun across the top of the limousine at him.

The security guard from Spencer stepped forward to aim his gun through the window at Tommy Cruze.

The mobster laughed. "Well, well, well, it looks like we have a standoff."

"I could shoot you now," Mac said, "and no one would shed a tear for you."

"And my men will shoot you."

"But you'll be dead," Mac replied, "and the contract on Archie will be null and void with no one to pay it."

Tommy Cruse laughed. "Is this woman really worth you getting killed over?"

"Yes."

"Bigger fool than I thought."

"Don't, Mac," Bogie said. "Let's all just take a deep breath and everyone back away."

"Yes, Mac," Tommy said in a mocking tone, "Let's all just take a deep breath and back away." He let out an insane sounding laugh.

Archie's hand was on Mac's arm. "Let's go, darling. This all was a bad idea."

"I suggest you take the little lady home and enjoy her company while you still can," Tommy Cruze said. "You won't have it for long." He laughed again.

His laughter was cut short when Archie shoved Mac's gun out of the way so she could reach in through the window to grab Cruze by the front of his shirt. Her handgun was in his face. Light blue, it resembled a toy. No one doubted that it wasn't.

"Now you listen to me, Cruze. I'd wipe that cocky grin off your face if I were you, because it ain't working. Neither are your big threats about coming after me, because I see them for the crock of horse poop that they are. You seem to have forgotten that I put your ass in jail for over ten years. This very morning, I killed two of your people. That's right. I blew them away with my little pink handgun, which is now in evidence." She growled when she said, "I really liked that gun, Cruze. All this blow hard bravado about how tough you are is a big fat waste of your hot air, because I know the truth. It's you who's afraid of me." She cocked her head in his face and glanced down inside the car. "What's that I smell?"

She sniffed. "Oh, I know that odor. It's the smell of fear. I smell it. Gnarly smells it. All of us here smells it. You reek of fear, Cruze. I suggest you go home and change your underwear before your men smell it, too."

She shoved him back into the limousine. While all of the men stood in shock at the petite, little blonde's display, she picked up Gnarly's leash and headed back down Spencer Lane to home.

In stunned silence, Cruze's driver and body guard climbed into the limousine and drove off.

Bogie said, "I don't know about you, Mac, but Archie scares me sometimes."

"She just scared the living daylights out of me."

❉   ❉   ❉

"Will you stop following me?"

It was an order, not a question.

As soon as Archie and her entourage got back to Spencer Manor, Mac launched into a recount of everything she had done wrong during their encounter with Tommy Cruze. She tried to ignore him and take her mind off her circumstance by unpacking her clothes and hanging them up in his closet.

Bogie and Hector were both calling in more security to keep Spencer Manor safe.

While Archie was uninterested in hearing what he had to say, Mac was following on her heels to make his point. He was so focused on Archie that he didn't notice Gnarly up on the bed, where he was not allowed to be, watching them circle around the master suite during the debate.

"I'll stop following you when you stop walking away from me and listen," Mac said.

Carrying an armload of clothes, Archie went through the dressing room to the walk-in closet. "I am listening to you." With one arm, she pushed all of his clothes aside to make room for her dresses. "You pulled your gun on him first, and that was okay," she said. "I pulled my gun on him, and that was wrong."

"You didn't just draw your gun on him, Archie, you called him out. You called him a chicken."

"I did not use the word chicken." She turned to him. The corners of her lips curled. Her emerald eyes twinkled. "Did you see how scared he was?"

"Any man is scared when a crazed woman sticks a blue gun in his face." He grasped her by the shoulders. "To tell you the truth, I'm more frightened by a woman pointing a gun at me than a man. Women tend to be more emotional. When you mix emotions and guns, bullets tend to fly."

She shook her head. "No, Mac. I've heard it before, but now I've seen it with my own eyes. Bullies are chickens. They cover up their cowardice with bravado like a child in a mask on Halloween. Their bullying covers up how scared they really are. Maybe they can even forget it themselves." She shook her finger, her nail dipped in rose-colored polish. "I called him on it."

"Yes, you did." Mac's tone was somber. "And his men saw it. That's why now he *has* to kill you. If he doesn't, his men won't respect him. If they don't respect him, then he can't rule the syndicate."

The cell phone vibrating in his pocket broke their stare down. The screen announced it was David. Mac put it on speaker phone. "Yeah, Dave?"

"We found the leak," he said.

"And?" Mac asked.

"She's dead," David reported. "She was the assistant at the marshal's field office in Cumberland. She sold Archie out and kept us in the dark about Cruze's release. Finnegan is looking at her financials now. It looks like she did it for cold, hard cash. When Finnegan called in about the hit on Archie, she ran and made the dumb mistake of calling Cruze's people for help. They helped her all right. They sent over one of their psychopaths to tie up the loose end. How are things there?"

"We had a run in with Cruze," Mac said, "live and in person."

"Is everyone okay?"

"I think Archie made Cruze pee his pants."

She giggled at the reference; however, David's tone was serious. "She didn't. Archie, I swear! You spent way too much time with Robin Spencer. How many times do I have to tell you? You don't go around agitating maniacs. It's not a good idea."

With a roll of her eyes, Archie went back to the closet with another load of clothes to hang up.

Mac asked, "Does Finnegan have any ideas about what Cruze would be doing here in Spencer?"

"One idea comes immediately to mind," David said. "Archie was the prime witness that sent him to prison. She was the eye witness who saw him commit the murder. In spite of Cruze's best efforts during the trial, he was never able to scare her into backing off."

"Which had to infuriate the hell out of him," Mac said.

"He's come to Spencer to personally oversee her death."

Chapter Six

David O'Callaghan and Randi Finnegan returned to Spencer Manor in time for a dinner of Cincinnati Three-Way Chili, an old family recipe from Mac's childhood. It was one of the few recipes he could cook on his own.

Archie and Mac had a lot of mouths to feed with the full house of security officers from the Spencer Inn and police officers, the deputy chief, police chief, and one US Marshal.

When David and Randi came through the front door, everyone forgot about the dinner and left the sunken dining room to go up to the living room to learn the details about the leak in the US Marshal's office. Randi carried an overnight bag that they had stopped at her home in Cumberland to collect in anticipation of a long haul protecting Archie.

"Unfortunately, we can't get any information from Ginger Altman," Randi said. "Cruze's people quieted her real good."

"Don't you people run security checks on your office help?" Bogie demanded to know.

"Hey, I didn't hire her," Randi shot back. "But I guarantee you that she wouldn't have been hired without passing a back ground check—I suppose all those stories about cops turning dirty are just urban legends."

"Considering that this was a witness who gave up her whole life as she knew it to put away one of the most dangerous men east of the Mississippi," Hector replied, "you'd think the US Marshal's office would have seen the importance of checking their people inside and out."

Randi looked like she was about to take both Bogie and Hector on single-handedly when David stepped between them and held out his arms to hold them back. "That's enough. I've had it up to here with everyone."

Bogie started to object. "She—"

"*She* didn't betray Archie," David said. "Finnegan is on our side. She cares as much about Archie as all of us. That's why she's here. What's been done is done. Now we need to focus on keeping Archie safe and getting Cruze back behind bars."

"He's right," Mac said, "We need to keep our heads clear and figure out how to stop Cruze."

Randi gestured at the cell phone she wore clipped to her waistband. "I have a call in to my contact with the FBI organized crime bureau. This afternoon, he told me that they've been keeping close tabs on Tommy Cruze's organization. After Cruze went to jail, his second in command, Ray Bonito, took over the operation. According to their sources, word is that Bonito isn't happy about being kicked down to second in command since Cruze got out. There's an internal war brewing, and Bonito is trying to get support from the men to back him. If that happens …" Her voice trailed off to let them to use their own imaginations.

Mac said, "Which makes it important for Cruze to keep face with his men. If they see him being taken down by a little spitfire …"

"I don't like Cruze being in Spencer," David said. "If he's here, so are his people. If a turf war breaks out, there's no telling where it will happen and who can get caught in the crossfire."

Bogie agreed. "We better cancel all time off until Cruze and his people leave town."

"An interesting thing that my source told me," Randi said, "Bonito is paranoid. He's been running things completely from behind the scenes and is never seen in public."

"Maybe there's a contract out on him," Archie said in a joking tone.

"Exactly," Randi said with a serious note. "Bonito liked being in charge. Cruze definitely sees him as a threat. So far, Cruze has been offering him the chance to step down quietly. That offer isn't going to be on the table for long."

Combing his fingers through his blond hair, David went to the stairs leading up to the bedrooms on the second floor. "I'm going to go take a shower and change."

Grumbling about the incompetence of the federal government in protecting its witnesses, Hector and Bogie returned to the dining room for their dinner.

"I'll show Randi up to one of the guest rooms," Archie told Mac, "while you show these guys how you eat Cincinnati Three-Way Chili."

After giving Mac a kiss on the cheek, she led Randi up to the second floor, which contained six bedrooms, two of which were suites with their own private baths. Gnarly trotted up the stairs ahead of them. At the top of the stairs, Archie turned to the right to go down the hallway at the end of which was the master bedroom suite that she was sharing with Mac. Gnarly trotted in the opposite direction to the other master suite, which looked out over the gardens of the estate and the lake on the other side of the point. At the end of the hall, Gnarly jumped up and, planting one paw on the door frame, with the other pushed down the door lever to open the door and slip into the suite.

Archie got halfway down the hall before she realized Randi wasn't behind her. Turning around, she saw that the marshal had stopped at the top of the stairs and was staring down the hallway into the suite in which Gnarly had entered. The king-sized bed was encased with a green silk comforter. The furniture was leather and suede.

Through the open doorway, Randi watched David, who had taken off his shirt, stretching his arms up over his head to loosen his back, aching from the long ride to and from Cumberland. Mesmerized, she gazed at his firm, taunt back muscles gracefully flowing down to his slender waist and tight buttocks.

"Like the view?" Archie hissed into her ear.

Startled, Randi gasped.

Gnarly, who was sprawled out on David's bed, whirled around.

David turned around and saw her. His toned, smooth muscular chest was scarred by a wound on his left breast.

Archie smiled when she saw Randi's cheeks turn red. "Maybe you should close the door, David."

He slammed the door shut.

Archie giggled over Randi's embarrassment. "There's nothing to be ashamed of. David is a hottie." She led her down the hall to the bedroom closest to her and Mac's suite.

"He hates my guts."

"David doesn't hate anybody's guts." She threw open the door and went inside. The guest room had a homey feel, but didn't contain as many of the personal touches that decorated the rest of the house.

Setting her overnight bag on the luggage stand, Randi noted that they had not stopped to pick up clothes for David to spend the night. However, he seemed to have already made himself at home in the suite down the hall. "Did someone pick up David's clothes from his house for him?"

"He's been staying here at the manor ever since his mom went into the nursing home," Archie explained.

"Why?" Randi opened her suitcase to take out her belongings.

Uncertain about how much of David's personal business she could reveal, Archie hesitated. "You know his mother has dementia—Alzheimer's?"

"He told me that she stabbed him with a fork and that was why he put her in a home." Randi took her toiletry bag and set it on top of the dresser.

"He ended up in the emergency room. That fork wound was deep," Archie said. "When David left the hospital, he came here and has never gone back to his mother's house. I guess it has too many bad memories."

"His father Pat seemed like a good guy," Randi said. "Why would David's mother want to stab him?"

Archie shut the bedroom door. "Violet suffered from emotional problems. Paranoia. Pills. Drinking too much. Suicide attempts. Several times, she ended up in the hospital. Once, Robin told me that Violet was in the hospital for a full year, and they didn't think she was ever coming home. Pat worked long hours and couldn't take care of David alone." She shrugged. "So, when Violet ended up in the hospital, he would bring David here and Robin Spencer would take care of him. This became his second home. Robin said he could come here anytime he wanted, for as long as he wanted." She added, "Mac has honored that. When David left the ER that night, he came here and has been here ever since."

Randi was staring out the window.

Wondering if she had betrayed David's privacy by telling Randi about his childhood, or maybe if she had given her some insight into his and Mac's relationship, Archie concluded, "So that's David's story."

"Thanks," she replied. "Now I know."

"Now you do."

✳   ✳   ✳

"Maybe we should have put Agent Finnegan in the guest house," Mac joked when he slipped under the covers next to Archie. "I don't think it's a good idea to have her and David under the same roof."

"Those two don't belong on the same planet." Recalling how mesmerized Randi was while watching David without his shirt on, she grinned. "I think she's got a thing for David."

"I have no doubt." Under the covers, he reached for her and slid over to hold her close. "It's called hatred."

"No, she likes him—a lot. She just isn't secure enough to let him know. So she pretends she hates him. In her mind, it's easier to accept that they can't get together because she's rejected him rather than him rejecting her."

"I really don't want to talk about David and Randi right now."

She turned to see that Mac was close. He had his arms wrapped around her. His eyes were soft as they gazed into hers.

The house was quiet, but no one was asleep.

Everyone was on alert.

Nighttime was the best time for Cruze's men to attack under the cover of darkness. Two of Hector's men were patrolling the estate with two of David's officers. Another one of his officers and a security guard were inside the house.

Gnarly was down the hall in David's room. Randi Finnegan was next door in the guest room.

"All this because of me," she murmured to him.

"You're worth it."

"Do you really think so?"

Mac brushed his fingers through her hair, cropped short to her head. He wondered how she had worn it before—before being in the wrong place to witness Tommy Cruze killing a man he accused of being with his wife.

Talk about life changing in the blink of an eye.

"Archie," he said softly, "today, when Finnegan told you to get in the car—when she was going to take you away—I felt like the core of my whole being was being ripped out of me."

"Mac, I'm not going anywhere."

He cupped her face in his hands. "Have you ever heard the saying that you don't realize how important something or someone is to you until they're gone?"

Emotion flooded her. Her eyes filled with tears. She nodded her head. She could see tears coming to Mac's eyes.

"That was when it hit me… I can't imagine you not being in my life."

"Me either," she mumbled.

He pressed his mouth against hers. When they parted, he held onto her tightly and whispered into her ear. "When this is over, will you marry me, Archie?"

Gently, she brushed her fingers across his face while gazing into his blue eyes. "Oh, Mac, …"

Chapter Seven

Unlike Mac, David didn't have any issues with Gnarly sleeping in bed with him, which was why the shepherd gravitated to his suite after he had moved in. Truthfully, David liked the feel of Gnarly's warm body next to his during the dark of the night. The four-legged companion chased away the ghosts in his mind.

The ghosts that haunted his mother's mind had been taunting him with threats that her dementia would be passed on to him since he had become old enough to notice them.

Robin and Patrick O'Callaghan had attempted to soothe the young boy's fears by pointing out how much he took after his father. Over and over again, they would remind him of his blue eyes, intense glare, tall, slender build, and commanding presence—all evidence of his father's genes. As he grew up, David would stare into the mirror and look for the signs of his father's genes overpowering those of his mother—the genes that carried her insanity.

It worked for a while.

Not so much since the night that Violet had stabbed him in the chest. In spite of being an elderly, wheelchair bound woman, she was strong enough to plunge the fork an inch deep into his breast.

When the doctor released him from the hospital, he went running to Spencer Manor—like when he was a teenager and his mother would have those screaming fits. The screams still seemed to be bouncing off the walls when he went to pick up his things the next day after Bogie had taken Violet O'Callaghan to the nursing home—never to return again to the home on Deep Creek Lake that she had shared with her late husband.

With his cold, wet nose pressed against David's hand, Gnarly nudged him from his stare out the window to let him know that someone was in the hallway. After grabbing his gun from the night stand, David climbed out of the bed and went to the door. "Who is it?"

He expected to hear Hector answer. Instead, it was Randi's voice. "It's me. You didn't come down to dinner. I was checking to see if you were feeling okay. Did I wake you?"

Cautiously, David opened the door a crack and peered out into the hallway.

She was alone. Still dressed, she did not appear ready to go to sleep yet. She carried two brandy snifters with liquor in them.

He opened the door wider.

She held up the drinks. "Peace offering."

Realizing that he was only dressed in a pair of sweatpants, he picked up his bathrobe from the foot of the bed. "I wasn't expecting any company."

She shrugged. "I don't think you have anything I haven't seen before."

After taking one of the snifters, he invited her into the suite and returned his gun to the night stand. "Only one. We need to keep our minds clear."

They clinked their glasses. Opting not to be close to the window where a sniper could hit them, David invited her over to the sitting area, which consisted of two leather wing-backed chairs in front of the fireplace.

Her cheeks turned pink when she said, "I wanted to thank you for standing up for me earlier."

Not recalling, David asked, "When?"

"When Bogie and Hector got on my case—"

He shrugged it off. "No problem… I should apologize for that comment I made about your husband running off to Alaska to get away from you. I'm not usually so insensitive… really I'm not."

"Not from what I see—"

"I guess there's something about you that makes me—"

"Why is that?"

David cocked his head at her. "Why do you have to be so tough?"

She blinked at him. "Because it's my job to be tough."

"But you're also a woman."

"There you go being sexist again. Where is it written that women have to be soft?"

"Well, if you want to be treated like a woman, then stop acting like a man."

She drained her drink and stood up. When she tried to go to the door, she found David blocking her way. He held her gaze. Uncomfortable with his penetrating look, she tried to avert her eyes. "You're in my way."

His eyes searched for hers. Finding them, he held her there. "Why did you come knocking on my door?"

"We need to call a truce," she said. "Archie has made it clear that she's not leaving. If I'm to protect her, I have to stay with her. That means we have to put up with each other. It's easier if we get along."

"I agree." His lips curled. "How well do you want to get along?"

She gazed up at him.

He stepped in closer to her.

She felt her heartbeat quicken. Her body felt hot. She didn't know if it was the blood coursing through her veins or the heat of his body close to hers. She looked up deep into his eyes. His hands were on her neck, lifting her lips to his.

The sudden vibration of her cell phone caused her to jump up and out of his reach.

Her shriek caused Gnarly to jump down off the bed. The German shepherd reached up with his paw to pull down the lever to open the door. With his snout, he pried the door open and ran from the room.

As if she feared the caller could see the flush she felt over her body, she brought the phone to her ear and stepped out into the hall to cool off.

David returned to his chair to finish his drink.

"That's great news," she said into the phone. "I'm going to be waiting by the phone. Call me as soon as you hear anything else." With a wave to David, she turned and headed down to the other end of the hall to knock on Archie and Mac's door.

"What news?" David asked while following her.

Tying his bathrobe shut, Mac opened the door. Wearing a dressing gown, Archie slipped into a chair next to the fireplace.

Randi waited for David to come in before announcing her news. "I just got a call from my guy at the FBI. They received word from a very reliable source that Tommy Cruze has ordered his chief enforcer to bring in a highly paid, very efficient hit man, and he wants to personally meet with this assassin tomorrow morning to give him his order to take care of a problem that he has. According to the source, he specified that this assassin is to have no problem hitting a woman target."

Mac grasped Archie's shoulder.

"Why is that good news?" Archie asked.

"Because we'll be there," Randi said.

"This task force has someone on the inside," Mac said.

Randi said, "They won't confirm or deny that. But since Tommy Cruze is in the area, and he's going to be at the meeting giving the orders personally, then it's fair to say that we have the situation under control."

"I'll believe that when I see Tommy Cruze dead," Mac said. "Then I will know things are under control."

Chapter Eight

Spencer Manor- The Next Morning

Mac never thought he would see the day where he would get claustrophobic in his seven-bedroom manor home. It wasn't so much claustrophobia as the need to get away, alone, out of the house filled with people.

With David at the end of the hall, Randi Finnegan in the bedroom next door, security guards and police officers on patrol outside and inside—all on alert—Mac needed space to be alone with his own thoughts.

It was the "on edge" part that was nagging at him.

More than once his two grown children, his son Tristan and his daughter Jessica, had come to Spencer Manor and brought several friends with them. There would be people sleeping in every room, including Archie's guest cottage. The last Fourth of July was a two-week long party with Mac making almost daily trips to the airport in McHenry to send college students home and pick more up from commuter flights to and from Dulles International Airport and beyond.

He hadn't felt as anxious then as he did now.

The threat on Archie's life had everything to do with it.

Mac gave up on sleep at five-thirty in the morning and got dressed in his navy blue running suit, complete with a jacket to protect him against the early morning chill.

Springing into action with the promise of an early morning walk, Gnarly began pawing at the bedroom door when Mac put on his old blue ball cap with the Washington DC police insignia above the bill.

"Going out kind of early, aren't you?" David called down to him from the top of the stairs. The pitter-patter of Gnarly's paws in the hallway and down the stairs had awakened him.

Mac wrestled with the excited shepherd to clip on his leash. "I couldn't sleep."

"I don't think anyone can," David replied.

Mac nodded his head in the direction of the room at the end of the hall where Archie was tossing and turning in his bed. "Archie finally fell asleep a little while ago."

"I'll keep an eye out for her," David assured him. "Take your time and get some fresh air."

"I should be back in an hour."

Mac opened the front door and Gnarly dragged him down the front steps and out the driveway to the end of Spencer Court. Upon reaching the main road, Gnarly took his master onto the hiking trail through the woods toward the bridge crossing Deep Creek Lake.

By the time they had hit the trail, Mac was running in sync with Gnarly's gait. They had struck a rhythm that allowed Mac's thoughts to flow. His heart raced when he remembered Tommy Cruze's smirk and his smooth tone when he mentioned Jessica. He suggested the order of raping and killing Mac's daughter as easily as if he were ordering a pizza.

Easily. Just like how easy it would have been for me to eliminate his threat to Archie and Jessica by killing him myself.

Mac didn't like that feeling. He liked to think that he—being the good guy—was incapable of killing with so little difficulty.

I'm not wired that way—or am I? Maybe that's what makes me such a good detective—because I'm wired with some of the same wires that the killers I chase possess.

The sun was beginning to shine on the lake to sparkle on the ripples across its surface, creating a diamond effect. Squinting against the reflection off the water, Mac reached into his pocket and pulled out his sun glasses to protect his eyes against the sun's rays. While clinging to Gnarly's leash with one hand, he fought to slip them on with the other.

"Hey, Mac!"

Unnerved by the intrusion into his thoughts, Mac broke their rhythm to look around for the source of the call.

Two elderly fishermen who had set up lawn chairs along the shore next to the bridge waved up to him. Mac only had time to wave back before Gnarly dragged him across the bridge.

When they reached the other side of the lake, Gnarly followed the sidewalk to turn the corner and trot down Route 219, past the local grocery store and gas station and through the traffic light before Mac pulled him to a halt.

The smell of coffee reminded him that he had not had his morning dose of caffeine yet. Beyond the shore of the tiny cafe, he could see Spencer Point basking in the glow of the morning sun. He and Gnarly had run a full four miles without stopping. "Want a croissant, Gnarl?"

Excited at the mention of food, Gnarly danced back and forth, leading Mac to the door of the café. It was as if he were saying, "Let's go! Let's go! Give me the croissant!"

The sign over the door read "Dockside Café." The red and white sign in the window said that they were open. After sitting the dog next to the door, Mac went inside to get his coffee and a fresh croissant for Gnarly.

The reception area included a gourmet coffee bar with serving counter. On the far side of the reception area, a spacious dining area offered customers a view of the lake and Spencer Mountain from inside or they could dine outside on the deck.

A girl of about six years old was sitting on a tall stool behind the coffee bar. Clutching a toy stuffed dog, she gazed at Mac with big, dark eyes that suggested surprise at seeing a customer so early.

"Good morning," Mac said.

"Good morning, sir." Carrying a computerized tablet, an exotic-looking woman with long black hair and dark eyes came in from out of the kitchen to greet him. She slipped the tablet onto a shelf under the cash register and directed her attention to their first customer of the day. She was dressed in a brilliantly bright blue and fuchsia colored dress that hung down to her ankles.

"One for breakfast?" She picked up a menu. "We aren't quite ready yet, but if you don't mind being patient, I will serve you a coffee … on the house."

Mac shook his head while holding up a hand. "No, I only came in for a coffee—black." From outside, he heard a bark.

Gnarly was peering at him through the window. The dog jumped up to plant his front paws on the window sill. His tongue hanging out of his mouth, he wagged his tail.

"And a croissant," Mac added.

Anticipating his breakfast, Gnarly continued to watch everyone's movements.

Hugging her toy dog, the girl moved to the window for a closer look at the dog that was about a hundred times bigger than the one in her arms.

"Stay away from that dog!" the mother yelled.

Startled by the shriek, Mac whirled around.

"So sorry," she smiled nervously at him. "You never can tell about…"

"I understand." Mac noticed that the daughter, still staring wantonly at Gnarly, returned to her chair. She held out her toy to Gnarly as if to introduce the two canines.

Behind the counter, the mother was grinding the beans for the coffee that Mac had ordered. "We only just opened. Coffee is not yet brewed."

"Take your time." Noticing pictures of Italian cathedrals and a map of Italy on the wall, Mac placed her accent: Italian.

"My family sent me over to live with my cousin and go to school when I was only eighteen." She grinned at him from over her shoulder. "He and his family had an Italian restaurant." A note of sadness crept into her tone. "Now, I run this small café with my daughter. Her name is Sari."

Mac strolled into the dining room. A serving tray containing the salt and pepper shakers, dishes of sugar packs, as well as bowls filled with cream containers, rested on a buffet against the wall inside the dining room. All of the tables in the café were bare. No servers or cooks appeared to be on the premises, except the mother and her young daughter.

"Here you go, sir." The woman smiled at him while handing him the coffee in a disposable cup with a lid and a white bag with the croissant inside. "Thank you so much for your patience, sir."

After paying for the coffee and croissant, plus a generous tip, Mac stepped outside where Gnarly almost knocked him down in his pursuit of the pastry. "Will you take it easy?" Mac demanded while holding onto a shred of dignity.

From off the sidewalk, a man in a dark blue running suit jogged across the small parking lot toward them. A grin crossed his face when he saw the man struggling with the dog trying to rip the paper bag out of his hand. The grin reached up to his eyes shielded by dark sun glasses. As he pulled open the door, he looked down at where Gnarly plopped down to devour the croissant. "Can see who's the boss in your house."

Mac glanced over at the runner donning a Toronto Blue Jay's baseball cap as he went inside the cafe. *Figures. A Baltimore Oriole's fan wouldn't be such a jerk.*

Gnarly sniffed the ground from where he had consumed the croissant. Satisfied that he had finished every crumb, he looked up at Mac, who was leaning against the side of the building while drinking his coffee. The dog sat up and whined.

Hearing the cry, Mac looked at him.

Eying the cup in Mac's hand, Gnarly cocked his head.

"No, you're not getting my coffee."

Gnarly hung his head and cried.

"You don't drink coffee."

He whined again—louder this time. Pleadingly, he placed a paw on Mac's foot.

"It'll stunt your growth," he argued.

Gnarly lifted his head and let out a long whine that ended in a bark.

"No."

Seeing that begging wasn't working, Gnarly stood up and barked out a demand that Mac turn over his coffee to him.

"Stop it."

When Mac refused to share his coffee, Gnarly tagged him forcefully in the chest with his front paws to knock the cup out of Mac's hand and onto the ground.

"You're not spoiled, are you?"

Gnarly was lapping up the coffee to wash down his croissant when Mac spotted a woman in a black running suit jogging from the hotel across the street. Her dark sunglasses concealed most of her face. On her way down from the sidewalk up by Spencer's main drag, she stumbled off the curb and almost fell to the ground before regaining her balance. She pushed her sunglasses back up onto her face before breaking into a run for the café door.

"Nora," a male voice called out, "wait up."

Mac looked across the parking lot in the direction of the call while the woman hurried toward the door.

"Where have you been?" the man asked.

"I went running," she answered from over her shoulder before the door shut behind her.

"But I thought we were going to spend every minute together." In contrast to the anxiety in his tone, the man was walking at a leisurely pace. While the majority of the residents and tourists of the resort town dressed down in casual fare, the stick-like man was dressed in an ill-fitting gray suit and white shirt with no tie. His clothes hung from his bony frame. As he approached the café, his appearance became even more bizarre.

While Mac and Gnarly watched, the man in the gray suit stuck his finger up his beak-shaped nose. After taking his finger out of his nose, he smiled a good morning to them. His rotten teeth were the same color as his suit.

Mac nodded a "how do you do?" before catching a whiff of an unpleasant odor that announced the approach of someone in dire need of a long hot shower with plenty of soap. Mac let out a cough while fighting the turn in his stomach that threatened to result in becoming sick.

Seemingly puzzled by the ill expression on Mac's face, the bird-nosed man smirked before going inside.

The Blue Jay baseball fan held open the door for the bird-nosed man to enter the café. Carrying his cup of coffee, Blue Jay fan touched the bill of his cap before heading back across the parking lot in the direction of the bridge to the other side of the lake.

"Are you ready to go?" Mac asked Gnarly, who was licking his chops.

He took up the leash and then stopped when he saw a white van parked directly across the street. David's black cruiser pulled into the hotel parking lot and stopped in the space alongside it. The SUV was a few seconds ahead of the black limousine that was stopped at the corner by the red light.

"We need to go, Gnarly," Mac said. *We need to go now.*

With that, the two of them ran across the parking lot, and hurtled the barrier between the café's parking lot and the real estate office next door. They ran down the street to the next traffic light to cross the intersection and jogged back up the other side toward David's cruiser.

Mac ducked behind the SUV in time to see the limousine pull into the parking lot for the Dockside Café.

Chapter Nine

"I take it things are happening," Mac said when the back of the white van opened to invite him and Gnarly to join the party hosted by two men whom he had never met.

In the van, crowded with audio surveillance equipment, one of the men was having a soft conversation with David, who was in his police chief's uniform.

"Who's watching Archie?" Mac asked Randi Finnegan.

"Bogie and half of the Spencer police force are protecting her," Randi said, "not to mention your security people." She added, "All of my charges should be so heavily guarded."

"It's going down now." David nodded out the front windshield.

Tommy Cruze's limousine was pulling into the Dockside Cafe.

"What a small world," Mac said. "I just came out of there."

Randi introduced Mac to the agent in the front passenger seat of the van. "This is Special Agent Sid Delaney. He's my inside guy with the organized crime bureau." She gestured at the other agent manning the audio equipment. "That's Tony Bennett."

"Tony Bennett?" Mac smiled at the agent. "Any relation?"

The young man grinned back. "As a matter of fact, we're cousins."

Mac blinked. "Cousins? I'm sorry, but you're kind of young to be Tony Bennett's cousin."

"Tony?" Now it was Agent Bennett's turn to be confused. "My cousin's name is Haley. Who are you talking about?"

Randi leaned over to tell him. "Tony's a famous singer— a little before your time." She told Mac, "Haley is a movie actress—a little after your time."

David reminded them of their reason for being there. "Tommy Cruze is meeting his contract killer in that café."

Agent Delaney pointed out the group across the street that had climbed out of the limousine. "You're not going to believe who's with Cruze."

They all crowded forward to see. In addition to the driver scoping out the landscape, Tommy Cruze was deep in conversation with a bald man with a bushy white mustache.

"Who is that?" Mac asked about their interest.

"Alan Richardson," Special Agent Delaney answered. "We've been trying to prove for a long time that he's more involved with Cruze's operation than purely with his legal counsel. If he's there when Cruze puts out the order for this hit, we'll have him on accessory and conspiracy."

"Richardson was the last call that Ginger Altman made on her cell phone," David said.

"Really?" Delaney asked with a pleased smile.

"Here comes the hit man," Agent Bennett said. "The show is about to start, lady and gentlemen."

Mac moved up toward the front of the van to gaze out the windshield. He recognized one of the two men going inside as the body guard, the enforcer, who had been sitting in the front of the limousine the day before.

The enforcer peered around the parking lot while talking with his companion, a muscular man dressed in a black. He had tattoos going up his neck. Both of their eyes darted around the parking lot. When they spotted the van, the men turned away to face the other direction.

Realizing that both the enforcer and the hit men were undercover federal agents, Mac smirked.

They were going into the café when the woman whom Mac had seen stumble in the parking lot earlier shot out through the open door with her bird-beaked companion close behind her.

"Nora, what did you expect me to do?" The group in the van could hear the scrawny man objecting through one of the federal agent's audio feed. "Do you want to see me killed? What was I supposed to do?"

"Be a man for once," they heard Nora answer before the agent wearing the mike went inside. The door closed to shut off the conversation.

Outside, Nora hurried across the parking lot in their direction with her companion lagging behind. As they passed the van on their way into the hotel, everyone ducked down and held their breath so that the couple wouldn't be aware of the conference inside—even Gnarly seemed to sense the need to be quiet.

"Coffee?" Mac recognized the deep, commanding voice of Tommy Cruze offering the new arrivals a drink before they started with the matter at hand.

"Black," one of the men said.

"Nothing for me," another voice Mac didn't recognize responded.

"Come on," Tommy ordered. "I don't trust a man who won't drink with me, even if it's only coffee."

"Then I guess we won't be doing business." They heard what sounded like someone standing up.

"Wait a minute," Tommy said. "Where are you going so fast?"

"I'm a busy man. I don't have time to waste on people I won't be doing any work for. Later."

Tommy laughed. The others at the table joined in before he said, "I like you. You have guts. I respect that in a man—but not in women—especially a woman who doesn't know who she's supposed to be scared of, or when. A woman like that needs to be taught a lesson—a good, long lesson that involves so much pain that she'll be begging you to put her out of her misery … which I don't want done until she's learned her lesson."

"We have a problem." Agent Delaney startled them out of the conversation.

A black SUV had pulled up near the parking lot entrance to the Dockside Café. Two men wearing jackets with "FBI" emblazed across the back in white block lettering got out.

"What is that about?" Randi asked.

Recalling the attempted hit on Archie, David said, "I don't think they're feds."

"No, they're not." Agent Delaney shook his head. "Those aren't government tags on that van. There's a hit going down."

Mac grasped the gun he wore in the waistband of his running pants. "The question is, who are they here to hit? The good guys or the bad ones?"

David threw open the door. "Doesn't matter. We need to stop them or we won't get enough evidence to nail Cruze."

Gnarly jumped out the door and trotted around to the back of the van.

As if the agents inside could hear him, Agent Delaney said into his mike, "Hurry up, guys. Get the goods on Cruze and get out of there."

Mac, David, and Randi jogged across the road in the direction of the parking lot. Each of them had taken out their guns and concealed them behind their backs.

His gold police chief's shield shining in the morning sun, David stepped up ahead of them. "Good morning," he called out in a cheery voice.

The man in the blue jacket who had fallen several feet behind his partner whirled around.

On David's left, Mac caught sight of the Uzi in the assassin's grip. "Gun!" Mac fired off three shots to drop the gunman with his hand on the trigger. A continuous spray of bullets went wild around the parking lot before the Uzi dropped out his hand.

While Mac dove to the left to take cover behind a car, David and Randi went to the other side to hide behind the assailants' van.

Unable to make it to the door, the remaining assailant fired off a spray from his automatic weapon while diving for cover in the space between Tommy Cruze's limousine and the café's catering van.

"At least they didn't get inside to blow our set up," Randi told David, who was calling on his radio for back up.

"Gee, like all these bullets flying in the parking lot isn't going to blow it." David called across the parking lot to Mac, "You okay?"

Mac gave him the signal of a thumbs up.

The federal agents' van was sitting helplessly across the street. Their parking space had a clear view of the café in order to keep tabs on Tommy Cruze. Now, since the assassin had a clear view of it, and there was no place for the agents to seek cover upon exiting, it had become a kill zone. Agents Delaney and Bennett couldn't come out to assist Mac, David, and Randi without getting cut in half by the Uzi.

"Back up is coming," David signaled to Mac at the same time that a spatter of shots came from behind the limousine when the shooter opened fire.

Glass rained down on them from car windows. Metal and gravel flew around them. Screaming, Randi ducked while David covered her as best he could. As fast and furious as the bullets were flying, their weapons were no match. They were outgunned.

As abruptly as the shooting started, it stopped.

For a moment, there was silence while Mac, Randi, and David held their breath.

Mac felt his chest. His heart was still beating as fast as it could.

Anguished screams came from the direction of the shooter. He sounded like a victim of a monster from some horror film—specifically, a werewolf movie. His cry was liberally mixed with snarling growls.

Mac rose to his feet and peered around from behind the car.

The bloodied body was sprawled on the ground in the middle of the parking lot where the shooter had tried to escape the ambush that had come up from behind.

His face covered with blood and the strap of the Uzi in his jaws, Gnarly trotted out from behind the limousine and over to Mac. The dog dropped the weapon at his master's feet as if it were a stick he had retrieved in a game of fetch.

"When you said back up was coming, I assumed they would be in a police cruiser," Randi told David, "not a dog collar."

"Are you okay?" Agent Bennett asked them. "If it wasn't for your dog coming up over the top of the van—I never saw anything like it, except maybe in a military special forces K-9."

Special Agent Delaney ran past them and into the Dockside Café.

David and Randi were examining the two dead assassins. Gnarly had ripped open the throat of the man who had them pinned. Blood had sprayed from the severed jugular vein and coated the sides of the van and the limousine.

"I guess the operation is blown." Mac knelt to examine Gnarly. Blood dripped from his jowls. "They can't get Tommy Cruze on soliciting murder for hire."

"Now it's a whole different ball game," Bennett said.

The woman who had served Mac his coffee came running out of the café with her daughter in her arms. Hysteria filled her face. "Help! Somebody help us!" A large handbag flapping from where it hung off her shoulders, she ran to Randi who hugged both her and the little girl.

"What's going on?" David asked Agent Bennett.

"People are dropping dead inside the cafe."

Chapter Ten

"Three dead mobsters inside and two dead outside." In the parking lot, Bogie shook his head to make sense of it all when he and the whole Spencer police force arrived on the scene.

The FBI agents had also called in their people, who were still moments away.

Mac saw that Randi was still comforting the café owner and her daughter. Clutching her toy dog, the little girl looked frightened, but wasn't at all as hysterical as her mother.

The US Marshal stepped across the parking lot to where Mac was filling in Bogie. "We need to get Leah and her daughter out of here before the media arrives. Cameras are going to be everywhere, and we need to get her to a secure location before that happens."

"Who's Leah?" Bogie asked.

Randi nodded over to the café owner. "Her daughter's name is Sari. With this happening in her café, and Tommy Cruze's organization involved—"

"There are those who will assume she was involved in some way and retaliate," Mac finished.

"Can I take them back to Spencer Manor in David's cruiser?" she asked Bogie. "I'm afraid with members of organized crime in the area—"

Mac clasped his hand on her arm. "Wait a minute."

"I don't have a minute."

"Leah and her daughter are your charges," Mac said in a low voice. When she tried to argue, he interrupted, "You're in plain clothes. David's in his uniform. But when she came running out of the café, she ran to you." He gestured at the dead assassins. "Who were they after? Tommy Cruze or her? Who's after her?"

"I can't tell you that." Randi glanced over at Leah, who was hugging her daughter as tightly as she could.

His arms folded over his chest, Bogie ordered her to answer. "I'm laying my life on the line to protect these young ladies. I have a right to know who from."

"The mob," Randi whispered. "Leah used to be married to someone very high up in organized crime, but he wasn't in Tommy Cruze's organization. Her husband was abusive, and she put up with it. After she had Sari, she decided to leave, but knew he'd never let her go. So two years ago she collected everything she could get her hands on, walked into the FBI offices, and offered it all in exchange for a new life for her and her daughter." She added, "Leah has provided us with invaluable information on all of the inner workings of some of the biggest crime syndicates on the West Coast. That's why we relocated her in the East."

Bogie unfolded his arms. "Did this Ginger who gave away Archie's location also know Leah's?"

Randi yanked her arm out of Mac's grip. "She certainly had access to it."

Mac squinted at Leah and her young daughter. "Don't you find it very interesting that Cruze chose *this* café to have breakfast at?"

Randi sighed. "Interesting isn't the word I was thinking of."

"I'm escorting all of you back to Spencer Manor." Bogie turned to Mac. "Will you explain to the chief?"

Mac nodded his agreement.

Bogie called to the German shepherd rolling on his back in the nearby grass to take care of an itch between his shoulder blades. "We'll take Gnarly with us so he doesn't contaminate the crime scene."

"Don't clean him up," Mac said. "He took down one of the shooters, so the feds will need to process him for evidence."

Noting the blood encrusted on Gnarly's snout and in his mane, Bogie held up his hands in surrender. "I don't want to be the one to tell Archie that she's going to have to cancel his appointment with Misty." He peered down at Mac from under his big, bushy gray eyebrows.

"Archie will understand."

"But will Gnarly?" Bogie asked.

"Gnarly's a big dog," Mac said. "He can handle it."

Gnarly was glancing back and forth between the two men with a questioning look on his face.

"Are you sure about that?" Bogie asked Mac before turning back to his cruiser.

Randi ushered the café owner and her daughter into Bogie's cruiser. Ignoring Bogie's direction for him to sit in the back, Gnarly jumped into the front passenger seat and refused to budge. Giving up without a fight, Bogie climbed into the driver's seat and sped off in the direction from which he had come only minutes before.

Mac watched them race across the bridge and roll along Lakeshore Drive. As they disappeared from sight, the van from the morgue and the medical examiner's car arrived. The medical examiner was covering the dead bodies up with white sheets when Mac went inside to learn about the other murders.

✳   ✳   ✳

Inside the café, Mac found David trying to gather information from the one remaining witness who had survived the incident.

The round table in the center of the dining room and the six chairs that had surrounded it were overturned. Bodies were scattered on the floor like fallen tin soldiers in a child's playroom.

Mac recognized the squat form of Tommy Cruze, sprawled on the floor with his arms and legs twisted like a Gumby doll. His eyes and mouth were open wide. A few feet away, his driver-slash-bodyguard was the same. One of his arms was twisted behind his back where he had landed on it. His lifeless eyes gazed up at Mac. Both men's chins, necks, chests, and abdomens were covered in blood that had spewed out of their mouths and nostrils.

Lying near the coffee counter was the man Mac had seen come in with the assassin.

Someone's missing.

"Where's the hit man?" Mac whispered to Special Agent Delaney, who was kneeling next to the mobster's enforcer. He recalled that less than twenty-four hours before, this same man was pointing a gun at his head.

"What hit man?" Delaney shot him a smirk.

Mac cocked his head at him.

"Richardson says this is everybody," the special agent said.

Mac gazed down at the body sprawled out at his feet. Unlike Cruze and his bodyguard, the enforcer, who had recruited the hit man tasked with killing Archie, was spotless. There wasn't a drop of blood on him.

Lauren Carr

Special Agent Delaney gestured over at the cash register where Alan Richardson was mopping his sweaty bald head with a linen handkerchief while David questioned him. "Maybe you can help your police chief get some useful information out of Cruze's lawyer."

The doors flew open and the morgue attendants came in with a gurney and body bag. Special Agent Delaney gestured at them. "Over here. This one goes first."

Mac whirled around to watch Delaney direct them in bagging the body and getting him out. *Before the ME can do his one scene examination? But—* When he saw Delaney cast a warning look in his direction, Mac turned back to the coffee counter.

"I don't know what you're talking about." With his handkerchief, Alan Richardson wiped down his bushy mustache. "There was no one else here."

"Are you sure about that?" David asked with a straight face. "Three dead men. They certainly didn't drop dead from natural causes. Someone had to have done something to make that happen."

Catching David's eye, Mac put on a straight face as well. To let Richardson know they were waiting outside would be to blow the undercover agents' covers.

"Unless you mean the owner and her creepy daughter," the lawyer responded.

"What's so creepy about her daughter?" Mac asked.

Richardson shot him a glance. "She doesn't talk. You say hello to her and she looks like she's going to jump out of her skin."

"Maybe she looks scared because she is scared," Mac said. "You're not exactly Mr. Rogers."

The lawyer turned to the police chief while cocking his head in Mac's direction. "Who is this guy?"

"Mac Faraday is a homicide detective," David said. "He works on contract with the Spencer police department on special cases."

Mac caught a wink from David in his direction. The police chief had lied as smoothly as if they had sorted it out before Tommy Cruze had dropped dead.

"Tell us what happened," David ordered Alan Richardson.

The lawyer wiped the beads of sweat from his bald head. "My client, Tommy Cruze, and I came here for a breakfast meeting with a couple of associates."

"What type of associates?" Mac stepped aside to allow the morgue attendants to wheel out the gurney with the enforcer in the sealed body bag.

Alan Richardson paused to watch the gurney leaving. His face grew pale. His flabby jowls quivered.

"Mr. Richardson?" David prodded him. "What happened here? Who were those men with the automatic weapons outside?"

"Were they after your client?" Mac asked. "Maybe settling an old score? Or was it a new one?"

"Tommy Cruze is—was—a legitimate businessman," Alan insisted.

"Yeah. Right," Mac responded.

"He was framed for the murder that he went to jail for," Richardson said. "The fed that led the investigation was crooked—and now he's sitting in Cruze's cell. The judge saw it for what it was and overturned the conviction."

"And how much did you pay that judge to flip the conviction?" Special Agent Delaney had come over to ask.

"Don't answer that, darling." A tall, leggy redhead in a white business suit filled the doorway leading in from the reception area.

Mac wasn't into buxom bombshells who looked like they belonged in the centerfold of a magazine. He preferred his women petite and sleek—the type he could pick up in his arms—like Archie. But, as he looked at the redhead, he thought that if he were into bombshells—here was one. He could see by the drop of Delaney's jaw that this woman was his type.

When the redhead stepped in, she gazed down at the floor in the direction of the dead bodies. Delaney reached out his arm to block further entrance. "You can't come in, ma'am. This is a crime scene."

"She's allowed," Richardson said. "Ariel is my attorney. We're business partners." He grasped her arm to pull her around. "She's also my wife."

Her eyes still on Tommy Cruze's motionless body, she said, "Richardson can't answer any questions without my being present."

"Mrs. Richardson," Mac said, "since you and your husband are partners, then I guess that means you worked for Tommy Cruze, too?"

"She never met Cruze." Alan stepped between them to block his view of her. "I met Ariel after Tommy went to prison. She's had no connection with him or his business in any way, shape, or form."

"While you were in with him up to your eyebrows," Special Agent Delaney said.

"Doesn't matter now, does it?" Alan replied. "You got what you wanted. Cruze is dead."

While Alan ranted on at the federal agent and David, Mac watched Ariel staring at Cruze's body on the floor. Feeling his eyes on her, she lifted her eyes to meet his. Fear filled them before she turned away.

Alan continued, "I wouldn't be surprised if those hit men outside wearing FBI jackets really did belong to you."

"If it wasn't for your agents being either crooked or incompetent," Ariel interjected, "that animal would still be locked up. But you couldn't put Cruze away and keep him there, so someone had to do the job for you."

"Like your husband?" David asked.

Pointing a long dagger of a fingernail in his direction, Ariel turned to the police chief. "You better watch who you go throwing accusations at."

"I had nothing to do with Cruze's extracurricular activities," her husband said.

"You're full of it, Richardson," Delaney said. "Cruze is dead. You aren't on his payroll anymore. So you can cut the crap and tell us who offed him. Or were you the target? Maybe Ray Bonito decided he was tired of being number two, especially after ten years of running the operation, and decided to eliminate the top man—and his lawyer—to clear the field."

"I wouldn't be surprised," Ariel replied. "Bonito is a certified psychopath. Not only that, but he was none too happy when Cruze's conviction was overturned. When you make an insane man unhappy, you have a gourmet recipe for a blood bath."

"Ray Bonito is crazy," her husband said. "I haven't seen him in over a year and a half. He's become paranoid, which happens to many men who get into bed with organized crime figures. After years of looking over your shoulder to see who's waiting to stab you in the back—literally—you can't help but become paranoid and cut yourself off from everyone." He added, "The only ones he'll have face-to-face meetings with are his most trusted men."

"And that doesn't include you?" Mac asked.

"You want to know how paranoid Ray Bonito is?" Richardson asked. "I'll tell you. Tommy Cruze couldn't even get in to see him. Ever since he got out, Tommy's been trying to have a face to face with Bonito—and Bonito works for Cruze, not the other way around."

Special Agent Delaney asked, "Are you saying Cruze was still running things while he was in jail?"

"Working remotely is all the rage nowadays," the mob lawyer said with a chuckle.

"Bonito set up this hit," Ariel said in a harsh voice while casting a glance at Tommy Cruze's body once more. "Ray Bonito is the one you should be questioning."

"What's Bonito's favorite MO?" Mac gestured at the two dead bodies being examined by the county medical examiner. "Firing squad or poison?"

Richardson shook his head. "Poison? That's much too tame for Ray Bonito." Looking around, he pointed at the two men twisted in death poses on the floor. "I haven't a clue about who did this. The only thing I can think of is the lady who runs the place. After all, everything we ate and drank came from her."

Examining the array of overturned coffee mugs, smashed creamers, and sugar packets scattered all over the floor where they had fallen when the table was overturned, Mac asked, "Was there anyone else here when you came in?"

"Besides that woman and her weird daughter—"

Richardson backed up when David abruptly stepped up to him. "That 'weird daughter' is a child. You don't know anything about her—the way she lives, where she comes from. So when you talk about that little girl, you do it with respect. Do you understand me?"

Ariel jumped to her husband's defense. "Do you know who you're talking to?"

Pulling her back from where she was chastising the police chief, Richardson nodded his head. Beads of sweat poured down the sides of his face to soak the collar of his shirt.

Mac pointed at a table for two against the window looking out on the deck. The napkins had been used, but the table was clear of any food or drinks. "Was someone sitting here?"

"When we came in," Richardson said. "A couple. But then, right after we sat down, they got into a fight and left."

"Fight over what?" Mac asked.

"I have no idea." Richardson shook his head. "Suddenly out of the blue, the wife had a meltdown and stormed out with her wuss husband chasing after her."

Mac recalled hearing the wife, Nora, on the audio saying that she wished he could be a man for once. Now Richardson referred to the husband as a "wuss." "Did you or Cruze or any of his people or associates say anything to them?"

Richardson shook his head. "None of us knew them or ever saw either of them before." He cocked his head at Mac. "Are you thinking that maybe they planted the poison that killed Cruze?"

"Tommy Cruze made a fortune out of making enemies," Delaney told him. "There's no telling what score that couple may have been settling."

"We didn't decide we were even coming here until this morning," Richardson said. "Those two were here when we came in. If they came to kill Cruze, then how did they know we were going to be here, and how did they do it?"

"Good question," Mac said while watching David answer his radio.

The police chief's eyes widened and his mouth dropped before he turned away and stepped into the reception area away from them. "Are you kidding me?"

Alan pointed a finger at the federal agent while saying, "I'm telling you…it doesn't take a brain surgeon to figure out what happened and who did it. It was that couple who was here and then left. They must have worked for Bonito."

Seeing David whirl around while pressing his radio to his ear, Mac excused himself to join him. The thought of Archie falling victim to the crime spree that had invaded Spencer gripped his heart. He tugged on David's sleeve to get his attention. "What's going on?"

"They have a DB at a bed and breakfast on Lakeshore Drive."

"Possible homicide?"

"Maybe accidental," David said. "Thing is, I can't leave this." He gestured at the two dead bodies on the floor in the middle of the café.

"Finnegan took the café owner and her daughter to Spencer Manor," Mac said, "and Bogie went with them."

"He's the only other one on the force with experience in possible homicides." David cocked his head at him and narrowed his eyes. "What are you not telling me?"

"Those assassins outside may very well not have been coming after Cruze."

David cursed.

His radio crackled. "Chief," the operator called out. "Who do you want me to send? Fletcher?"

Mac tapped David on the shoulder. Once he had his attention, he tapped his fingers against his own chest. "I can go. You just told Richardson that I'm on contract with the Spenser police. I've investigated hundreds of murders, and I'm still certified by the state as an investigator. I can handle one little DB at a B and B."

David looked Mac up and down and noticed that he was still in his running sweats. After a heavy sigh, he told him, "Okay. But you can't go like that. Take my cruiser, swing by the station, and take a quick shower. I have an extra set of clothes in my locker. They'll fit you. I'll have Tonya give you a badge and service weapon."

Chapter Eleven

"Gnarly, there you are." Archie came out onto the front porch to greet Bogie's cruiser when it rolled through the Spencer Manor entrance. Once again, she was dressed in her soft gray suit for an outing at the Spencer Inn after dropping Gnarly off at the Doggie Hut. When she saw the German shepherd, covered in blood, jump out through the cruiser's open window, she shrieked. "What happened to you?"

"He took down a hit man," Bogie told her before opening the rear door to let his other passengers out. "You don't want to see how the other guy looks."

"Mac—" she gasped.

"Mac's fine," Bogie said. "But there's a mess at the Dockside Café. Tommy Cruze is dead."

Archie sighed with relief.

"That's the good news," Bogie said. "The bad news is that since Gnarly took out one of the dead hit men, he's now covered with evidence. The feds are going to be coming out here to process him. That means you have to cancel his appointment with Misty."

"Do you know how hard it is to get an appointment with Misty?" Archie's hands were on her hips. "I'm supposed to leave him like *this…*"

Hanging his head like a guilty child, Gnarly sat before her.

"Would it make you feel better if I went back to the Dockside and killed Tommy Cruze a second time?" Bogie offered.

"It's not me I'm concerned about. It's Gnarly." She pointed to the dog, who had lain down. With a long, mournful whine, he rested his head on her pumps. "Look at him. He's devastated. He loves Misty. You should see him when he leaves the Doggie Hut after one of her deep body massages. She makes him feel so handsome." She stomped one of her feet. "Oh, I hate Tommy Cruze for doing this to Gnarly. If he was still alive I'd go shoot him myself."

"I'd hate to be Cruze right now." The deputy chief went into the house.

After digesting that bad news, Archie noticed Randi Finnegan and two new faces.

"More refugees from the mob," Randi said. "This is Leah Juliano and her daughter, Sari." She went on to explain that they had been placed in the area two years earlier after being put in the program.

"Well, hello, Sari." Archie knelt down by the little girl who had squirmed out of her mother's arms and was showing Gnarly her stuffed dog. "You're a beautiful little girl. How old are you?"

Sari's eyes met Archie's for only a moment before she turned her attention back to Gnarly.

"Sari doesn't talk," Leah said.

"That's too bad." Archie rose to her feet. "Why not?"

"She just stopped talking one day." Leah looked up and around at the stone and cedar mansion. "Is this your house?"

"I live here," Archie said. "It's complicated."

"Sleeping with the big man for money, huh?" Leah laughed. "That's not complicated. It's the way of the world."

Giving up on trying to like the woman Randi had brought to Spencer Manor, Archie asked, "What would be the odds of a witness hiding from the mob having a mob hit go down in her establishment? Who would have thought?"

"I never saw any of those people before in my life," Leah said forcibly.

"I wasn't saying—" Archie said by way of an apology.

"Come, Sari." The café owner pulled her daughter by the arm up to her feet. "We need to wash your hands. That dog is filthy." Without invitation, Leah dragged her daughter inside the house.

With an apology in her eyes, Randi nodded at Archie. "I think it's the culture clash. Leah can be—"

"Rude." Archie added, "It's not culture. It's lack of manners."

"She'll be relocated within two days," Randi said. "With so many mob figures in the area now, I'm afraid of taking her to the Spencer Inn or any public place."

"She and her daughter can stay," Archie said.

"Thank you, Archie," Randy said. "I knew I could count on you. You're such a class act."

"I'm not doing it for her," Archie said. "It's for her daughter." She whirled around on her heels and went inside to call Misty to beg for another chance for Gnarly.

❊   ❊   ❊

In the upscale resort town of Spencer, Maryland, where many of the town's residents were listed in "Who's Who", the small police station resembled a sports club. Located along the shore of Deep Creek Lake, the log building that was home to the police department sported a dock with a dozen jet skis and four speed boats. Its fleet of police cruisers was top of the line SUVs painted black with gold lettering on the side that read "SPENCER POLICE." For patrolling the deep woods and mountain trails, they had eight ATVs. Like the cruisers, all of the vehicles were black with gold trim.

David was on the mark when he surmised his clothes would fit his older half-brother. After a quick shower in the police chief's private bathroom on the top floor at the station, Mac slipped into a pair of dress slacks, a button-down shirt, and a blue sports jacket that he had found in David's locker. Mac chuckled when he discovered that David's shoes, however, were one size too small. That meant he had to wear his worn running shoes.

Tonya, the desk sergeant, smiled up at him when he came downstairs. "My, my. If you had blond hair, I would have thought you were the chief."

Knowing that she was unaware of the familial relationship he shared with David, Mac only grinned.

Tonya had lived on the lake her whole life. Many suspected that the long hours she put in at the station were an excuse to not go home, to where two of her three grown children had returned with their offspring after a short time spent in the outside world.

"Gnarly's not riding shotgun with you on this case?" Tonya was a huge fan of every dog. Sometimes, Mac felt like she was simply going through the paces while making small talk until they arrived upon the topic of Gnarly and his latest escapades. She had three dogs of her own that she doted on more than her kids. The dogs were more self-sufficient.

"Not this time," Mac answered.

"Doc Washington is meeting you at the scene." She handed him a pen to sign for his gold police shield, that of a detective, and police-issued gun, a Colt semi-automatic. "So what's the word with you and your mother's lovely assistant?"

Mac paused with the pen an inch from the paper. His eyes met Tonya's. She arched an eyebrow in his direction. In the two years he had known her, he had never known the motherly desk sergeant to miss a thing.

"Tommy Cruze is dead," Mac said. "That made our day."

"Made a lot of people's day." She lowered her voice. "Now that the contract on Archie has most likely gone away, is she moving back into the guest cottage or is she going to …" She cast him a naughty smile.

"We'll see." He felt his cheeks warm.

"Oh, I should have known," Tonya laughed. "You're exactly like the chief. Never kiss and tell. Though Bogie did tell me not only did Archie move into the Spencer Manor's main house, but also that she moved into your bedroom, which only has one bed."

Mac joined in her laughter. "The fact that Archie and I are very close was never any secret."

"Well, I'll tell you this," she tapped him on the chest to make her point, "I'm expecting a wedding invitation when you two have your big, swanky social event of the year at the Spencer Inn in the main ballroom. I'll even buy a dress for the occasion."

"Don't worry. Every officer on the force will get an invitation, and we'll expect them all to come."

Before Mac realized what he had said, Tonya let out a whoop. "I knew it!" She jumped back and pointed at him. "You did ask her, and she said yes! I could tell when you walked in that you had a glow about you. Tell me how you asked her. Did you get down on one knee? Did she cry?"

Suddenly overwhelmed with tears of joy, she rushed around her desk to take Mac into a bear hug. As soon as she regained her voice, she returned to firing off questions about the proposal: when, where, and how big will the diamond be.

While she was firing off questions, Mac shushed her. Finally, she quieted down so he could tell her, "I haven't told David yet. So don't tell anyone."

"He'll be happy," she replied with confusion. "Why wouldn't you tell him?"

"I haven't had a chance," Mac said. "Besides, he may feel like he's intruding on us living at the manor."

"I didn't think about that," she said. "Once he sells his house, he'll be able to move into a place of his own."

"The way the market is, and as old as that house is, it may be forever before he can sell it," Mac said. "I'm going to offer him the guest cottage."

"Doesn't Archie use the guest cottage for her office?" Tonya asked.

Mac clipped the police shield to his belt. "She can use the study, where Robin used to write her books." Seeing tears in Tonya's eyes, he feared that she would spill the beans before he had a chance to personally tell David. "Remember, this is our secret. I don't want David to hear this through the grapevine. I want him to hear it from me."

"Is Gnarly going to give Archie away?" Tonya wiped a tear from her eye. "He does have to be in the wedding. You can't not let Gnarly take part in it."

"There's someone else I need to break the news to."

＊　＊　＊

Vacation rentals, ranging from cozy and rustic to luxurious estate living, lined the shore of Deep Creek Lake. There's something for everyone.

Some homeowners converted their estate homes into bed and breakfasts to help ease the financial burden of owning a home at such an exclusive address. For some, it was the only way they could own on Deep Creek Lake. Other homeowners enjoyed meeting new people from all walks of life in the pleasant setting. In exchange for a room with a view of the lake, the guest would share a filling breakfast with the homeowner, who, intimate with the goings on, could advise where, and where not, to go.

Located along a quiet cove in the Spencer corner of the lake, the Skeltner Cove Bed and Breakfast was a sprawling, three-story log home. A private dock and beach were among the amenities it offered its guests. The county medical examiner's van was parked in the road at the end of the wooden plank walkway.

When Mac pulled David's cruiser into the driveway, he saw that the sign for the bed and breakfast had a notice hanging from a hook underneath it that read "NO VACANCIES."

On his way inside, he paused to admire the view of the lake from the porch. The bridge was a little over two miles away. Across the water, the Dockside Café was so close that he could make out the flashing lights from the emergency vehicles.

"Great view, huh?" a woman's voice startled Mac out of his focus on the scene across the way. Before he turned around, he placed the voice. It was Dr. Dora Washington, the medical examiner, who had come out of the house while his back was turned. "I see David had to call in his reserves."

As always, Mac was struck by her flawless figure and blue-black hair that she always wore in a silky ponytail that spilled down to the middle of her back. She looked more like she belonged on the cover of a fashion magazine than cutting up dead people in the morgue.

When he had first met the medical examiner, after getting beyond her physical beauty, Mac was struck by how brilliantly smart she was. Dr. Washington had nailed Mac and David's sibling relationship by their second meeting based purely on their eye color, cheekbones, and jaw-line. During a consultation in her office, she bluntly asked David for confirmation of her assessment. She had the class to keep that information to herself.

"Not your average tranquil lakeside living." Mac gestured to the inside of the house. "Are you finished doing your thing?"

"Yes. Now I'm waiting for you," she said. "I told them not to move the body until you got a look at her." The corner of her lip curled into a smirk. "It will seem like old times for you."

"Homicide?"

She flipped her ponytail back over her shoulder. "I don't make that call until I open 'em up." She turned around to head back inside.

Mac followed her. "And I don't make it until I take a look at the scene and speak to the witnesses."

After stepping across the threshold, she turned left into a foyer stairwell. The dead woman was still resting in a heap at the bottom of the stairs with her feet and legs up above her head. The blood splatters on the hardwood steps and along the wall in the long stairwell were telling. Out of respect, the medical examiner had covered her with a white sheet.

After slipping on his evidence gloves, Mac squatted down next to the body and lifted the sheet to examine her.

She resembled a discarded rag doll. Her pink nightgown was worn and faded. Her hair was thin with bald patches on her scalp. Her arms were withered and thin to resemble skin draped over bones.

"She's been dead a little over an hour," Dora said while he peered at the dead woman from every angle. "I pinpoint the time of death at between six-forty-five and seven o'clock. It looks like she bounced down the stairs with her head hitting every step the whole way down." The doctor was not exaggerating. Her face and head were bloody and scarred.

Mac cocked his head while looking at the scrapes and scratches on her thin arms. *Defense wounds.*

"Who is she?" He removed the paper bag that Dr. Washington had encased her hands in to preserve evidence. Strands of dark hair were embedded under her fingernails along with black fiber.

"Mary Catherine Skeltner," she said. "Half of the couple that own this place. Husband is back in the kitchen. I told him to wait for you to get his statement."

"She put up a fight before going down the stairs." Mac showed the medical examiner her hands.

"Very good." She smiled down at him. "It must be in the genes."

They heard hushed voices and footsteps coming from the dining room into the foyer. Swiftly, he put the bag back on her hand and sealed it with the rubber band.

"I saw the cruiser pulling in," the male voice was saying as he approached the foyer from behind Mac. "Now that the police detective is here, I'm hoping that this can be taken care of as quickly and painlessly as possible."

"Russell Skeltner," Dora said, "I'd like you to meet Mac Faraday. He's the detective working for the Spencer police department."

Mac rose to his feet.

"As you can see, Detective Faraday," the husband said, "it's pretty clear what happened. My wife slipped and fell down the stairs. Accidental death."

"An investigation needs to be conducted before that decision can be made." When Mac turned around, he recognized the blue running suit and Toronto Bluejay's ball cap. It was the jogger from the Dockside Café. Mac offered his hand. "We meet again."

"Really?" Russell Skeltner shook his head. "I'm afraid—"

"Coffee shop this morning," Mac reminded him.

A wide grin crossed Russell Skeltner's face. "The runner with the dog. German shepherd. He stole your breakfast."

"Actually, he didn't steal it. I bought it for him."

"That's not how it looked—"

Tired of his attitude and the smirk on Dora's face at the reference of the infamous Gnarly winning yet again, Mac nodded in the direction of the dead woman lying at their feet. "What happened here?"

A somber expression filled Skeltner's face. "My wife was killed falling down the stairs."

"You seem less than upset about it," Mac noted.

Russell Skeltner sucked in a deep breath and folded his arms across his chest. "Mary Catherine has been sick for years. Cancer. They did everything to save her. Before she came down with it, she was a vibrant woman. Athletic. We'd go running together every day. After zapping her with everything imaginable, they saved her life, but it ended up being a life not worth living." He pointed up the staircase. "You can see for yourself. She was taking thirty different pills a day. For the last two years, she has been bedridden and spaced out—sleeping twenty hours a day."

He ran his hand over the front of his athletic suit. "This morning I went running, like I do every day. Before I left, I set a glass of juice on her bed stand so she could wash down her pills when she woke up. When I came home an hour later, I found this, and a spilt glass of juice upstairs."

He offered his theory. "She spilt her juice and tried to come downstairs to get another glass, but fell and killed herself." He concluded with a wave of his arms. "Accidental death."

Mac looked from him to Dora, whose face was as devoid of expression as that of a professional poker player, and back to the husband of the dead woman lying in a pool of blood between them.

With each second of silence, the muscles in Russell's face tightened with impatience.

"I need to see your wife's bedroom," Mac finally said.

❋   ❋   ❋

While Dora went to work photographing the body and the scene for her records, Mac followed Russell Skeltner to the kitchen in the rear of the house and up the back staircase to the bedrooms on the second floor level.

"Do you have any guests staying here this weekend?" Mac asked in a pleasant tone. Even though the question was conversational, it was meant to determine if there were any other suspects.

"We haven't had guests since Mary Catherine got sick," he replied. "She always wanted to have a B and B on the lake."

At the top of the stairs, a county forensics officer was taking pictures of the stairs and each blood splatter on the way down. The Spencer police department was rich, but small, which meant they had to use the services and labs of the bigger departments around them for the more serious crimes.

Russell Skeltner led Mac down a hallway at the end of which was the master suite. The door was open to reveal a cluttered bedroom. Numbered place markers and rulers littered the room where the forensics officer, a young woman who Mac noted appeared about the same age as his son in college, had marked evidence to suggest what had led up to the woman's death.

"We were only here a few years and doing pretty good until it got too difficult for her to manage." Standing next to the doorway, Russell gestured for Mac to step inside.

The room contained a television blasting a reality program featuring a has-been teen pop star, a bed tray overturned on the floor, and a glass resting in the middle of an orange juice spill. There were clothes scattered about on the bed, a chair, and the floor. On the bed stand was row upon row of pill bottles.

The bathroom door was open to reveal a sink and counter that was cluttered with more pill bottles and women's cosmetics.

Mac noticed that the indentation in the mattress was in the center of the bed. There was a blood smear on the pillow case and a drop of blood on the bed poster next to the night stand. Both had been marked by the crime scene officer. The blood smear was over two inches long.

"The blood smear is old," Russell Skeltner told Mac when he noticed him studying it. "Mary Catherine would get nose bleeds—side effect from some of her meds."

"Where do you sleep, Mr. Skeltner?"

The husband's head snapped in Mac's direction in response to the question. "I sleep in one of the rooms at the end of the hall. Mary Catherine slept all hours of the day with the television blaring twenty-four-seven. It was impossible for me to sleep in the same room with that." He added, "But that doesn't mean I didn't love her."

With no response to the answer, Mac knelt down to examine the hardwood floor. Mary Catherine Skeltner had been sick and bedridden for so long that she did not have the time to devote to cleaning—especially her floor. The hardwood floor contained a layer of dirt and dust that had built up. Mac turned on his penlight to study the drag pattern on the floor leading from the bed to the hallway.

When he saw the beam catch on something to create a brilliant spark of light, Mac felt a jolt as his heart seemed to skip a beat. *What is that?* He lowered himself onto his hands and knees to get a closer look at the object resting against the side of the leg of the bed stand.

"I heard the ME tell you that the time of death was between six-forty-five and seven o'clock," Mac could barely hear

Russell saying. "I left the house at six-thirty to go running like I do every morning."

Mac resisted the temptation to touch it. "Mr. Skeltner, how's your eyesight?"

There was a moment of silence before he answered. "Twenty-twenty. Perfect. Why?"

"How about your wife?"

Another pause. "Terrible. She wore glasses. As you can see, she left them on the night stand. Probably another reason she fell down the stairs. She was so hyped up on drugs—"

Mac sat up to see that a pair of eyeglasses with thick lenses was indeed resting on the bed stand. "Then I guess she didn't wear contact lenses."

Another pause.

When he didn't receive an answer, Mac, still on his knees, turned to look up at Russell Skeltner. The two men's eyes met.

"No, Mary Catherine didn't wear contact lens," Russell answered.

Mac called down the hallway to the forensics officer. "We have a contact lens here on the floor that needs to be processed into evidence. It's not the victim's or husband's."

"My God," Russell gasped. "Mary Catherine was…murdered! I can't believe—" He fell back against the wall. "Every day, I go running along the shoreline and cross the bridge to go to the Dockside Café for coffee. Whoever did this must have realized my schedule and…I can't believe this is happening."

"Mr. Skeltner, you need to step out of this room into the hall in order for us to contain the scene." Mac ushered him out into the hallway to allow the forensics officer in to photograph and collect the contact lens.

While the forensics officer was taking pictures of the lens from various angles, Mac continued studying the drag marks on the floor. There was one clear path in the layer of dust—

leading from the bed and through the doorway out into the hall.

"Did you see the piece of her nightgown?" the officer pointed at a piece of material that had caught and been torn from a piece of clothing. "She was definitely dragged on her back to the top of the stairs."

Pink! Mac smiled. *Mary Catherine Skeltner's nightgown is pink!*

"Takes me about twenty to twenty-five minutes to jog to the café every morning," Russell Skeltner was telling Mac even while he was trying to concentrate on the drag marks in the hall. "Then, I jog back after drinking my espresso next to the lake. I always get there right when they open." He stepped away from the wall to tell Mac, "That was where we met this morning."

Mac looked up from where he was studying the torn material that had been ripped from the nightgown Russell Skeltner's wife had been wearing.

"My wife's time of death is the same time as when you and I met in front of the Dockside Café." A wide grin was filling Russell Skeltner's face. "Guess you can't ask for a better alibi witness than a homicide detective, can you?"

Chapter Twelve

Mac could feel Russell Skeltner peering out the window from inside his home—laughing at him. *I hate killers, especially smart killers who think they've gotten away with it.* He resisted the urge to slam the door of David's cruiser. *Don't give him the satisfaction.*

Replaying the different scenarios in his mind, Mac was clutching the cruiser's door handle when he noticed a movement in the other direction out of the corner of his eye. It was so far in his peripheral vision that he almost missed it. When he turned to look over his shoulder, he saw the curtain move in the window of the log cabin across the road.

Leaving the cruiser in the bed and breakfast driveway, Mac strolled over to the cottage. A yellow tabby cat greeted him when he stepped onto the walkway. After escorting the visitor to the door, the feline rubbed against Mac's leg until the door was opened by a tiny elderly woman dressed in a rose-colored house dress. The cat scurried inside.

"Hello, ma'am." Mac showed her the police shield he wore clipped to his belt next to his service weapon. "I'm Mac Faraday with the Spencer police department. I'm investigating the death of Mary Catherine Skeltner, the woman who lives across the road from you."

The old woman peered up at Mac with wide eyes. "Pat? Chief Pat?" A wide smile crossed her face, pushing her wrinkled cheeks up to make her eyes narrow slits of grayish-blue.

Mac felt a solemn smile come to his lips. He had seen several pictures of his birth father. The resemblance was striking. "No, Mac. I'm Mac Faraday. I live on—"

"They told me that you died several years ago. Your son David is supposed to be chief now."

Concluding that setting her straight would be a lost cause, Mac moved on to the reason for his visit. "I was wondering if you had noticed anything going on across the road this morning."

"Did you say Mary Catherine was dead?"

"Yes, ma'am, I'm afraid so."

Her face scrunched up in a scowl. "Her husband did it," she said in a harsh tone.

"Why would he kill her?"

"Because he didn't like living with a sick woman," she said. "Everything was fine when they had money and he could buy all his toys—expensive running shoes and travel all over the place to run-run-run-run, that's all he does is run—going to this marathon and that one and leaving his poor wife all alone and sick. I'm surprised he didn't kill her before now." She pointed a gnarled up finger at him. "I know you'll catch him, Chief Pat. He won't get away with it. You'll catch him—like you always do."

"Did you see him go running this morning?"

"Every morning." She nodded her head. "He went out running while I was in the kitchen putting on the tea kettle."

"What time was that?"

"Six-thirty," she said. "I get up at six-thirty every day. I don't need an alarm. I just wake up—have for years from when I used to teach school. Taught over in Oakland for forty years."

Mac frowned. "Did you see anyone else come by the house across the road after Mr. Skeltner left?"

"A boy on a bike," she answered. "The bike was silver. He was wearing black sweats with a hood up over his head." She stepped outside and pointed across the road to where she saw him. "He rode up and then got off and walked his bike around back behind the house. That was about fifteen minutes later. I know because I let my tea seep for fifteen minutes—" She tapped Mac's chest to make her point. "—*after* I put in the tea ball. I was pouring my tea when that boy rode up."

"About how old was this boy?"

Her face scrunched up in deep thought, she stared at the finger she was pressing against his chest. "Teenager. Maybe middle teens. Sixteen?"

Following the line from her finger poking him in the chest to the home across the road, Mac turned. "On a bike, huh?"

After climbing into the cruiser, Mac slowly drove along the road that followed the lake shore to the bridge and across to the café. He had difficulty keeping his eyes on the road while searching the bushes and hiking trails. Russell Skeltner could have hidden the bike to ride back to kill his wife, and then speeding back to hide it, all in order to get to the café in time to establish an alibi.

Only Russell Skeltner was much too tall and solidly built to be mistaken for a teenaged boy.

Maybe it was a teenager looking to steal some of Mrs. Skeltner's drugs. Nah! Russell Skeltner had to be behind it somehow.

At a pull-off right before the bridge, Mac spied the two elderly gentlemen who had called to him while he was jogging that morning. They were now packing up their gear. Year round residents of Spencer, they would fish from the same spot every morning when he would run by. As they had that morning, they would also notice everyone who crossed the bridge.

"Hey, there!" Mac waved to them after parking the cruiser in the dirt boat launch where one of the fishermen had parked his old truck. "How're the fish biting?"

Spying the cruiser, the two men exchanged quick glances before strolling up to where Mac was sitting in the car. "Hey, aren't you Mac Faraday?" One of them peered at him. "Robin Spencer's boy?"

After Mac confirmed that he was, they both looked over the SUV, noting the gold lettering that identified it as a Spencer police cruiser. "Since when are you working for the police?" one asked. The other inquired if Mac had lost all of his millions of dollars in the stock market.

"No, I'm working as a consultant for the Spencer police department." Mac assured them by showing them his police shield. "Only on this one case. A woman died suddenly this morning at the Skeltner Cove B and B—"

"Mrs. Skeltner?" The one fisherman jabbed his buddy with his elbow before telling him, "She was real sick with cancer."

"Is that the woman whose husband goes running by here every day while we're fishing?"

"Saw him just this morning," the other man replied. "Not long after you went by with Gnarly. How is Gnarly?"

"Gnarly is fine," Mac assured him.

"Why isn't he helping you on this case?" the old man asked in an accusatory tone.

Stunned by the question, Mac could only shake his head and shrug.

"Did Mr. Skeltner run by before or after I caught me that foot-long catfish?" the other man scratched the side of his head.

"It was either before or after," his companion answered.

Looking at Mac, the fisherman nodded his head. "Definitely before or after I caught that two-foot long catfish."

"Poor guy," his friend shook his head. "Wife sick all those years, then goes into remission only to die. When did it happen? How'd she die?"

"Shortly before seven o'clock," Mac answered. "By any chance, did you see someone ride by on a bike about that time?"

They both nodded. "Dressed in a black hoodie. He rode by heading in the opposite direction," one replied. "Couldn't miss him. He was speeding because when Skeltner was running up on the bridge, he almost hit Skeltner or something. I don't know what. All of a sudden, Skeltner yelled and was swearing at the kid on the bike."

"I saw Skeltner make an obscene gesture at him," his buddy confirmed with a nod of his head. "Didn't see what he did, but it really ticked Skeltner off."

Mac blinked. "You mean you saw them both at the same time?"

Nodding their heads quickly, one asked, "Why? Is that important?"

"Yes."

✳   ✳   ✳

"Russell Skeltner had his wife killed." Mac followed David from one desk to the other through the police station while making his case.

After returning from the cafe, the police chief was busy doing the mundane administrative chore of passing out messages, notices, and other types of office drudgery. Even though he could delegate the duties to Tonya, he preferred to do most of them himself.

"Well, that's going to be pretty hard for you to prove," David laughed while shoving an invitation to a police-fire-fighter ballgame into his hand, "considering that you're his alibi and the neighbor saw some kid in a black hoodie sneaking in while he was out running."

Folding up the notice without reading it, Mac shot back, "Then he had the kid in the black hoodie kill her for him while he was out setting up an alibi. Wouldn't be the first time."

"Just your luck that you happened to be on hand to become that alibi," David said with a smirk.

"They may be able to collect DNA from the contact lens," Mac said. "The problem is getting a suspect to compare it to."

"Why are you so convinced Skeltner is in on it?" David asked. "The woman was strung out on drugs. It could have been a kid after her meds."

"Skeltner didn't even try to appear remorseful about her being dead," Mac said.

David stopped and turned to him. "Did you say she had cancer?"

Mac nodded his head. "For the last three years."

"After years of watching his wife suffer, maybe Skeltner felt relief over her being out of her misery," David said in a gentle tone. "I'll admit that I felt relief when Dad finally passed. It's hard to watch a loved one suffer."

With a swallow, Mac pushed the image of the father he never met suffering a long, painful death and focused on the dead woman he had examined at the bottom of a flight of stairs. The image of Russell Skeltner's cocky smile came to the forefront. "Maybe he decided to help her along by having someone come in to kill her while he was setting me up to alibi him. Whoever it was, he's missing a contact lens, and we've got it."

"I'll call forensics to make sure they don't sit on that evidence." The paperwork dispersed, David jogged up the steps to his office.

Without waiting for an invitation, Mac followed him into his office. "What did you find out at the Dockside Café after I left?"

"The feds are taking the lead in both the shoot out and the apparent poisoning." David flipped through a stack of envelopes left in the center of his desk. "No surprise there. As thrilling as it is to be in charge of a multiple homicide, I really don't relish being involved in a mob case." He waved an envelope at Mac. "But from what little I know about organized crime, with Tommy Cruze dead, the contract on Archie is no more. Who's going to pay for hitting her? My guess is that she's safe now, but I'm not calling our people off security detail until we get a confirmation from the feds."

"Neither am I." Mac sighed with relief. "But it looks good." They were both safe. "Do you believe Richardson and his wife when they say Ray Bonito was behind the hit men in the parking lot?"

"Tommy Cruze was a legitimate businessman. Why would anyone want to hit him?" David said in a mocking tone. "Delaney agrees that it's most likely Ray Bonito. He ran the day-to-day operation while Cruze was in jail. When he got sprung, Cruze was expecting to take up where he had left off, and he wasn't known for taking no for an answer."

"So Bonito decided to send a hit squad to take Cruze out of the picture permanently," Mac said.

"That's the way they do it in the mob." Unwilling to deal with the stack of paperwork, David dropped the envelopes onto his desk.

Recalling Randi Finnegan's sudden departure with the café owner and her daughter, Mac said, "Or that hit squad could have been after someone else."

"You mentioned something about that earlier." David's head jerked up from the pile of mail. "What were you talking about?"

"You were inside when Finnegan scurried the café owner Leah and her daughter out of there."

"That's right," David said. "I thought they were removing the little girl from the scene."

Mac's eye caught that of the police chief.

"Are you kidding me?" David demanded to know. "Don't tell me that the café owner—"

"Her name is Leah," Mac said. "At least that's the name Finnegan told me."

David gripped his hips with his hands. "Is there *anyone* in Spencer who's *not* in the witness protection program?" He grabbed the side of his head while shaking it. "Then those gunmen could have been going after her. Who are they hiding her from?"

"A West Coast crime syndicate."

"Great," David said with heavy sarcasm. He wiped his hands against each other and then waved them both in the air as a gesture of tossing the matter aside. "Glad it's not our problem."

"The hit men outside could have been after either the café owner or Cruze," Mac said. "It's also up in the air as to who was the intended target of the poisoning. Who planted it? Richardson to take out Cruze? Whose side is Richardson really on? Cruze's or Bonito's?"

"Not our problem," David repeated, with a shrug. "Let's deal with what is our problem. You say Skeltner hired the guy on the bike to kill his wife while he set you up to be his alibi. Find the guy on the bike, or at least the bike."

"That should be easy," Mac said. "Here on Deep Creek Lake, there should only be a few hundred bikes."

Chapter Thirteen

"Oh, no!" Archie cried into the phone. "You can't do that! Can't you give me just another hour? Forensics should be here any minute."

"I'm sorry, Archie," Misty replied. "But my schedule is full and I have other clients waiting. This Pekingese has been trying to get in for three weeks."

"A Pekingese? Not a Pekingese."

Gnarly's head snapped up and around from where he was involved in a staring contest with Sari. He was lying in his favorite spot on the loveseat. Clutching her toy collie, the little girl sat on the sofa across from him.

"I feel for Gnarly," Misty told Archie. "Really, I admire him for being so heroic, but I can't hold appointments again and again indefinitely. Once things settle down over there, call in and reschedule."

Even though she understood, Archie was heartbroken for the German shepherd when she hung up the phone. "I'm sorry, Gnarly." She reached over the back of the loveseat to pat him on the top of the head. "Next week, I'll call and make another appointment for you."

Leah came up from the dining room with a plate of cookies and a glass of milk for Sari. "Would you like a snack, sweetie?"

The little girl sat up to peer at the plate of sugar cookies. The dog raised his head to take in the goodies only one long jump from his snout.

"Gnarly, no," Archie said in a firm tone.

Gnarly trained his eyes on the woman holding the plate of cookies.

Leah eyed the hundred pounds of fur and teeth. "Does he always look so mean?"

"He isn't really. Gnarly will behave himself," Archie said more to the dog than to her.

Together, the two women went into the dining room to join Randi, who was on her cell phone.

Archie could see one of Spencer's police officers out on the deck talking to one of the security guards from the Spencer Inn. Upstairs, Bogie had made it his duty to fix Mac's toilet. It was the first time she had ever seen a plumber packing a Colt semi-automatic in his tool belt.

"I guess the café is going to be closed for a while," Archie told her.

When Leah opened her bag and took out a tube of lipstick, Archie saw a smart phone resting on top of her wallet. "Yeah, I guess so." Leah stopped reapplying her lipstick to glance over at Randi. "We're blowing this joint. Within forty-eight hours it will be a new city and new identities."

Archie looked up into the living room where Sari was eating her snack. "Must be so hard for your daughter—being in the program at such a young age."

"She'll get used to it," Leah said with only a small drop of compassion.

"When did she stop talking?" Archie asked.

"Her father used to always say that children are to be seen and not heard," Leah said. "I guess one day she decided to make him happy and stop talking." Slipping her lipstick into her bag, she shrugged. "He never complained about her being too noisy after that."

"Have you tried therapy?"

Her hand still in her bag, Leah glared up at Archie. "Why? She's happy. As long as she's happy, then I'm happy. If everyone is happy, why mess with it?"

❋   ❋   ❋

In the living room, Sari clutched her stuffed dog tightly while eating one of the cookies her mother had brought to her. Her eyes met Gnarly's. The two of them stared at each other as if they could penetrate through each other's eyes to read each other's thoughts.

With a look over her shoulder, Sari saw that her mother was at the dining room table talking to the other two women. Silently, she slipped off the sofa, picked up a cookie, and, holding it out far in front of her, slowly moved across to the loveseat until the cookie was in front of Gnarly's nose.

Unsure, Gnarly lifted his head to look up across the living room. Archie was still engaged in a conversation with Sari's mother. Archie was seemingly unhappy with how the conversation was going. His brown eyes came back to focus on the child offering the goodie.

"Nice doggie," she whispered so low that only he could hear.

Gently, he took the cookie from her hand, stood up, and turned around on the loveseat so his back was to Archie and Sari's mother.

As soon as he had taken the goodie from her hand, Sari ran back to the sofa to climb back up on it.

✳   ✳   ✳

Randi hung up her cell phone and pointed it at Archie. "The marshal's office wants to wait for a confirmation from someone on the inside that the contract is cancelled before releasing you from protection. Better to be safe than sorry. Once we get that confirmation from one of our undercover agents, you'll be free to come out from under the radar."

The marshal then turned her attention to Leah. "We're going to release a statement to the media that a young mother and her little girl were killed in the poisoning. That way, if you and Sari were the targets, they'll think the hit was a success."

"Do they know who those men with the submachine guns were working for yet?" Leah asked. "Was it Mario?"

"We're still trying to identify them," the federal agent replied.

"How about what happened inside the café? Did you see what happened to those men?" Archie was asking Leah.

Her dark eyes wide, Leah shook her head frantically. "I have no idea what happened," she said. "I was in the kitchen cooking their orders when suddenly there was screaming. I heard dishes and furniture crashing. Sari came running into the kitchen. When I went out, men were on the floor—coughing up blood, twisting, and screaming. They were shaking something awful—" She covered her face. "I once saw—It reminded me of—" Breaking down, she dropped her head into her hands.

Randi told Archie, "Leah's husband had been known to use poison."

"It's a terribly painful way to die," Leah whispered. "I've seen dinner guests in our own home die after sharing an after-dinner cocktail with Mario. They start coughing up blood, shaking and twisting and grabbing their heads—poison that attacked the nervous system. That's what it was." She clutched her chest. "Suppose it was planted there for me. He would have used that poison to let me know—"

Randi shook her head. "If it was Mario, it would have been a more direct attack. Like the men with the machine guns."

"But how—" Archie started to ask when Gnarly let out a bark. Leaping over the back of the loveseat, he charged for the door.

"Who is it?" Grabbing her purse, Leah jumped up from her chair.

Archie stopped her. "It's Mac. Gnarly always barks at Mac like that. It's Gnarly's way of reminding Mac that this is his house and he's is only letting him stay here."

Gnarly was jumping on the door when Mac eased it open to make him back up. When he spotted David behind him, Gnarly rushed between Mac's legs to greet the police chief. It was only due to a quick move on his part that Mac avoided landing face-first on the floor.

Archie rushed into Mac's arms. "I'm so glad you're home. It scared the life out of me when Bogie said there had been a hit at the café."

Mac embraced her tightly in his arms. "I guess Gnarly is good for something."

David was easing the dog's paws from his shoulders to the floor. When he saw Randi coming up from the dining room, David's eyes narrowed into a glare. "Finnegan."

She stopped to shoot back an equally vicious glare. "O'Callaghan."

"I need to have a word with you."

Randi eyed Mac. "You told him."

"Of course I told him," Mac said. "This is a major murder investigation in our town. Those were two hired assassins who meant serious business. I couldn't let David go on working on the assumption that Tommy Cruze was their target when it could have been someone else." He glanced over at Leah, who was clutching Sari.

Seeing the fear in the little girl's face upon the two men's entrance, Archie went over to Sari and knelt down. Mac saw the grip of her blue Ruger stick out from under the back of her shirt. "Sari," Archie asked, "would you like me to show you the room where you and your mommy will be staying tonight?"

When her mother nodded her consent, Sari slid off the sofa. When Archie reached for her hand, she pulled away and hugged her stuffed dog to her chest.

Leah explained, "Sari doesn't like it when strangers touch her." She offered a nervous smile. "It's hard for her to trust anyone enough to open up to them." She knelt down to her daughter. "You can go with Ms. Archie. She's a nice lady. Deputy Chief Bogie is upstairs. He's here to protect us. It will be okay." She added in a firm tone, "Just don't go too far."

Silently, Sari followed Archie up the stairs. Once they were certain that she was out of earshot, David turned to Randi. "Don't you think I had a right to know that a major mob target was living under my nose?"

"Leah and Sari live in McHenry," Randi said. "That's not Spencer territory. The Garrett County sheriff knows about her. Besides, you won't have her under your nose much longer. We're relocating her and Sari. It will take a couple of days to get the relocation all set, but then we'll be gone."

"Don't you think I had a right to know about it this morning when you were in the van and you knew that a major crime boss was marching right into her place of business?"

"Come on, O'Callaghan," Randi replied with a laugh. "You know damn well how the government works. Nobody tells anybody anything."

As much as it pained him, David admitted in a soft tone that Randi was right.

"Right now we all need to put our egos in check and concentrate on the matter at hand." Mac stepped in between the police chief and marshal to separate them. "We have four dead men—"

"Five," David corrected him.

"Four," Mac said. "The fed was faking. He was alive when they took him out. That's why Delaney wanted him out of there so fast."

"How did I miss that?" David muttered.

Hearing him, Randi smirked when she asked, "What did you say?"

"When a fed tells me to look to the left, I make a point of looking to the right," Mac said. "Cruze and his body guard coughed up blood. The fed didn't. My guess is he faked being dead on the off-chance that he was the target. They aren't going to be looking for a dead man."

"A man came running through the kitchen and out the back service door when people started screaming," Leah said. "I saw him come in with the man you said was a federal agent. Was he working undercover for the FBI, too?"

Reminded of the civilian amongst them, Mac and David exchanged glances before Randi ordered Leah, "Forget you heard that."

"Hey, I'm out of here and in another part of the country in three days." Shaking her head, Leah held up her hands in surrender. Mac saw a cell phone clutched in her palm. "As far as everyone is concerned, Sari and I were two victims of that poisoning."

"Another local restaurant bites the dust," David said. "I pity the fool who buys the Dockside Café with all the so-called victims added to the actual body count."

"Unless we find out what really happened," Mac said. "Okay, we know they were poisoned, but how?" He turned to Leah.

She clutched her chest. "I didn't do it."

"We're not saying that you did," David said.

Mac noticed that Randi, who had turned away, was silent in defending the café owner. "I'm sure forensics is testing everything to find the source," he said. "But I think we can narrow it down the old fashioned way. I noticed that they didn't have their food yet. So it wasn't in the food."

"I was in the kitchen cooking their breakfast orders when it happened," Leah told them.

"Then the poison must have been in their drinks," David said.

"What did they have to drink?" Mac asked her.

"Coffee," Leah said. "Only one of the men didn't have anything, the one who came in last with the undercover operative. He was the man who ran out through the kitchen." She added, "And orange juice. I had served them orange juice when I took their orders."

Mac rubbed his finger across his lips. "Did they all drink the orange juice?"

"All of them, except the agent who ran."

"Did the bald man with the mustache have orange juice?" Mac asked.

After she nodded her head, David said, "Richardson wasn't poisoned, so it wasn't in the juice."

"It was in the coffee," Mac said.

Randi said, "They all had coffee."

"Different people drink coffee different ways," Mac said. "Some use cream, some use sugar, some use both cream and sugar."

"It was in either the cream or the sugar," David said. "The cream was in those little plastic disposable tubs."

"The big fat man and one of the other men who died had cream in their coffee," Leah said before shaking her head.

"The man who came in last, with the man who ran out, he drank his coffee black—no cream or sugar."

"But he faked his death," Mac muttered.

"The two men who died, Cruze and his bodyguard, both had cream in their coffee," David said. "It was in the cream."

Mac turned back to Leah. "What about the couple who left? What did they have?"

"Nothing," Leah said. "The man insisted that his coffee had to be fresh. So I brewed a fresh pot. I was bringing it in to him when his wife threw a hissy-fit and they got into a big fight and left. They didn't have anything."

"They left, and suddenly people started dropping dead," David said. "Did they dodge a bullet?"

"—or fire it?" Mac asked.

They all looked up when they saw Bogie coming down the stairs. His uniform was wet.

"What happened to you?" David asked.

"From the upstairs windows, you get a clear view around the lake," Bogie explained. "While I was watching, I busied myself by fixing the clog in Mac's toilet." He turned to Mac. "It was wedged down there pretty tight. So I took the toilet up off the floor and got it for you." He pulled a yellow rubber duck bath toy out of his pocket.

"What—"

Before anyone could react to the surprise, Gnarly leapt over the back of the loveseat in one bound, grabbed the rubber duck out of Bogie's hand, and tore up the stairs with it in his mouth.

"I don't like that … dog," Leah said. "I don't like the way he looks at me."

"Gnarly's not vicious," David said. "Possessive of his stuff, but not vicious."

Randi put her arm around Leah to comfort her. "Leah is afraid of dogs."

With a sigh, Bogie said, "Guess I better go put the toilet back together again." He turned to Mac. "Want to lend me a hand? After all, it was your dog, and it's your toilet that he flushed his duck down."

"Gnarly," Mac muttered to the dog that had run up the stairs, "I'm going to kill you."

❅   ❅   ❅

"What's Leah's story?" Mac demanded of Randi after she had shown the café owner her guest room upstairs.

After Leah was comfortable, Randi rejoined David and Mac in the study where they were enjoying a before-dinner cocktail. After the day they had had, they felt they deserved it.

Of all the rooms in the manor house, Mac felt most comfortable in Robin's study. There he felt the essence of the woman who had given birth to him.

Robin Spencer's famous mysteries had been penned in the most cluttered room in Spencer Manor. Built-in book-shelves containing thousands of books collected over five generations took up space on every wall. Robin had left her son first editions of all her books. First editions that famous authors had personally inscribed to her, and books for research in forensics, poisons, criminology, and the law also lined the shelves. With every inch of bookshelf space taken, the writer had taken to stacking books on her heavy oak desk and tables, and in the corner.

Portraits of Spencer ancestors filled the space not taken up with books. After almost two years, Mac was still in the process of learning many of their names and histories. Some appeared to be from the eighteenth century. Others wore fashions from the turn of the nineteenth century and on.

The most recent portrait was a life-sized painting of Robin Spencer dressed in a white, strapless formal gown from the 1960s. She looked like a young Elizabeth Taylor. When he

Lauren Carr

had first seen the picture, Mac was taken aback by how much Robin resembled his grown daughter, Jessica.

The portrait of the demure-looking author filled the wall between two gun cases behind the desk. One case contained rifles and shotguns, while the other had handguns. Some of the guns had been handed down through the Spencer family. Others, the author had purchased for research.

Robin had acquired other weapons during her mystery writing career. The coat rack sported a hangman's noose and a Samurai sword hung on the wall.

In a chair in the far corner of the room, Uncle Eugene watched all of the comings and goings. A first aid training dummy, Uncle Eugene had been stabbed in the back, tossed off rooftops, and strangled on numerous occasions—all in the name of research. When he wasn't being victimized, he sat in an overstuffed chair in the corner dressed in a tuxedo with a top hat perched on his head. With one leg crossed over the other and an empty sherry glass next to his elbow, Uncle Eugene looked like he was taking a break while waiting for the next attempt on his life.

Leah and her daughter would be sleeping in the guest room across the hall from Randi. The master suite would be on one side of her, and David at the other end of the hall.

"She'll be gone in forty-eight hours tops," Randi said. "I certainly appreciate you letting her hide out here until we leave."

"Don't mention it." Mac handed her a snifter with cognac. "I noticed when I brought up the poison that Leah insisted she didn't do it, but you didn't jump in to defend her."

"Neither did you," Randi said.

"I only met her this morning," Mac said. "You've been working with her for how long? You know her. You know her past. Don't tell me that you don't suspect that she slipped rat

130

poison into Cruze's cream out of self-defense when she saw him come into her place?"

"And you wouldn't have killed Cruze if given half a chance," Randi said.

Mac looked to David for his back up, which he didn't offer. Instead, he was staring at Randi with a suspicious glint in his eyes.

"I don't know about Leah," she said in a harsh whisper. "I've never been able to put my finger on it. I've concluded that it's because she does come from a completely different world than me or any of us. Her father was an assassin with one of the most notorious crime families in Europe. Her mother, an Italian, sent her over here to the United States to get her away from the family business. What her mother didn't know was that the cousin she had sent Leah to live with had started an American branch of their now international crime organization. When Leah got married, she thought her husband was a successful businessman. She had no idea what business he was in until after she had Sari."

"Who are her friends?" Mac asked.

"She doesn't trust anyone enough to have friends." Randi's furrowed brow and squint reflected confusion. "None that she speaks of anyway. She's a totally different animal than Archie has been in the program. I've concluded that it has to do with why people come into the program. You'd be surprised how many criminals and criminal types end up in the program. That's how they come into the evidence they give us. Then, we have witnesses who are innocent, law-abiding citizens who literally are in the wrong place at the wrong time—"

"Like Archie," Mac said.

"And chose to do the right thing," Randi finished with a nod of her head. "Leah was raised in a crime family. She was surrounded by drug and illegal arms dealers, crooks, and killers. She's got a totally different wiring than we do."

"If she doesn't have any friends, then why does she carry a cell phone?" Mac asked.

"Maybe for protection," David replied. "I know a lot of women who don't carry cell phones to talk to their friends all the time, but only to use if they need help."

While Randi agreed with David, Mac had a nagging feeling that Leah wasn't all she appeared to be. *Randi is right. Leah comes from a completely different world—a world where killing comes easy.* "Would Leah put the lives of innocent people at risk to poison one man?"

"The feds have taken the lead on the murders at the café," David said. "So we really don't need to focus on solving them."

"Except that I don't like the idea of keeping a possible killer under my roof," Mac said. "Are the feds even looking for that couple that ran out of the café before Cruze collapsed? They were in the dining room after Leah went back into the kitchen to prepare their orders. They could have planted the poison in the cream. Tommy Cruze had collected a lot of enemies. He's hurt a lot of people. Any of them could have paid off one of Cruze's people to give them a heads up of where he was going, and then arranged to get to the café first to set up his murder." Excited by the prospect that came to his mind, he added, "The fight could have been staged. We need to find that couple."

"Have you been listening to me, Mac?" David replied. "The poisoning is not our case. It's the feds' case. They don't like it when locals poke their noses into their cases—believe me. They can be more territorial than Gnarly."

Randi said, "Well, I am a federal agent and I'm going to investigate this lead. If those hit men that Gnarly took out this morning were there for Leah and Sari, we need to find out who knows where she is and who sent them. If the poison was meant for Leah, we need to know that, too." She clasped the weapon in her holster with one hand while heading for the door. She paused in the doorway before turning to Mac and David. "Are you two coming?"

David looked over at Mac. "I can see you chomping at the bit to take this on."

"I got a good look at both of them," Mac said. "I think they're tourists. They came to the café from the hotel across the road."

"Sounds like a good place to start," Randi said. "What are we waiting for?"

Chapter Fourteen

Gnarly ended up going along for the ride after Leah ordered them to take him because she feared for Sari's safety.

Usually, the German shepherd would jump at the chance to go with Mac or David, especially in the police chief's cruiser. Such wasn't the case this time. Gnarly refused to come when Mac called for him. Eventually, Mac had to lead him by his collar to the car. While urging the dog into the back seat, Mac saw Sari peering out the front window at them. When Gnarly turned back to look at the house, she waved. Mac could see that it was Gnarly she was waving to.

With Randi filling the front passenger seat, Mac had to climb in back with Gnarly. "If I remember Cruze's murder trial," Mac said, "he was tried for the murder of Dr. Reynolds, not his wife."

Randi nodded. "The investigators were never able to prove that Cruze killed his wife, but her car was found in a secluded rural area with two shell casings inside and a giant blood splatter on the seat. DNA proved the blood to be a match with Harper Cruze. No evidence could be found to put Cruze or his people at the scene. Richardson claimed she had left Cruze. Without a body, no one could prove who was right."

Mac muttered, "So she could have survived."

"If she is alive," David said, "after a decade in jail for killing her lover, Cruze would have to have her at the top of his list of most wanted dead."

Randi looked into the rearview mirror back at Mac. "How old would you have guessed the woman of this couple to be?"

"Late thirties, early forties," Mac replied. "How old was Cruze's wife when he went to jail?"

"Late twenties."

David said, "Then that would make her about the right age."

"Why come after him?" Mac asked. "Why come near him?"

"Same reason as Archie," Randi said. "Kill or be killed."

Mac agreed. "I guess Cruze would know if she was really alive and out there."

David pulled the cruiser into the hotel lot and parked the cruiser next to the lobby entrance. "Only thing is, according to Alan Richardson, it was only this morning that Cruze decided to go to the café." He unsnapped his seat belt. "So how would this woman, who may or may not have been his wife, know he was going to be there?"

"Same way the FBI knew he'd be there," Randi said. "Someone on the inside."

Mac leaned forward toward her seat. "If Cruze's wife is alive and in the program, now would be a good time to tell us."

Randi turned around in her seat. "I don't have a membership roster of everyone who's in the witness protection program."

Mac peered closely at her face. When he had first met her the day before, he had thought she was hard looking. She would be called a handsome woman—not unattractive, but not pretty, either. Up close, with her face illuminated by the parking lot light, he could see that her features were pretty. She had high cheekbones and dark eyes. With the right make-up, she could be striking.

Having spent a career working with numerous female police officers, Mac was aware that attractive women who played up their feminine features were taken less seriously than women who played them down. It was a subconscious fact of life, not sexism. Men instinctively want to protect pretty women. Spending too much time out in the field worrying about the "pretty woman" can distract you from someone who might be trying to kill you.

"You didn't answer his question, Finnegan," David said.

Randi broke the stare to lock eyes with David. "Even if I knew, I couldn't tell you. You both know that. Why do you even ask?"

David looked over the back of his seat to Mac as if to ask his opinion.

Tired of waiting for someone to open the door to let him out, Gnarly stomped his front feet and groaned.

"Okay," Mac said to the agent, "but if I find out that you're holding out on us…"

"What?" she challenged him with a razor-sharp glare back at him. "What are you going to do?"

David threw open his door, climbed out, and opened the back door of the cruiser to release Gnarly and Mac. "Let's start with the desk clerk."

"Oh yeah," the desk clerk nodded his head quickly when Mac described the couple who had escaped the massacre at the Dockside Café.

Seemingly bored with the interview portion of the investigation, Gnarly yawned and plopped down with his head resting on Mac's feet.

"The odd couple," the clerk said.

Having seen the couple up close, Mac understood the clerk's reference.

Randi and David exchanged glances. "Odd couple?" Randi asked.

The clerk, a young man with thick, dark eyebrows and a goatee, laughed. "I've been working here for five years. By the end of my first, I figured out the people who check into this place. I can spot a couple married to each other like that." He snapped his fingers. He leaned over the desk to whisper, "I can also tell who's meeting with someone who isn't his wife."

"Tell us about the odd couple." With a circular motion of his finger, Mac urged him to get back on topic.

"Well, you know how a lot of couples look like they belong together? You can tell by looking at them that they match in some way. They mesh." He shook his head. "Not those two. This morning, I came in for the first shift, and she went running out the door looking like an Olympic athlete. He came stumbling down around seven o'clock looking like something the cat dragged in—and smelled like it, too." He shot them a wicked grin. "My guess, he must have money to have snagged a looker like that." Seeming to have a second thought, he shook his head. "But she doesn't strike me as the trophy wife type. Not that we get that many here. Couples like that check in up at the Spencer Inn." He looked at Mac, dressed in a sports jacket over a pair of dress jeans. "You look more like the Spencer Inn type."

Not revealing that he owned the Spencer Inn, Mac chuckled. "I'll take that as a compliment."

"Do you have the odd couple's names?" David asked.

"Gordon and Nora Crump from Lancaster, Pennsylvania."

"What room are they in?" Mac asked.

"Two-oh-four," the desk clerk answered without checking. "But they aren't there. They went out to dinner a couple of hours ago."

Confident that the desk clerk would know the answer, Mac asked, "I don't suppose you know where they went to eat."

"She asked me." The young man grinned. "She had heard someone talking about a Southwestern restaurant on the lake. The Santa Fe Grill and Cantina. I gave them directions to it. They were all dressed up. He even looked like he took a shower…maybe."

❋   ❋   ❋

"The odd couple?" Randi repeated after they had climbed back into the cruiser.

"Odd." David maneuvered the cruiser on the twisting road along the lake.

"Why is it so hard to believe that a beautiful woman can fall for an unattractive man?" Randi asked with an accusatory note in her tone.

"The clerk wasn't saying that Gordon is unattractive," David said, "but that they didn't look like they have anything in common."

"How can you tell that by looking at a couple?" she asked.

"He's right," Mac called out from the back seat. "I saw them. They don't look like they belong on the same planet, let alone in the same bed."

David turned the cruiser up an entrance ramp that climbed up a slight hill into a crowded parking lot.

The Santa Fe Grill was a very popular Southwestern restaurant. Adding to its popularity, it sported a boat dock where guests would pull in for outdoor dining. Loud Southwestern music blared from the outdoor speakers to practically drown out the guests that filled the outdoor café. Inside the restaurant, there was an outdoorsy feel with high ceilings under which the guests' chatter could bounce and echo to mix with the music.

After climbing out of the cruiser and opening the back door for Mac and Gnarly, Randi said, "It's going to be almost impossible to find them in this crowd."

The blast of six gunshots fired in rapid succession followed by a woman's scream drowned out Mac's reply.

David pointed beyond the rows of parked cars toward the restaurant's main entrance. "Over there!" he shouted over the screams while pulling his gun from its holster.

Gnarly was already on the run. He charged at the sound of the first shot. Like a salmon fighting to swim upstream, he dodged around the fast moving legs to get to where Gordon Crump was sprawled out in what would be a flower bed during the summer months with his wife Nora kneeling over him.

"Did you see who shot him?" Randi grasped the hysterical woman's shoulder.

Jumping at the agent's touch, Nora looked up at them and covered her mouth with her hands.

"Did you see where the shooter went?" David searched the crowd for someone with a weapon.

Not answering, Nora gazed at the police chief standing over her.

Behind them, car horns were blaring. Patrons not wanting to be part of the scene, or possible victims, were frantically seeking escape routes. Some cars were making impromptu exits over curbs and down the hillside to the main road.

"Is he still here?" Randi asked the dead man's wife.

She pointed out at the exit ramp. "There! That's him in the black car."

Craning his neck to get a look at the driver of the black car that had turned out onto the lake shore road, David raced back to his cruiser while calling in a description of the vehicle speeding away.

Seeing that Gnarly was hot on someone's trail, Mac had opted to follow the barking dog. As he was dodging the courtyard bench, Mac noticed a rack with a silver bike chained to it. *Silver bike!* Mac paused long enough to note it. *Could it be the same killer? What could be the connection?*

He turned the corner of the building to the back of the restaurant to witness a flock of kitchen help who had been lounging outside scattering at the appearance of the canine hot on a trail. Determining that his prey was not amongst them, Gnarly was clawing and barking at the staff entrance.

"Hey, man!" someone called to Mac, "What's wrong with your dog?"

With no time for conversation, Mac threw open the door to let Gnarly scurry in. Cooks and servers were yelling and jumping up onto counters to avoid the dog galloping straight through the kitchen followed by a man with a gun. Mac weaved through frightened cooks and servers while fighting to keep the shepherd in sight.

Gnarly followed the scent into the dining room, turned a corner and stopped at the men's restroom door.

"Is this where he's hiding?" His gun poised to shoot, Mac opened the door for Gnarly to charge in. Mac thrust his arm through the doorway with his finger on the gun's trigger. Inside, he searched each stall for the shooter before determining that Gnarly had led him astray. "No one's here, Gnarly." Mac holstered his gun. "I'm afraid your nose misled us this time."

His nose to the floor, Gnarly turned in circles until he came to the sink.

"Come on." Mac clapped his hands to get the dog's attention. "David needs our help."

Instead of going to him, Gnarly bolted under the sink to the trash container and rammed into it. It fell over with a loud metal clang.

"Gnarly!" Mac yelled. "What are you looking for? Did someone dump an old donut in there?"

While his master chastised him for the mess he was creating, Gnarly stuck his head inside the trash can. Dragging a black running jacket, its hood clutched in his teeth, he backed out. As he extracted it, the jacket became unfolded and a handgun fell onto the floor. After dropping the jacket to the floor, Gnarly let out a round of boisterous barks at Mac. When he was finished telling him off, the German shepherd sat down, peered at the jacket and gun, and then back up at Mac.

"Not bad, Gnarly," Mac admitted. "But that still doesn't get you off the hook for clogging up my toilet."

The reminder of the toilet caused Gnarly to hang his head in shame.

Chapter Fifteen

Mac gets to go play cop and mobster, and I'm sitting home like the little woman waiting for her man to come home.

Archie tossed her e-reader onto the sofa and turned around to look at Bogie, who was reading a Zane Grey novel he had found in Robin's library. It was an autographed first edition that the author had purchased at an estate auction years before. "It's not fair," she told the deputy chief.

"Life isn't fair." Bogie turned a page. "Haven't you learned that yet?"

"I guess I should have learned that twelve years ago when I gave up my family and went into the program," she said. "How ironic. I did the right thing, but I ended up on the run."

Bogie looked up from his book. "But look at where it landed you."

"If it was really fair, I'd be out there with Mac and Gnarly chasing down the truth instead of here."

"Hey," Bogie objected. "I may not be as handsome as Mac and Gnarly, but I can still be pretty good company."

"It isn't that." Archie looked around the spacious living room. As luxurious as it was, she felt like a caged lioness wanting to be out on the hunt with her lion. "Maybe a nice, long soak in the tub will make me feel better."

Upstairs, she noticed that the door to Leah's room was open. *I should at least try to be civil. After all, she is my guest.* She paused in the open doorway while weighing the consequences of not saying hello.

Leah was sitting in the chair by the window with her smartphone in her hand. Her fingers flew gracefully across the screen while she texted away.

"Hello," Archie interrupted her communication.

Startled, Leah thrust the phone behind her back. "Don't you people knock before entering someone's room?"

"The door was open and I was going by on the way to my room." Archie replied. "Is everything okay?"

"Yes."

The two women stared at each other.

"Good night," Leah said in a forceful tone.

"Same to you." Archie moved on down the hallway.

❋   ❋   ❋

"Did you catch him?" Marshal Randi Finnegan hurried over to ask David after he parked the cruiser along the curb in front of the restaurant.

David saw Nora Crump sitting in the back of one of the fleet of cruisers that had arrived at the scene in response to his call. They were still waiting for the ME. He tried to contain his disgust when Gordon Crump's widow tore her eyes away from the dead body to look at him.

"No." David whizzed by the marshal to go up to speak to Nora.

Randi let out a quick breath. "Do you mean he got away?"

"Yes."

She followed him. "How?"

"He just did." David whirled around to tell her. "I'm not super cop, you know."

"Why is your face red?"

"Because I've had a lousy day, that's why." He turned to Nora. "Tell me what happened here tonight."

The widow's eyes bugged at his sharp tone. Her mouth hung open. Her eyes darted to Randi.

"David," Randi said, "the woman lost her husband."

"I'm sorry." With a sigh, David covered his face and started again. "I'm sorry for your loss. Can you tell me what happened?"

One of his officers came out of the building to tap him on the arm. "Chief, Mr. Faraday found something inside that you ought to see."

"Just a minute, Oakley." David held up a finger to the officer as an order to wait. At that moment, he wanted a statement from Nora Crump about what connections she had that would cause three men, one her husband, to suddenly end up dead. His arms folded across his chest, he peered down at her.

With frightened eyes that resembled a deer crossing the road in the dead of night only to be caught in the high beams of a racing truck, Nora gazed back up at him. "I don't know," she said in a small trembling voice. "We had dinner. We were having a good time. We came out to go to our car and this man suddenly came out from the courtyard and walked right up to Gordon and shot him. Not just once. He kept shooting, even when Gordon was down on the ground…and all I could do was stand there. I don't know… Did I scream? I felt like I was screaming, but I don't remember if I did or not."

Randi asked, "Did he ask for anything? Your husband's wallet or watch?"

"No." She gasped. "He did say something right before he started shooting. When he came up to us, he said, 'Hey,

Gordon.' Gordon stopped. Then, I saw the gun. This man—he was wearing a dark running jacket and a hood up over his head so I couldn't see his face. He said, 'This is for Tommy Cruze.' That was when he started shooting." She covered her ears. "I don't know how many times he shot. He wouldn't stop shooting."

David asked, "Did your husband do business with Tommy Cruze?"

She sobbed. "Business? Maybe." She shrugged. "We never really talked about his business dealings. But I do remember taking a phone message at home once from some guy who said his name was Tom Cruze." She offered a weak smile. "I remember it because I made a joke asking him if he made movies. You know? The movie star." Her smile fell. Tears came to her eyes. "'But the man on the phone didn't see the humor in it. His voice was so hard when he said, 'If your husband knows what's good for him, he'll call me back.'" Tears rolled down her face. "Who is this Cruze guy? Why would anyone kill Gordon? I mean, who would want to kill someone who sells toilets?"

"Toilets?" Randi asked. "What did your husband do?"

"Gordon owns a kitchen and bath supply store."

While David and Randi exchanged puzzled expressions, the officer whispered in the police chief's ear. His eyes lit up before he told the officer, "Take Mrs. Crump down to the station and make her comfortable."

"Do you want me to take her statement?" Officer Oakley asked.

"No, I'll take it." David turned around to go into the restaurant. "Call Bogie on his cell and tell him what's going on."

"Do you want him to come down here?"

"No," David said with a sharp tone. "I want him to stay with Archie Monday. This isn't over yet."

❊   ❊   ❊

His arms folded over his chest, Mac was standing guard in front of the men's restroom door when David and Randi came in. "Took you long enough," Mac called to them.

"I was talking to the victim's wife," David said.

The corner of Mac's lip curled. "Did you catch the perp pulling out of the parking lot?"

"No." The word was a sharp snap at him.

Randi told Mac, "He's very sensitive about it."

Mac unfolded his arms. "He should be. Nora Crump sent him on a wild goose chase."

"You make that sound like she did it on purpose," Randi said. "You saw her. Her husband was gunned down in front of her. She was in shock—still is—and confused."

"Oakley told me you found the murder weapon." David gestured at the bathroom door. "It's in there?"

"The shooter didn't get in the car and run. Gnarly followed his trail around behind the restaurant, and in through the kitchen entrance to here where he dropped the gun and his jacket." Mac opened the door for them to peer inside. "Then, he mixed in with the crowd running out to see what happened."

Slipping on his evidence gloves, David stepped inside and knelt to examine the jacket and gun on the floor next to the garbage can.

"The gun was wrapped up inside the jacket." Mac followed him inside after ordering Gnarly to stay out in the corridor. "Gnarly pulled it out onto the floor."

Careful not to disturb any possible fingerprints, David picked up the gun and sniffed it. "It was recently fired. We need to contain this scene and get forensics in here."

The forensics team was already coming in with their cases of equipment. After ordering them to search the men's room for possible evidence of the shooter, David and Randi went back outside to collect statements from possible witnesses who had stuck around instead of running.

"So we meet again," one of the forensics officers, a petite redhead, said before following her partner into the men's restroom.

"Again?" Mac asked.

"Skeltner Cove B and B," she reminded him. "Mary Catherine Skeltner was dragged out of her bed and tossed down the stairs." She clutched the handle of her crime scene kit with both hands. "Got any suspects yet?"

"One," Mac said. "Unfortunately, he has an alibi. Have you had a chance to process the evidence yet?"

"Well, you guys have been keeping us pretty busy," she said with a slight smile on her lips. "But, we do have one piece of good news for you."

"I could use some good news."

"Whoever killed her, we got her DNA," she said in a coy tone.

"Her?"

"Her," she replied. "So if your suspect is a man, then he isn't your guy. At least he doesn't belong to that lens you found or the hair we collected from under the victim's fingernails."

Her reply caught Mac's interest. "Our killer is a woman with dark hair and she wears contact lenses."

"It was a daily disposable lens with enough human tears on it to lift a DNA profile." She peered inside the bathroom. "We also got fibers from a black material under her fingernails." She caught Mac's eye before looking back down at the jacket on the floor. "The same type of material that this jacket is made of."

"A witness saw our chief suspect riding a silver bike," Mac said. "There's a silver bike at the rack outside."

She grinned at him. "If the treads to that bike's tires match the tread marks we collected at the scene, then you might be able to make a case for these two murders being connected. But then, I'm not the detective. My job is to only examine the evidence and give you the report." She went into the bathroom.

"Very interesting."

Mac turned to go secure the bike he had seen when he realized that Gnarly was nowhere around. *I swear I spend half of my time at crime scenes looking for that animal.* Calling out for Gnarly in a coarse whisper, Mac went into the dining room.

The murder had cleared out the restaurant that was usually packed on the weekends. Those who had finished giving their statements to the police had hurried home to their loved ones.

Only one employee, a brunette dressed in the form-fitting red and black dress of a Mexican senorita, was still in the dining room. She was sitting next to the fireplace crying softly while stroking Gnarly, who was resting his head in her lap. While wiping her nose with a napkin with one hand, she stroked the top of Gnarly's head with the other.

Neither of them moved when Mac came up to their table. "I hope Gnarly isn't bothering you."

Startled, she clasped her hands to her bosom and whirled around. Appearing equally startled, Gnarly looked up over his shoulder at Mac as if to accuse him of interrupting a very good petting.

Apologizing for scaring her, Mac pulled out a chair from the table next to her and straddled the back to sit down. "I guess the murder scared away all of your customers."

The windows looking out into the parking lot were lit up with blue and red lights from the emergency vehicles. Seeing that Mac wasn't dragging him off, Gnarly returned his head to the pretty woman's lap. She resumed petting him.

"If you weren't with the police," she sniffed, "would you be hanging around if you didn't have to?"

"No," Mac said. "I'd rush home to hug my family." He cocked his head at her. "Why haven't you left?"

"One of the police officers—his name tag said Fletcher—told me the chief would want to talk to me." Her eyes filled with tears. Weeping, she dropped her head and clutched Gnarly closer to her. As best as he could, Gnarly inched in to give her a canine version of a hug with his head pressed against her breast.

Mac asked her in a quiet tone, "Did you see what happened?"

She brought her hand down from where it was wiping her eyes. She hugged Gnarly. Quickly, she nodded her head. "I can't believe I saw a man…killed."

"Can you tell me what you saw?"

She lifted her eyes from where she was staring down into Gnarly's face. "Are you here to take my statement?"

"One of the other officers will do that," Mac said. "But I am working with the Spencer police on this case. Did you actually see it happen?"

Nodding her head, she pointed at the window. "I was at the window looking for them…I was their server, and the man had left without his credit card. It was strange. Suddenly, his wife had to leave. I had only just served him coffee, and she got all anxious that they had to go. I couldn't ring them up fast enough."

Recalling the café that morning, Mac asked, "Did they have a fight?"

She shrugged her shoulders with one hand up in the air in a gesture of confusion.

"All of a sudden, they had to leave," Mac recalled.

"*She* had to go," the server corrected him.

"Did she get a call on her cell phone?" Mac asked. "Maybe something happened…"

"I didn't see her using the phone," the server replied. "She was mostly taking in the crowd and the view outside."

"What about the husband?" Mac asked. "The man that got shot?"

"He was talking non-stop," she said. "It was both sad and funny at the same time. He was talking away to her, and you could see that she wasn't paying any attention to him." She shuddered. "I remember thinking what a weird, disgusting…" Tears came to her eyes. "I feel so bad. He smelled… it wasn't cologne, it was body odor, and he kept picking his nose. I kept thinking how gross—Now he's dead." Sobbing, she collapsed her face into Gnarly's mane. "I feel so bad now for thinking that."

Gently, Mac patted her shoulder. "They were having coffee …"

"He ordered coffee for dessert." Wiping her nose, she sat up. "Double cream and sugar. I heard her tell him that one day all that fattening cream and sugar was going to kill him." Her voice shook. "Five minutes later…"

"Did they walk out together?"

"No," she said. "They decided to leave together. I got their check and he gave me the card. I rang it up and took the booklet to them. As soon as I got there, she got up and told him to come. I was still clearing the table when they took off. Then I saw that he had left the card. I went to the reception area to catch them and I looked out the window and… saw it …"

Mac sat forward. "What did you see happen?"

"She was crossing the access lane to the parking lot," she said. "The killer, he was wearing a black running suit with a hood on it, passed her coming toward the restaurant from the parking lot. They walked right past each other and he came up to where her husband was stepping off the curb to follow her. Suddenly, he pulled out a gun and shot him." She covered her ears. "I can't tell you how many times he shot him. It seemed to go—he went down with the first shot, but the man in the hoodie stood over him and kept on shooting. Then he ran around behind the restaurant and the wife came running up to her husband."

"Where was she while her husband was being shot?"

The server paused to think before answering. "I wasn't watching her. I can't say for certain—I think she was behind the killer—on the other side of the road."

"She wasn't standing next to her husband when he was shot?" Mac asked.

Quickly, she shook her head. "I saw her running up while the killer was running around toward the lake."

The three of them sat in silence. Mac and the server were digesting what had happened—she from memory, Mac visualizing what she had described.

Nora Crump was ignoring her husband while taking in the crowd…coffee with double cream and sugar …"one day all that fattening cream and sugar will kill you …" he could see her saying. *The poison at the Dockside Café was in the cream.*

"Show me where they were sitting." Mac jumped up from his seat so fast that both the server and Gnarly were startled.

Choking on her tears, the server pointed at the very table from which Mac had pulled out the chair to sit down.

"Where was the wife sitting?" Mac asked her.

"In the chair that you're sitting in."

Mac turned around the chair and sat down at the table. The fireplace would have provided a warm ambiance for the couple. Looking around, Nora Crump also had a view of the mural of a Southwestern scene on the wall next to the fireplace; a view out the window at the outdoor café, which was closed for the season; one of a corner of the lake; one of the courtyard directly on the other side of the window; and one of the corner of the parking lot.

What made you suddenly leave? What did you see? Was it the killer? Were you running to or from something?

Mac was still gazing through the window when David came rushing in from outside. "There you are!" the police chief called to him. "Come on. We've got to go."

Frightened by the anxious tone in David's voice, Mac assumed something had happened to Archie. "What's happened?"

David waited for Mac to get close before whispering, "The feds got a location on Ray Bonito. Randi got us permission to be there when they grab him."

Chapter Sixteen

Something isn't right with that woman.

Archie had come into the kitchen to prepare a nighttime snack when she spied Leah's smart phone on the floor next to the doors opening out onto the deck. She had seemingly dropped it while slipping it into her pocket before taking Sari down to the dock to feed the ducks before putting her to bed. After picking up the phone from the floor, Archie studied the screen.

What's up with her? Why did she react the way she did when I caught her texting? Was she sending a note to a married man she was having an affair with? Or was it someone from her family that she had left behind when she went into the program? Someone she's not supposed to be contacting.

With a pang in her heart, Archie recalled all the loved ones that she had to leave behind, many of whom she didn't have a chance to say good-bye to, when she went into the program more than a decade before. Now, Randi had said they were faking Leah's and Sari's deaths before relocating them.

If Leah is so concerned for their safety, then who is she texting? The whole idea behind the program is to go deep under-

ground. It doesn't work if you have any contact at all with your past. Not only does it jeopardize your safety, but also the safety of your loved ones. If whomever you are running from even suspects that someone you love has been in contact with you, they are liable to be tortured or killed to get information about your whereabouts.

With one eye on the dock, Archie slipped the smart phone into her pocket, stepped out onto the deck, and hurried down to her guest cottage.

Many a child had fed the ducks down on the dock in the morning or evening as the sun was going down. The feeding would always be accompanied by childish squeals of delight. Not so this evening, Archie noted while trotting down the path to her stone cottage. *Sari won't even talk to the ducks. How sad.*

Watching for Leah and her daughter to come up from the dock, Archie placed her hand on the door knob. With the other, she clutched the phone concealed in her pocket.

"Everything okay?"

Her gasp ending in a shriek, Archie whirled around while pulling her blue Ruger out from behind her back to aim it into Hector's face.

"It's only me!" The security manager threw up his hands. "Easy, Archie."

With a sigh of relief, Archie lowered the gun and replaced it in the waistband behind her back, under her shirt. "You should warn people before sneaking up on them."

"You should warn people before pulling a gun on them," Hector countered.

"If I gave killers a warning before shooting them, then they'd get the drop on me."

"Point well taken," Hector said. "What are you sneaking around about?"

"I'm not sneaking around," Archie said.

"You're lying."

"I am not." She threw open the door. "I need to get some folders from my office."

Before she could hurry inside, Hector grabbed her by the arm. "I need to check it out first to make sure it's secure."

"Be my guest." She stood back.

Hector pulled his gun out of his holster and stepped inside. The beating of her heart sounded like a clock timer in her ear while she watched Leah and Sari down at the dock. Silently, the mother and child sat on the dock. Sari would throw food to the ducks that were crowded beneath her feet while her mother, uninterested in the feeding, glanced around at the scenery.

"All clear," Hector announced.

"Thanks," Archie said while hurrying inside.

While the bodyguard waited, Archie ran through the small kitchen and down the hall to her office. Once inside, she dropped down to her knees in front of a plastic storage cart that contained five drawers and yanked open the third drawer down. That was where her organization ended. The drawer contained a wide variety of cell phones, from flip to slide to smart. Her breath quickened while she clawed through the phones until she found the style and model she wanted. She uttered a gasp of satisfaction when she found it.

The next drawer down contained the cord that would attach the two phones.

She plopped down onto the floor and went to work.

"Ducks all fed?" Hector called out in a cheery voice that made Archie jump.

Cool it, Archie. You're as jumpy as a schoolgirl getting her first kiss. She continued to download and copy the settings from Leah's phone to the clone phone she was creating. *Just ten more seconds.*

"Where's Archie?" She heard Bogie call out to Hector.

"She's getting something out of her office."

She could hear their voices moving closer.

The screen on her phone read "Cloning Complete." She detached the cord and tossed it onto the floor next to her desk. She slipped Leah's phone into one pocket while dropping the clone into the opposite pocket.

"All done," she sang out while coming out of her office and closing the door. "I was about to pour myself a cocktail. Do you two want some?"

"Love one," Bogie said, "but we're on duty. I'll have a cup of hot tea if you don't mind."

Hector opted for a cup of coffee.

Archie led them up the path, across the deck, and into the kitchen where she opened the cupboard to take out the packages of loose leaf tea.

"I just got off the phone with Tonya at the station," Bogie said. "The husband of that couple at the café this morning was murdered."

"Seriously?" Archie stopped with the tea kettle in mid-air on its way to the stovetop. She turned to stare out the deck doors off the back deck to the dock, which was home to the speed boat and two jet skis. Since David had moved in, he had been riding her jet ski more than she did.

Leah and Sari came into the kitchen. Hugging her toy collie dog close to her chest, Sari had changed into an over-sized nightshirt that Archie had offered to her to use for pajamas. It hung all the way down to the little girl's ankles. The events of the day had not allowed them time to pack any clothes or belongings from home.

Recalling her staring at Gnarly when he was in the room, Archie turned to her when they came in. "Gnarly should be home soon, Sari."

"Sari doesn't like dogs." Leah's hardened tone grated on Archie's nerves.

"Are you sure about that?" Archie looked down at the little girl staring with a longing look in her eyes out at the lake. "She doesn't act frightened of Gnarly."

"You can't trust dogs." Leah glanced around the room. "Have you seen my phone? I can't find it."

"No, I haven't seen any phone laying around," Bogie said.

"We'll be on the lookout," Hector said.

Archie took the phone from out of her pocket. "Right here." She held it out to Leah. "I found it on the floor next to the door."

Leah snatched the phone from Archie's hand. "I don't think so."

"What?" Archie blinked.

"I think you took it."

"Now wait a minute." Bogie stood up to his height.

"She's been snooping on me and Sari ever since we got here."

"If Archie's snooping on you, maybe it's because you need to be snooped on," Hector replied.

Ignoring the two men challenging her, Leah shook her phone in Archie's face. "You stay out of my room and my business, or you're going to find yourself in a lot more serious trouble than you had with Tommy Cruze."

"You're a guest in my home," Archie remind her. "That means I can go anywhere I want, anytime I want."

"Well, if you want to keep that pretty face of yours pretty," Leah said in an icy tone, "you'd better think twice before getting in my way."

"Is that a threat?" Bogie's hand was on his gun.

"Yes," Leah answered. "And what are you going to do about it?" She smirked at all of them. "I have the US Marshals watching my back. Because of me, they've broken up the biggest and baddest crime organization on the West Coast. Like you and your little play cops with your puppy-dog can even touch me."

≛   ≛   ≛

"Both of the assassins this morning had several texts from two cell phone numbers," Randi Finnegan explained to Mac from her seat in the front of the cruiser. "One of them was a pre-paid phone which has since been shut off. That one had the place and time that Tommy Cruze was going to be at the Dockside Café."

David was speeding as best he could on the dark, twisting dirt road going up to a remote section of Spencer Mountain. They were away from Deep Creek Lake in an area that Mac had never visited.

On the seat next to him, Gnarly was equally curious with his snout up against the window. Mac wondered how well dogs really see in the dark.

"Our people tracked the GPS for the other number to a cabin on Spencer Mountain," she said, "They've known for quite a while that Bonito owns a hunting cabin up on the mountain."

"Hunting's not allowed in Spencer," David said.

"Bonito doesn't care about little laws like that," she said with a smile in her voice before turning serious. "Turn off your lights. They're going to be surrounding the place to go in when their man gives the signal."

"By man, I guess you mean the agent that had escaped the café during the poisoning?" Mac asked.

Randi turned back around to face frontwards. "I don't know what you're talking about."

Leaning forward to peer through the windshield to navigate on the dark wooded road, David eased the cruiser onto a side road and through the brush. He parked off the road behind a black van that Mac didn't see until after the police cruiser had come to a halt.

Agent Delaney appeared none too happy when Randi led them to where he was crouching behind some bushes. On the other side, Mac could make out dim lights in a log home. Even in the dark, he could see by the rustic setting and shabby outdoor furniture surrounding it that the place was several decades old. It did not fit with the modern estate homes located down along the lakeshore and on top of the mountain where treetops were trimmed to afford clear views of the lake and valley below.

With no lake view, this cabin was located and built to not be seen.

In the darkness, Agent Delaney didn't notice Gnarly until he moved in to sniff the gun he was wearing on his hip. "You brought the dog?"

"He turned out to be pretty handy this morning," David said.

Recalling that Gnarly had taken out the hit man who them all pinned that morning, Agent Delaney nodded his head. "Sorry, I forgot." He turned to Gnarly. "Welcome to the team. One rule: Don't get cocky out there."

Gnarly uttered a noise from deep in his throat and sat down. Eying the agent, he licked his chops.

"Cocky is his middle name," Mac said.

"What's going down?" David asked. Noting that a team of agents were moving in on a cabin that was in Spencer, Maryland, his jurisdiction, he added, "and why am I only finding out about this now?"

"Because we didn't know this was where Ray Bonito was hiding out," Delaney said. "We thought he had abandoned this place years ago after Cruze was put away."

"He's right," Randi said. "If I knew that Bonito or any of his people were still active in this area, I would never have agreed to locating any of my charges here."

"This place was burned as a mob safe house back when Cruze was put away," Delaney said. "I guess after such a long period of no activity, we forgot about it, and Bonito figured it was clean again to bed down."

"Sounds like you guys need to work on your long term memory," Mac said.

"You'd be surprised at how long my memory is," Delaney replied.

"What's happening now?" David repeated his original question.

"Our hit man—" Delaney began.

"The one who escaped the poisoning at the café," Mac said.

Delaney cast Mac a dirty glance before continuing, "He started calling back the number that one of the assassins had on his cell phone. He claimed to be TO'd about a hit going down while he was on the premises and demanded restitution for his silence, or he was going to the authorities. It took several calls, but he finally got a text from the number saying to come here to collect."

Mac shook his head. "I don't like that idea. Sounds to me like your man is walking into a setup. Why would they pay him?"

"Because the cover on our man is a first-class assassin. Bonito may be a psychopath, but he's also smart. He'll want our man working for him. He'll bring him on board, and we'll get all that we need to put him out of business."

"Richardson says he's a total paranoid," Mac said. "The only people who have direct contact with him are his most trusted men, which didn't even include Tommy Cruze. The only reason he'd let your man come out here is—"

The sound of gunfire completed Mac's statement.

"It's an ambush! Move it! Move it! Move it!" Delaney called to his men, who were already moving in on the dark cabin.

As the agents moved in, shots were fired at them from the cabin.

Randi was moving in when she saw a dark figure pop up from behind a wood pile. The killer was so close that she could see his laughing eyes trained on her as he aimed his handgun at her. Seeing the barrel of the gun an arm's length from her face, she froze. *Do something! You're acting like a complete newbie.*

The blast deafened her. She waited for the pain that she expected to hit her body before darkness took over.

Blood spilled out of the gunman's mouth before he collapsed down on top of the wood pile.

The noises around her echoed when she saw David come from behind the wood pile to grab her by the arm. "Don't just stand there! You need to take cover! Now!"

The rapid fire of a machine gun drove them down behind the water well. She could smell David's musky scent while he covered her with his body.

The series of gunfire was quickly reduced down to a spattering of shots from here and there as Bonito's men were quickly eliminated. It was as if they had taken a code. No one was going to be taken alive.

Mac had counted a half-dozen. The count was then reduced to one man. Swinging an Uzi left and right in front of him to clear his path, he raced out the back door.

It was like a re-broadcast of the morning before, this time with a sea of federal agents being held at bay by one man. He had everyone pinned. With their semi-automatic handguns, the federal agents were out gunned.

"Any ideas, hot shot?" Delaney asked Mac while they crouched behind a rusted-out truck on blocks.

Before Mac could answer, the gunman rose and drove them all down while he ran towards the trees. Mac dove for the ground and aimed for the running legs. They were quick moving targets, but it was his only shot before they lost the maniac in the deep woods. There was no telling what he would do to innocent local residents in his desperation to escape arrest.

Under the truck, he could hear the pitter-patter of dog paws in the bed of the truck. *Gnarly! What's he up to?*

His answer came when he heard the gunman scream. There was a flurry of gunfire. Gnarly yelped. Mac heard a thud.

Silence.

Mac felt his heart in his throat. Crawling out from under the truck, he envisioned finding Gnarly a lifeless, blood-soaked fur bag after trying to take down the gunman.

In the darkness, he saw nothing.

"Where'd they go?" he heard Delaney ask from beside him.

One of the agents said, "I saw the dog jump out of the bed of the truck and tackle the guy, and then they both disappeared."

"If anything happens to that dog, I'll be sleeping in the guest room for the rest of my life," Mac muttered. "Gnarly!" His call was answered by a whimper from out of the darkness. "Anybody got a flashlight?"

Delaney was already shining a pen light in front of him while they made their way through the dark toward the woods where they had last seen the gunman.

"Gnarly!" Mac called again.

The bark and whine came from in front of them. Delaney shone the light down to the ground.

If they had gone only a couple of steps further, they would have fallen into it—the grave—freshly dug for the agent who had pushed Bonito too far. It ended up being the grave of the gunman, who had landed on his own gun, which cut him in half.

Gnarly stood on his hind legs with his front paws up on the side of the grave which was too deep for him to crawl out of nor was it long enough him to be able to gain the speed to jump out.

Mac couldn't help but laugh. "What did you get yourself into now?"

Gnarly backed up and tried to jump out of the pit, only to manage to get his front legs on the rim. Unable to gain traction with his back legs, he tumbled down to land on his back on top of the dead gunman.

"I guess you need my help, huh, Gnarl?" Mac laughed.

Answering him with a snarling bark, Gnarly dropped down and dug in the dirt.

"What are you going to do? Dig yourself out?" Mac laughed again.

Gnarly stood and stretched up the side of the grave with something in his mouth.

"What's that he's got?" David knelt next to Mac.

Delaney directed his light on Gnarly, who had something clutched in his teeth. They all moved in to get a closer look at the prize Gnarly had dug up in the bottom of the grave.

It was a decomposed arm with the hand still attached.

Chapter Seventeen

"You're letting that filthy dog sit in my seat?" Randi Finnegan's voice went up two octaves when she came around the corner of the cruiser to find Gnarly in the front passenger seat with the window open.

"Hey, he deserves it," David said while scratching the dog behind both ears. "He's taken out two hired assassins in twenty-four hours. Better than what you accomplished back there."

Too mad for words, she rammed her knee into David's groin, causing him to buckle over and fall to his knees.

"Am I going to have to separate you two?" Mac asked when he hopped over a fallen tree to join them, only to find David down on his knees.

"I'm going to have Delaney drive me back to the manor." Randi whirled around to go hunt down the agent.

"Are you okay?" Mac watched David slowly pull himself up to his feet.

"Sure," David answered in a pained tone. "I didn't want to have any kids anyway." Steadying himself against the side of the cruiser, he made his way around to the driver's side and climbed in.

"What did you do to Finnegan now?" Mac asked after climbing into the back seat.

"What I always do to women. I opened my mouth without thinking." He started the cruiser. "How's Delaney's man?"

"Got hit in the shoulder," Mac answered while fastening his seat belt, "which is better than the guy who shot him. He got one in the forehead."

"Any idea who the hand belongs to?"

"Could be one of a dozen people," Mac said, "that they know of. That's not counting the guys they don't know about."

"But no thoughts about where Bonito is," David said.

While looking over his shoulder to ensure that the way was clear for David to back out onto the mountain road, Mac shook his head. "They found the cell phone. It forwarded the texts from another phone, which, from what they were able to determine here, had been shut off."

"He could have called from anywhere in the world." David spun the wheel to turn the cruiser around to head back down the mountain to Spencer Point. "Most likely, he's not even in the area."

Seeming to agree with him, Gnarly turned around in the front seat, planted his front paws on top of the back of the seat, and uttered a low bark.

"Yeah, Gnarly," Mac said to the German shepherd, "That's something to think about." He asked David, "Are you heading back to the station?"

"I still have a few questions for Nora Crump," David said. "Something doesn't smell right about her husband's murder."

"That bad smell started when she sent you on a wild goose chase," Mac said.

"Did you ever have a witness send you on a complete wild goose chase?" David asked.

"Only those who were in on it," Mac said. "Who was in the car she sent you after?"

"I said I didn't catch 'em."

"You lied."

David caught his eye in the rearview mirror. "What makes you think I lied?"

"Two things." Mac held up his index finger. "You're too good to lose a suspect. If they had outrun you, you would have hunted all night for them. You came back too soon to have lost them." He held up a second finger. "You're mad about it. What happened? Was it a car full of nuns and you pulled your gun on them?"

"No." With a heavy sigh, David concentrated on the road.

"You can tell me." Even in the back seat on the passenger side of the cruiser, Mac could see the firm set of David's jaw. "What happened?"

"It was a car full of drunken women on their way home from a bachelorette party," David finally said. "They offered me seventy-five dollars to strip for them. When I told them that I was the chief of police, they giggled."

Mac burst out laughing.

"They had a designated driver. She had the decency to be mortified and kept trying to get them all in line, but they were drunk out of their gorges. When I refused to strip, two of them tried to tear my clothes off. They were grabbing for things they had no right grabbing." He raised his voice over Mac's humor. "It's not funny, damn it!"

Mac bit his lip. "You're right. It's not funny." He chuckled. "They should have at least offered you a hundred."

"Of course you can laugh about it." David pulled over to the side of the road, put the cruiser into park, and whirled around in the seat. "Look at you. Mac Faraday. The Lord of Spencer Manor. Simply because of the accident of your birth, you get respect from people who haven't even met you."

"You get respect," Mac argued.

"Seventy-five dollars to take off my clothes!"

"Which you didn't do, I assume."

"Look at me, Mac!" David said. "Stab wound from a little old lady in a wheelchair who happens to be my mother, who hates my guts, and hiding in my big brother's home because I'm too much of a wuss to handle the nightmares in my own home!" He whirled back around to face the front. Mac suspected he didn't want him to see the tears in his eyes.

"No wonder," David said in a low voice. "I wouldn't respect myself, either."

The two of them sat in awkward silence.

When David reached for the gear shift to put the car into drive, Mac reached up to clasp his shoulder. "Yeah. Look at me. I'm sitting in the back seat of a cruiser while my dog is sitting in the front because he doesn't respect me enough to let me sit up there."

With a whine, Gnarly dropped down onto the seat and buried his face in his paws.

"You're talking about a dog, Mac. Big difference."

"I respect you."

"You feel sorry for me."

"No," Mac said. "You're feeling sorry for yourself right now—anyone would with what you're going through with your mother. I went through the same thing when my wife left me. If my own wife, the woman who had vowed for better or worse, who knew me better than anyone on the face of this earth, had so little respect for me that she would take another man into our bed, then how could anyone else respect me and my badge?"

David hung his head. "I guess there are similarities."

"I know it's tough, David." Mac squeezed his shoulder. "But you're not alone in this. I've got your back. Archie has your back. Bogie has your back." He chuckled. "Even Gnarly has your back. You're never alone."

"That's hard to remember sometimes."

"Remember it," Mac said. "Have faith that when you come out on the other end, you're going to be stronger for it."

"If it doesn't kill me first." David put the cruiser into drive and pulled out onto the road to continue down the mountain.

After a long silence that made his head ache with the tension David was going through, Mac leaned against his seat belt to ask him, "Did you know that Gordon Crump drank his coffee with double cream?"

Slowly, careful to keep one eye on the road, David turned his head to look over his shoulder at Mac.

"Considering that he was at the Dockside Café this morning," Mac said, "where two men were murdered with poisoned cream, I find that very interesting. Don't you?"

David pressed his foot down on the gas pedal.

✳   ✳   ✳

To have your spouse murdered is hard enough. Homicide detectives understand that. However, they must also face the reality that, in many cases, it is the spouse who has committed or commissioned the murder.

When Mac looked through the two-way mirror at Nora Crump, looking like a wrung-out rag in the interrogation room, he thought of how many times he had questioned the wife of a murder victim. Most of the time, he felt like a heartless monster for suspecting someone who had lost the love of her life to violence. The only thing that alleviated his guilt was the thought of how many times the wife ended up being the very one behind her husband's death.

With the case file that he had put together since the murder four hours before, David threw open the door. "If you want to be in on this case, you might as well be in on the fun."

Mac followed David out into the hallway and then over to the next door to go into the interrogation room.

Nora looked up from where she was staring down at her hands on the table. There was no recognition in her red, swollen eyes when she saw Mac come in, or when David introduced him as the squad's homicide detective. Mac surmised that she didn't notice him that morning when she hurried past him and Gnarly on her way into the Dockside Café.

David sat down in the chair across from her.

"I'm sorry for your loss, Mrs. Crump." Choosing not to remind her of their brief meeting, Mac took the seat at the end of the table.

David began by opening the file. "Mrs. Crump—"

"Don't call me that please."

David jerked his head up from the case file. "Excuse me?"

"Don't call me Mrs. Crump. I hate that name."

"What do you want me to call you?"

"Nora," she answered.

David and Mac exchanged puzzled expressions. Sharing the same O'Callaghan eyes, their furrowed brows held an identical appearance with the left brow arched in question.

"Okay," David finally said to her. "Nora, we have a problem."

"Is all this about my sending you after that car and it not being the killer?"

"Partly," David replied.

"I told you—my husband was just shot right in front of me." She touched a blood stain on her shirt. "I have his blood on me. He took his last breath in my arms. The last thing I noticed was where the man who shot him ran off to."

"Actually," Mac cleared his throat, "most people, when someone is right in front of them shooting down people, won't ever take their eyes off of the guy with the gun, if only to ensure that they don't get shot next."

Nora gazed at him. "I was in shock," she said. "I don't remember everything that happened."

"Like that you were standing right next to your husband when he was shot?" Mac asked.

"I was."

"We have witnesses who said you were several feet away," Mac said, "and that the killer walked right past you to go up to your husband and shoot him."

The fright in Nora's eyes transformed into anger. "Was someone you loved ever killed right in front of you?"

"Yes," Mac replied to her stunned dismay, "and I remember vividly every move, every sound, every instant. Because when it happened, everything went into slow motion, and I replayed it over and over and over again until it was seared into my memory. So don't give me that bull about you not remembering."

Her voice was cold. "Not everybody is the same. So I'm different from you. When I face trauma, I block it out."

"Why did you leave the restaurant?" Mac threw her off-balance by asking.

"Same reason anyone leaves a restaurant," she replied. "I was done eating."

"The server said that you suddenly got into such a big hurry to leave," Mac said, "that your husband left his credit card behind because he had to run to keep up with you."

Nora's eyes glazed over with deep thought.

"I thought this was a pleasure trip," David said, "a nice, pleasant dinner date with your husband. Why would you suddenly need to leave?"

She opened her mouth. Nothing came out. She swallowed.

"Now is the time to tell us everything," Mac said.

"But I don't know everything," she said in a low voice. "That man in black—he was wearing a hood up over his head—he shot my husband. I know people saw him do it."

"Who was he?" Mac asked.

"He worked for Tommy Cruze," she said.

"Who happens to be dead," David said.

"What?" Covering her mouth with her hands, she gasped.

"Tommy Cruze was at the café across the street from the hotel where you and your husband are staying," David explained. "Witnesses saw you and your husband there this—yesterday—morning. Shortly after you left—"

"Abruptly," Mac interjected, "much like you did last evening."

"Tommy Cruze and his body guard dropped dead," David said. "They were poisoned."

"But the man who shot Gordon said he worked for Tommy Cruze," she said. "'This is for Tommy Cruze.' I heard him say that."

Mac looked from her to David, who was looking back at him.

"Maybe…" she started.

"What?" David urged her to continue.

"I guess it's possible," she said in a low voice. "I guess it makes sense."

"What makes sense?" Mac asked.

She moved her chair in closer to the table. Placing her hands on the table top, she leaned in to explain, "Gordon inherited a very successful kitchen and bath supply company. His father was real smart. They had three stores when he passed. But then Gordon…" her voice trailed off. "My husband had issues."

"What type of issues?" Mac was unable to keep the suspicion out of his tone.

"Gordon lacked his father's charisma. Most everyone did business with him because they loved the guy. He was everyone's friend. Gordon was…" She sighed. "It didn't take long for all of the business's regular customers to go elsewhere. Two out of the three stores were closed within two years. We were clinging to the last store by a thread. I wouldn't be surprised if Gordon did something stupid."

"Like what?" Mac asked.

"Make a deal with the devil," she said. "I have no idea what this Tommy Cruze was into, but I do know Gordon was getting threats. He owed someone a lot of money, and if he didn't pay up…I only found out by accident. Gordon claimed not to be afraid, but I was." She nodded at Mac. "Yes, I did leave suddenly last night because I felt like someone was watching us. It felt like—I got so scared that I couldn't take it any longer—us sitting there in a public restaurant in the open like that—so I told Gordon that we had to go. I wanted us to get back to the hotel and lock the door."

"What happened at the Dockside Café?" David asked her.

"I had no idea what this Tommy Cruze looked like," she said. "We were sitting there in the café. Gordon had taken some containers of cream out of his pocket." She demonstrated taking something out of her pocket. "I had no idea that he had them. I asked him what he was doing with cream in his pocket. He told me to shut up. He put them in the bowl. He told me that we had to go. I wanted to stay, but he said it was time to go. So we got up and left—and left that bowl with the cream that he had put in it on the table." She sucked in a shuddering breath. "I guess Gordon thought his problem would be gone if he got rid of Tommy Cruze, but he was wrong."

She looked down at her hands, folded on top of the table. "Even though he was dead, Tommy Cruze still killed him." She choked. "Just like Gordon's dumb luck."

Chapter Eighteen

Archie and Bogie were sitting on the front porch steps in the dark when David's cruiser pulled around the circular driveway and parked.

"We were starting to get worried about you when you didn't come home with Randi." Archie kissed Mac and wrapped her arms around his neck when he stepped out.

"I hear I've been missing all the excitement while babysitting." Bogie opened the door to let Gnarly out. "Even the dog is getting more action than me."

"We'll be getting you back out there soon enough." David noticed Randi saunter out onto the porch. She had her bathrobe wrapped around her. "The feds wiped out what appeared to be Bonito's closest men up on the mountain. They're moving in on him. He's going to be wiped out soon enough."

Wagging his tail at Sari who was pressed up against the window inside the living room, Gnarly was standing up with his front paws on the sill.

Mac opened the door in time for Leah to come flying down the stairs to intercept Sari and sweep her up into her arms before Gnarly was able to give the girl a big, wet kiss on the face. "Sari, what are you doing up?"

Startled by Leah's lunge between him and Sari, Gnarly snarled and snapped at the woman.

"Did you see that?" Leah turned around to Mac while clutching the girl in both of her arms. "He was going to bite Sari."

"No, he wasn't," Mac said. "You jumped in between them and scared him."

"Is that blood he has on his face?" She hurried over to Randi who stepped in with Archie, Bogie, and David. "I don't want to stay here any longer."

"Why?" Randi asked. "You're safest here until we can get your new identity set up."

"That dog is dangerous." Leah pointed at Gnarly, who was wiping his face on the afghan draped over his loveseat. "He tried to bite Sari. I don't feel safe here. I want to leave now."

"Most likely Gnarly tried to kiss her," Bogie chuckled. "He loves children."

Randi responded to Leah's shocked expression. "I know how terrified you are of dogs, but Gnarly isn't like other dogs. I've seen it myself. Sari is completely safe with him."

Gnarly's grunting drew their attention to the loveseat where the dog was sprawled on his back, his hind legs spread apart to expose him in his full glory, while twisting and scratching an itch between his shoulder blades. Abruptly, he rolled over onto his stomach and let out a series of barks as if to announce that he felt much better.

"Either that dog gets locked up someplace, or we leave." Leah whirled around and raced up the stairs. At the top of the stairs, Sari tossed her collie dog over the bannister without her mother noticing. Like a secret admirer seeing a rose tossed to him from the balcony, Gnarly leapt from the loveseat to catch the toy in his teeth and ran down the stairs to his hiding spot behind the sofa in the study.

"I really don't like that woman," Archie said. "Sari so wants to be friends with Gnarly, and Gnarly likes her, too."

Randi Finnegan said, "It's my job to keep her not just safe, but also comfortable, considering all that she's given up to help us. If she's afraid here with Gnarly, then I should move her."

It was exactly as Leah had called it. She had the US Marshal at her beck and call for snitching on her ex-husband. Her blood boiling, Archie clenched her teeth while exchanging a quick glance with Bogie, who sighed heavily while running his fingers over his mustache.

"I'll make arrangements for the three of you to stay in a suite at the Spencer Inn," Mac said to Randi. "Between security and David's department, you'll all be safe there."

"We'll go first thing in the morning." Randi's eyes fell on David's.

They met for a short moment before David turned away. "I'll go call my people."

❀   ❀   ❀

Randi Finnegan believed in traveling light. You never know with witnesses in the program when you're suddenly going to have to be on the move. In fact, there had been more than one time when she was forced to move with only the clothes on her back. With the chief of the police down the hall, the deputy chief sleeping on the sofa in the living room, and eight armed guards, four police officers and four trained private security guards patrolling outside, she felt reasonably safe.

That was not to mention the German shepherd who also seemed to be on watch roaming from one bedroom to the next, except for Sari's room. Leah had closed and locked the door after Randi assured her that they would be moving the very next morning.

Randi was packing her clothes for the move to the Spencer Inn when there was a knock at her door. Assuming that Gnarly wasn't smart enough to knock, she tucked her handgun into the pocket of her robe and opened the door a crack to find David O'Callaghan on the other side. He was clad in his bathrobe and lounging pants. Through the opening of his robe, she saw that his chest was bare. He was cradling two brandy snifters in one hand.

"Peace offering," he said.

Without a word, she opened the door and gestured for him to come inside. Silently, he held out one of the snifters to her. She took it and closed the bedroom door.

When their eyes met, he raised his glass in a toast. "I'm sorry for making light of what happened tonight. I work with men so much that I can forget how to be a gentleman."

"I'm not asking for special treatment—only a little sensitivity would be nice."

He clicked his snifter against hers. "To sensitivity."

"To sensitivity." Eying him over her glass as she sipped the smooth cognac, she noted how blue his eyes were.

After partaking of the cognac, David wet his lips before saying, "I have a confession to make."

"You want to finish what we started last night," she replied.

He laughed. "That wasn't what was I going to confess."

Her cheeks felt warm.

"Though—" he pointed at her, "don't let me forget that we do want to talk about that." He sat down on the edge of her bed. "About tonight, when you froze—"

"I didn't freeze."

"Yes, you did.

"If you had given me a chance—"

"You had icicles hanging from your nose you froze so bad," David countered.

Now her face felt hot. He was right, and she hated him for seeing and knowing that he was right. As good as he looked to her sitting on the edge of her bed in his bathrobe, with his chiseled chest so close she could reach out and touch it—touch him—and feel the heat of his flesh on her hand; she wanted him gone, and the truth about him having saved her life along with it.

"I've been there," he said in a quiet voice.

"Been where?" she whispered back.

"I froze," he said. "I had been in Iraq and Afghanistan. I had command of fifty-five men under me. Yet, with all that—a couple of years ago, in Washington, DC, of all places, I came face to face with a twelve-year-old boy pointing a Beretta into my face and laughing as he was about to pull the trigger." David paused to take a sip of his cognac. Closing his eyes, he sighed. "All I could think about was that he was some mother's son. I couldn't move… Mac saved me… He shot that boy in the back…killed him. It was him or me. Just like tonight. It was him or you."

She sat down on the bed next to him. "Thank you."

"Don't mention it. We'll never talk about it again." David gazed into her eyes.

She felt as if he were examining her inner being.

"I'm not going to tell anyone about what happened," he said, "and I promise not to tease you about it anymore."

"I'd like that."

"I thought you would." He caressed her cheek. "Do you want to talk about that other thing you wanted to talk about?" He moved in closer to bring his lips towards hers.

"Not really," she replied. "I think we've talked about it enough."

"Same here." He covered her mouth with his.

✻　✻　✻

The deputy chief was sprawled out on the sofa. He was covered with a multi-colored afghan that Robin Spencer had received as a gift from a fan in Arizona. His mouth hanging open, Bogie snored loudly.

Gnarly led Sari across the floor, careful not to make a sound as they made their way to the hallway and the stairs down to the ground floor where the home theater contained an assortment of treasures that he had stashed behind the last row of seats. There was also a big box of popcorn and a microwave in which to pop it.

His secret friend opened the door. Her mouth dropped open when she saw the size of the movie screen.

Gnarly placed his front paws on the counter and stretched his neck to knock over the box of popcorn. Grabbing it up into his mouth, he carried it over to Sari and nudged her until he tore her attention from the movie screen.

Effortlessly, she interpreted his message. Taking a bag from the box, she went over to the microwave. While she popped the popcorn, Gnarly went over to the control center and picked up the remote in his mouth.

It took three minutes to pop the popcorn. Within five minutes, the secret friends were stretched out on the floor. Gnarly had the stuffed dog between his front paws, and Sari clutched the rubber duck in one hand. Between them, they shared a bowl of popcorn while watching an old Benji movie.

Chapter Nineteen

"I don't like Leah."

"You don't like anyone who doesn't like Gnarly." Mac came out of the bathroom to find Archie in his bed—wearing the top to the pajamas of which he was wearing the bottoms. Thinking about how much better she looked in it than him, he turned off the light and crossed the room to climb into bed next to her.

"Gnarly doesn't like her either," she said while letting him pull her over to his side, "and he is an excellent judge of character."

"Look at who you're talking about," Mac said. "Where did that rubber duck come from?"

In an effort to sound innocent, Archie's voice went up a whole octave. "You must have gotten it for him."

Mac shook his head. "Gnarly is up to his old tricks again. He stole it. I could have sworn I saw a rubber duck in the Phillips' kids' wading pool when they invited us over last week."

"Mac," she argued, "I'm sure that's not the only rubber duck in all of Deep Creek Lake."

Lauren Carr

"Should I call the Phillips to ask them if their four-year-old son is missing a rubber duck?"

"No!"

"So Gnarly did steal it and tried to hide it from me by flushing it down my toilet."

"Mac," she said, "he's a dog. How was he supposed to know that it would clog your toilet? Give him a break."

"Like you're giving Leah a break?"

Catching the meaning behind his playful grin, Archie sighed and folded her arms across her chest. "Now I feel guilty."

He wrapped his arms around her and kissed her on the cheek. "For covering up for Gnarly or for suspecting Leah of being a bad person?"

Another thought crept into her mind. "She's been texting someone—someone she's not supposed to be texting. When you're in the program, you're to cut off all contact with your past."

Seeing that she was not going to give up on talking about something other than them, he sighed and fell back onto the pillows on his side of the bed. "Maybe she's texting friends that she has made since entering the program. She's been in the program for two years. She's got to have made some friends in that time."

"She dropped her cell phone on the deck and accused me of stealing it when I gave it back."

"Did you steal it?" Mac asked her.

"No!" she replied. "But you should have seen her. She flat out accused me of stealing it."

He cocked his head at her. His eyes narrowed, and he peered at her face. She shifted to avoid his gaze. "Did you clone her phone?"

"Yes."

"Hah!"

Archie picked up the phone from the night stand. "She must have suspected that I did that, because ever since I made the clone, her phone has been off."

"What do you think she's doing that you had to clone her phone?"

"I have no idea, but she's up to something," she said. "She's definitely up to something."

"You're in the program and you text people," Mac said. "Why are you suspicious about *her* texting?"

"The feds released a statement saying that she and Sari were dead," she reminded him. "If she was serious about wanting to keep her daughter safe, then she would behave like she was dead. That means not reaching out to anyone from her old life. If she's supposed to be dead, who is she texting?"

Archie looked down at where Mac was resting his head on her shoulders. He smiled softly up at her. "You're right," she said. "I'm reaching. I don't like her and would like her to be guilty of something."

"That's what David is saying about Russell Skeltner," Mac said. "I think he had his wife killed because I simply don't like the guy."

"Is David right?"

"No." He rolled over onto his side and gazed up into her emerald green eyes. "I don't care if he does have an alibi and if the contact lens belonged to a woman. Skeltner's as guilty as sin."

"And Leah is up to something." She rolled over to face him. "I intend to find out what before she leaves."

"I have no doubt that you will," he said. "And while you're finding that out, maybe you can help me by digging into Russell Skeltner's past to find a motive for him killing his wife."

"Yes, sir, detective, sir." She saluted him.

As their laughter subsided, she brushed her hand across his cheek. He kissed her fingertips. Gazing at her slender hand, his soft expression turned to one of deep thought.

"What are you thinking so hard about?" she asked him.

"Ray Bonito." Mac looked over at her. "Cruze's lawyer says he's completely paranoid—like Howard Hughes paranoid. Even Cruze couldn't get in to see him."

"He probably has reason to be paranoid," Archie said.

"Do you remember Ray Bonito from the trial?"

"Never saw him," she replied. "The marshals kept me as far from Cruze's people as possible."

"He wasn't there the night of the murder?"

"No." She shook her head. "The police got all of Cruze's men who I saw at the murder."

"What do you remember about Cruze's wife?"

"Oh, I remember her all right," Archie said. "She was an associate professor in business administration at the university. She used to come into the library."

"A professor?" Mac sat up. "I pictured her as the clichéd blonde gun mole."

"No, she was a gorgeous redhead," she recalled, "and very smart. She taught business law."

"Law? Really?"

Archie's eyebrows almost met in the center of her forehead. "What are you thinking?"

Mac was out of bed. Without putting on his bathrobe, he threw open the door and ran down the hall to knock on David's door.

"Mac, what did I say?" Archie called to him from the bed.

"Everything!" Mac called over his shoulder back at her while pounding on David's bedroom door. "Get your laptop. We have some research to do." He turned back to the door. "David, wake up. I put it together."

The door down the hall flew open. "What's all the racket about that can't wait until morning?"

Turning around, Mac found himself face-to-face with Randi Finnegan. He also caught a glimpse of her naked breasts before she realized that her bathrobe was hanging open. He was still finding his voice when she flew back into the bedroom and David came out into the hall.

Wearing only his lounging pants, David was clutching his gun in his hand. "What's happening?"

Mac worked his mouth for a moment, while peering beyond David to where Randi was impatiently waiting on the bed. "I figured it out."

"What out?"

"Who hired those hit men at the cafe?"

David glanced over his shoulder back at Randi. He turned back to Mac. "Do we have to go now?"

"I need Archie to hunt down the evidence," Mac replied, "so I think you two have some time to get into something less comfortable."

On the top floor of the south wing of the Spencer Inn, Alan Richardson stepped off the penthouse elevator with his two bodyguards. After an early morning workout at the resort's athletic club, it was time to call room service for breakfast.

The high-priced lawyer and his bodyguards paid little attention to the two linen carts in the corridor. The housekeeping staff was cleaning the other suites on the floor—two staff employees in the corner suite across the hall, and another pair at the other end of the corridor.

Richardson opened the door and stepped into the suite with one of the bodyguards behind him. The guard instinctively pulled his weapon when they spotted Mac waiting in the chair in the corner of the living room.

"Not even a hello before shooting me," Mac replied at the sight of the gun.

The guard kept his weapon aimed at him.

"What are you doing in my suite?" Richardson stepped into the room.

"Actually," Mac replied, "this is my suite." He gestured at their surroundings. "I guess you didn't do your homework. I own the Spencer Inn. Therefore," he waved in the air the key card he had used to let himself in. "I can go anywhere I want—whenever I want." After putting the key card down on the table, he picked up the mimosa he had been drinking when they came in. "Have a mimosa …on me." He gestured to the pitcher and glass on the bar.

Richardson ordered the gunman to put away his gun. "I'd rather you leave, even if you do own this hotel. There is an expectation of privacy when you check into a hotel—and right now, you're invading it." He crossed to the door and opened it. "So I would invite you to leave."

"I know where Tommy Cruze's wife is."

Alan Richardson froze. The guard looked from the lawyer to Mac and back again.

Mac flashed a smirk at Alan Richardson. "Now your line is to tell the guard to wait outside while we talk about this in private."

The lawyer ordered the guard. "Outside. Don't let anyone in until I come tell you." Once the guard was out in the hall, Richardson closed the door and rushed to stand over Mac. "What the hell are you talking about?"

"Where's your wife, Richardson?"

"Out," the lawyer replied. "What does she have to do with any of this?"

"I remembered something during the night," Mac said. "At the café yesterday morning, when your wife came in, one, she could not take her eyes off Cruze. Yet, you said she had never met Tommy Cruze."

"He was an ugly brute, and he was dead," Richardson said. "That's why she couldn't take her eyes off him."

"Two,'" Mac said, "you referred to the hit men as those men posing as FBI agents." He cast a smile in Richardson's direction. "You were inside before they arrived, and during the shootout. How did you know they were wearing FBI insignias on their clothes?"

"One of your people mentioned it," Richardson said.

"Maybe," Mac said, "but I like my idea better. You knew because you and your wife set up the hit."

"Why would Ariel get involved in any conspiracy to hit Tommy Cruze?" Alan Richardson laughed loudly. "She had never even met him."

"Nose job, cheek and breast implants, but that wasn't enough to fool a face recognition program into not seeing that the woman who you now claim to be your wife is really Harper Cruze." Mac sat up. "That's why you two had to take him out. You weren't lying all those years ago when you said Cruze's wife had left him before he got home to kill her. She had escaped." Grinning, he pointed a finger at the lawyer. "You helped her. We called the FBI to ask about the blood that was left in the car." Mac shook his head. "No body tissue. If she had been shot, there would have been body tissue mixed with the blood. She faked her death to frame her husband for killing her, and then you defended him just enough to make it convincing, but not enough to keep him from going to jail."

"How many of those drinks have you had?"

"Like I said, I own this Inn." Mac took a cell phone from his pocket and tossed it onto the coffee table. "I found the burn phone from which the phony FBI agents received the text giving them the time and place to hit Cruze. You texted your wife with the location, and she texted the hired killers from this burn phone."

"No jury will ever hear any of that," Richardson said. "Your search was illegal, and that cell phone will be tossed out of evidence."

Mac continued, "During the night, we collected DNA from the dishes that Ariel ate from last night and sent it to the lab. They compared it to Harper Cruze's DNA. It was a match. Harper Cruze had dinner in this suite last night before running—maybe to get away from me. I saw how she was staring at Cruze's body yesterday morning. It wasn't just horror—it was relief—that comes from a long war being over."

"Ariel had nothing to do with any of it." The lawyer poured a mixture of the mimosa from the pitcher into a glass. "Would you believe I introduced them?" He lowered himself onto the loveseat across from Mac. "I warned her from the very beginning—when she started dating Cruze—that nothing good would ever come from it. But she found him exciting—she loved men who were forceful and aggressive—until she found out how forceful and aggressive he was." He sipped from the glass. "By then, it was too late. She was in deep and couldn't get out—not alive."

"So you helped her fake her death and then defended Cruze of murdering the man she was having an affair with." Mac sat forward in his seat. "Tell me, just between us—did you purposely lose that trial?"

"I didn't have to with Kendra Douglas testifying," the lawyer said. "You should have seen the prosecution's witness. That woman was determined and unshakable. Cruze knew he was buried the second she took that stand." He sat back in the seat and laughed. "Do you want to know the totally ironic part of the whole thing?"

"What?"

"Harper wasn't having an affair with Reynolds," he whispered. "They were only friends."

Mac wasn't surprised. "She was having an affair with you."

"Cruze focused on Reynolds because he was handsome and had a reputation with the ladies. He never suspected it was his dull, workaholic lawyer."

This shocked Mac. "You had to know Cruze would kill Reynolds."

"Collateral damage." The lawyer went on, "I was the one who suggested the Dockside Café. I set up the hit with the assassins, trusted associates of Bonito."

"What if that couple hadn't left?" Mac asked. "What if your paid assassins hadn't been stopped by the FBI and went in? Would you have let them kill—"

"Their instructions were to only kill Cruze and his bodyguard. I had to kill him. It was kill or be killed." The smug look was gone. "Cruze was so intent on revenge when he got out of prison. He never bought that Harper was dead. Over the years, he had become convinced that everything, Kendra Douglas witnessing the murder, Harper's disappearance— everything was an elaborate con job to frame him and put him away. When he got out, he was obsessed with getting revenge on everyone for everything." Richardson paused to sip his drink. "I thought that if I was able to uncover where Kendra Douglas was so he could concentrate on her, that would satisfy him."

"So you dug around until you found someone in the US Marshal's office willing to give up Kendra Douglas's location," Mac said.

"Everyone has their price," the lawyer said with a smirk.

"And if they become a lose end," Mac said, "all you have to do is make a phone call, and they're dead."

Mac was surprised to see Alan Richardson's face go blank.

"Ginger Altman," Mac said, "with the US Marshal's office. When they started closing in on her, her last phone call was to your office. A short time later, she was dead—killed by another one of Bonito's people."

"Yes, I had her killed, too." Alan Richardson gazed down into his glass. "I did it all to protect Ariel. I love her. I'm sure you'd do the same thing for your woman."

"Yes, I can see why you believed you had to do it," Mac said. "It was only a matter of time before Cruze saw Ariel and recognized her. If not by looks, then by a glance, or the way she tilted her head."

"All you have on me is conspiracy to commit murder," the lawyer said. "Once a jury finds out who the target was and why, they'll refuse to convict me."

"What about your wife?" Mac replied. "She had to know."

Alan set the glass, now drained, down on the coffee table between them. "I have represented members of organized crime for twenty years. I know where all the bodies are buried. You'd be surprised what the feds would be willing to give up in exchange for what I have to offer." He sat back in his seat. "One woman for a dozen of the FBI's most wanted."

"I'm not in the position to promise anything," Mac said. "All I want is to know what happened at the café."

"I told you what happened at the café," Alan said. "We went in. We ordered coffee and breakfast. Suddenly, people started dropping dead."

"You forgot about the couple that left before Cruze dropped dead."

Startled, Alan nodded. "Maybe because they left before things started happening."

Resting his elbows on his knees, Mac sat forward. "Their names are Gordon and Nora Crump."

"Names don't ring a bell."

Even though Mac was suspicious, he could see that Alan Richardson's confusion was sincere. "Had you ever seen them before?"

"Never laid eyes on them before in my whole life." The lawyer shook his head.

"You said they got into a fight—"

"They did."

"What about?" Mac asked.

"No idea," Alan said. "I wasn't interested in them. What does it matter what they were fighting about?"

"The husband is now dead," Mac told him. "His wife claims he had some business dealings with Tommy Cruze."

The shock on the lawyer's face was genuine. "If he did, I knew nothing about it."

"A witness to the murder says the killer said, 'This is for Tommy Cruze,' right before he emptied his weapon on him."

Alan Richardson shook his head so hard his jowls shook. "We had nothing to do with that. They were long gone of their own volition before our men arrived."

"Maybe there was another connection," Mac asked.

"We wouldn't even know where to find them."

"Come on," Mac laughed. "You're a crime boss. You have connections. Spencer and Deep Creek Lake is a small community. How hard could it be—"

"Why would we want to kill some strange looking couple bickering over him being a wimp?"

Mac jerked his head. "What did you say?"

Alan gazed at him with question in his eyes.

"You said they were bickering about him being a wimp."

A slow smile formed on the lawyer's lips. "I remember now… what they got into a fight about…Louie, Cruze's bodyguard, took their cream."

"Cream?" Mac repeated.

Alan nodded his head. "We ordered coffee all the way around. The woman poured our coffee for us. We had sugar, but no cream on the table. But there was a bowl of those little tubs of cream over at that couple's table, so Louie went and got it. When the husband didn't say anything, the wife had a fit."

"Then she left." Now the slow grin came to Mac's lips. "Cruze and his bodyguard used the cream… and then died."

The cream Gordon Crump had left on the table!

Chapter Twenty

FBI Agents Sid Delaney and Tony Bennett were waiting at the police station when David O'Callaghan and Mac arrived with Alan Richardson in custody.

In the early morning hour, most of the officers were assembled to get their assignments from Desk Sergeant Tonya before going on patrol. This was the second shift for most of them since Tommy Cruze and his crew had arrived in town. Gordon Crump's murder the night before did nothing to slow things down.

"What is this?" the senior special agent's tone was over-flowing with annoyance.

"Alan Richardson has confessed to hiring the two assassins at the Dockside Café," David announced.

"That's our case," Tony Bennett said. "You aren't even supposed to be investigating it."

"I was following up a lead in another murder case when Richardson confessed," Mac said.

Agent Delaney regarded Alan Richardson with a mixture of both disbelief that he confessed to anything willingly, and annoyance that it was to the local police chief and not him. "Is that true?"

"I want a deal," Richardson said.

"Be serious," Delaney said.

"I am serious," Richardson said. "I have a ton of information that will close up a lot of your open cases. You'll get it all. You can even put me in jail. All I want is immunity and protection for my wife, Ariel."

Delaney looked from Alan Richardson to his partner to David and Mac, then back to the lawyer. "Where is your wife?"

"She's driving back to our place in Philadelphia," Richardson said. "I called her before we left the hotel. She'll meet your people in Philadelphia and call me when she is at a safe house and under protection. Once I know you have her and she is safe, then I'll start talking. I'll give you everything you need to bust the biggest mobsters on the East Coast."

"Put him in the car and we'll take him back to Washington," Agent Delaney told Tony Bennett.

"This should be interesting," Agent Bennett said before taking the lawyer by the arm and leading him out.

Special Agent Delaney glared at Mac and David in silence.

After the door shut, David said, "You don't have to thank us."

"Thank you?"

"You're welcome," Mac replied with sarcasm.

"We have a serious problem," the special agent announced while looking from one of them to the other.

"Well, it just got better," David said. "I have a feeling Alan Richardson is going to make your career in ways you could only imagine. He's been representing mob figures for his whole career."

"Now all we have left is the poisoning inside the café," Mac said.

"Whoever did that put a lot of thought and premeditation into it," Delaney said. "Our forensics people said every tub in that bowl that had been on Cruze's table was tampered with. The paper cover over the tub had been peeled off to mix the poison into the cream, and then the tub was resealed. No one would have noticed without looking for it."

"Well, at least you finally have Alan Richardson's confession to hiring those two assassins to take out Cruze," David said. "We still have Gordon Crump's murder, as well as Mary Catherine Skeltner."

"I also have Ray Bonito's murder to solve," Agent Delaney said. "Oh, and identifying the double-crossing inside man who set up the ambush last night."

David and Mac exchanged puzzled glances.

"Ray Bonito?" David asked. "Was he the—"

"Body in the grave." Delaney nodded his head. "DNA confirmed it."

"Any idea when he was killed?" David asked.

"We're still working on trying to pinpoint the last time he was seen alive by anyone," Delaney said. "What gets my hackles up is that we collected the dead men's cell phones and found an exchange of communication with who we thought was Bonito, and more than one text saying that our guy was a fed and to eliminate him ASAP. Someone blew his cover, and I want to know who."

David gestured to the parking lot outside where Delaney's partner had taken Alan Richardson. "Could have been—"

Mac was already shaking his head. "Richardson had no idea that the hit man was an agent."

"If it wasn't Richardson, then that means the rat who burned our guy has to be someone on the inside." Delaney said. "I'm investigating my men, but I can already tell you that

I doubt our rat is among them." He shook his index finger in David's face. "You better hope like hell that I do find our rat on our side, because once I'm through looking there, I'm going to start looking in your camp."

"My men aren't dirty!" Lunging, David riled like a papa bear.

Fearing that the police chief was going to physically attack Delaney, Mac yanked him back by the arm. "We'll investigate our own camp, thank you very much."

"You do that." Delaney stepped up to tell David to his face.

The two men's penetrating glare cast an electrical vibe throughout the room that captured the officers' attention.

"Who's going to investigate you?" Delaney asked in a low tone. "After all, your men weren't in our van to see my man… you were."

Mac pushed in between them to break the glare. "You can investigate O'Callaghan as much as you want. He's clean. I'd stake my life on it."

"Well, my man staked his live on it, and he's got a bullet in his shoulder and the cover that he's spent three years setting up is burned. He's lucky. In that ambush, it could have been a lot worse. No one blows my operation without getting called on it."

"Bring it on," David challenged him.

"I will."

With that parting shot, Delaney, under the glare of the whole Spencer police force, departed.

"Here I thought he'd be happy that we brought in Alan Richardson," Mac said in a breathless voice.

"This is not good," Tonya said. "Having the feds mad at us is not good at all."

"No, it's not," David said.

"Maybe the agent blew his own cover and didn't realize it," Tonya said.

Mac shook his head. "Cruze trusted him enough to ask him to take out Archie. As of yesterday morning, his cover was secure. It was after the murders at the café…" *The men received the information that the agent was a cop via text!*

Mac remembered the conversation he had with Archie the night before. *"If she's supposed to be dead, who is she texting? She's up to something."*

"I need to go home," Mac said with a desperate tone. He grabbed his gun from its holster. "Tonya, call the manor, and tell Randi not to leave with Leah. They are to stay until we get there." He grabbed David by arm. "We need to get out to the house now."

"What is it?" David asked.

"I'll tell you on the way."

Mac was rushing for the door when it flew open so hard and fast that he thought the federal agents had returned. Instead, Ariel Richardson walked in. Her beautiful face was contorted in anger. Her eyes were red rimmed and wide. The gun she had aimed at Mac's face appeared equally menacing.

He backed up from the door.

"I came for my husband."

Lauren Carr

Chapter Twenty-One

The hardest part of being a research assistant or editor—the two things that Archie had made her life since being abruptly torn from her old one— is lack of movement.

Archie had learned to focus all of her attention on the task that she was given. Whether it was how autopsies were performed at the turn of the nineteenth century, or digging into the background of a murder suspect who appeared completely innocent to everyone else on the planet, she would virtually dive into her computer and the Internet—only to come up for air sometimes as much as ten hours later, exhausted and hungry, and with cramped muscles from lack of movement.

As the years went by and her muscles had grown older, she found that she had to force herself to break from the concentration and do some walking.

After hours of digging through various social media sites to unravel the mystery of Russell and Mary Catherine Skeltner, Archie left the study and went in search of a snack upstairs in the kitchen.

She was startled by a witch's cackle bursting forth from the home theatre across the hall.

Archie slowly pushed down on the door handle and stepped inside. Loud music hit her in the ears and face as the crescendo of the thrilling soundtrack from *The Wizard of Oz* burst forth from the room. Specifically, it was the scene of the flying monkeys filling the sky around the Wicked Witch's castle.

"Oh, Gnarly, I'm scared," a little girl's voice came from out of the darkness.

The dark scene from the old movie filled the movie screen in the theatre. Lounging sofas made up four rows of seats for the viewing audience.

The terrifying music was mixed with a little girl's squeal. "I'm so glad you're watching this with me, Gnarly."

A dog-like groan responded to her.

When her eyes adjusted to the dark in the room, Archie discovered Bogie, sacked out on one of the lounges, sound asleep. Sari and Gnarly were sprawled out on the floor in front of the screen. Sari laid on top of Gnarly with her arms wrapped around him. In front of them was a giant bowl tipped over and spilling popcorn across the floor. Both of them were feeding from the bowl and the popcorn on the floor.

"I know they're not real, but those monkeys always scare me." Pointing to the screen, Sari told Gnarly as if he had never seen it before. "But Toto escapes from the castle and goes to get help."

Gnarly was more interested in the handful of popcorn she had in her hand. She opened it to let him lick up the pieces from her palm, after which she licked the remnants that his tongue had missed.

"You're the best friend I've ever had." She hugged him closer. "I know you'll never hurt me." She kissed him on the top of the head. "I love you, Gnarly."

Gnarly returned her kiss with a lick on the face and mouth.

So she does talk! Just not to us. "Sari," Archie called as she came forward out of the darkness.

The little girl whirled around and stared up at her.

"I see you and Gnarly are watching *The Wizard of Oz.*" Archie knelt down next to her.

Saying nothing, Sari clung to Gnarly.

"That was my favorite movie when I was growing up. Do you know who I loved the most in the whole movie?"

Sari stared at her without saying a word.

"Toto," Archie said.

The two of them eyed each other.

"I know you can talk, Sari," Archie said. "It's okay that you only want to talk to Gnarly. He's a good listener. But if you ever want to talk to someone who will answer back, you can talk to me. I'm a good listener, too."

The message in the little girl's eyes ordered Archie to leave them alone.

"Maybe you'd like some ice cream to go with the popcorn?"

Sari turned to the dog and asked, "Do you want some ice cream, Gnarly?"

"His favorite flavor is vanilla," Archie said. "Would you like some hot fudge sauce on yours?"

Sari nodded her head.

"Two ice creams coming up." Watching the little girl return to hugging Gnarly, Archie backed out of the theater.

The cell phone in her pocket vibrated to signal a text. She took it out of her pocket to see that it was the clone for Leah's phone. She was sending a text to multiple recipients—all of whom were only named by initials. *Scatr & la lo untl I contact u*

Hurrying back into the study, Archie reached into her pocket for her cell phone and dialed the number for Mac's cell. After three rings, it went to voice mail.

"Rats!" she stomped her feet.

Scatter and lay low until I contact you!

Recalling the text message, Archie's eyes raised when she heard a scream and a gun shot from the bedroom two floors above.

"Your husband isn't here," David told Ariel Richardson, who had ordered everyone (Tonya, David, Mac, and two officers who had not yet left to go on patrol) to gather together in the center of the reception area. They were all holding their hands up for her to see.

"You're lying!" Ariel's well-cultured tone from the day before now held a hysterical edge to it. "He told me that he was coming here with you."

"But when we got here, the feds were waiting," David explained in an even tone. "The attempted hit is their case. That makes your husband their witness. They're taking him to Washington right now. They left about a half-hour ago."

Mac tore his eyes from the barrel of the gun to look into Ariel's eyes. He had seen that look before, usually in the faces of women who felt that they had lost it all. They had nothing more to lose. *This is not good. This is not good at all.*

"Your husband is making a deal with the feds," Mac said. "He loves you very much and wants, above everything else, to keep you safe."

"Alan won't last a single day if he so much as speaks to the feds," Ariel said. "They can't protect him. No one can protect him. That's why I'm taking him with me and we'll run away together—we can go underground and start a new life."

"Ariel," David said while stepping toward her, "we know how dangerous the people your husband worked with are—"

"You know?" she shrieked. "You don't know anything. I lived with them. They have connections everywhere—into everything. There is no place that they can't reach you."

While David had Ariel's attention, Mac, keeping turned to the side, slowly reached down to touch the button on his cell phone. Unable to see the keypad, he could only hope that he tapped the side that would do a redial of the last number he had dialed, and that the phone would be on speaker phone.

"Do you know how long it took me to find a rat in the US Marshal's office to get me Kendra Douglas's location in the Witness Protection Program?"

"You?" Mac asked. "It was you?"

"The caller ID on Ginger Altman's phone was Alan Richardson," David said. "But since you're his wife—the phone is in his name."

"You set up the hit," Mac said. "Those two hit men at the café—"

"I told Alan about it after I had set it up so that he could make sure he found an excuse to leave before they got there," she said.

"Then *you* hired the hit men," Mac said.

"They thought they were doing a job for Bonito," she said. "Texting is great that way. With no voice and a phony ID on the phone—"

"You can easily hide your identity," Mac finished. "When I confronted him with the evidence, he took the blame to protect you."

"Alan was always such a gentleman." Tears rolled down Ariel's cheeks. "He saved my life."

"Ginger Altman," Mac said, "the leak at the US Marshal's office who gave you the whereabouts for Kendra Douglas—I guess it was you, not Alan, who arranged to have her killed when she became a threat. Your husband didn't seem to know about it when I mentioned it."

"She called the office and demanded money to run away," Ariel said. "I met people like her all the time when I was married to Tommy. Once you start paying them for their silence, they never go away."

"Alan is confessing to everything," Mac said, "everything that you did—to protect you."

"That is why I'm going to save him now." She aimed the gun at Tonya. "You have five minutes to turn over my husband, and then I'm going to start shooting your officers one by one."

❊ ❊ ❊

Years of training had Bogie instantly awake and on his feet the second he heard the gun shot from up above. He almost tripped over Sari and Gnarly while running for the door. Before throwing it open, he turned to Sari, who was clinging to Gnarly. The German shepherd was ready to charge as soon as Bogie opened the door.

"Gnarly, stay with Sari," Bogie said. "Whatever happens, make sure she's safe."

Whirling around, Gnarly gently took Sari's wrist into his mouth and led her to the other side of the room to disappear into the darkness of the theater.

Cracking open the door, Bogie peered out. He could see Archie at the top of the steps.

"Randi is bleeding," he heard Archie say. "You need to let me call a doctor. She needs help."

"If you want to help her," he heard Leah yell, "you'll go get Sari and give me the keys to your car. If I see any cops following me, then she's dead! Tell her!"

Bogie heard a muffled response that sounded pained.

He tapped the button on his radio. "Tonya," he said in a loud whisper. "This is Bogie. We've got a hostage situation here at Spencer Manor." He heard no response.

"Bogie!" Hector Langford's voice called out into his ear. "Are you able to respond? We heard a shot. Is everything cool inside?"

It took several seconds for Bogie to realize that the Spencer Inn security manager was calling to him on his ear bud.

"No," Bogie answered. "We have a hostage situation. Leah has shot Finnegan and taken her hostage. She is demanding her daughter and safe passage out. I repeat, Leah is armed and has taken Finnegan hostage. I'm not getting any response on my radio from the station."

"That's because something is going down there," Hector said. "I got what sounds like a butt dial from Faraday. Some woman sounds like she's taken them all hostage and is threatening to shoot everyone."

"Damn!"

"I've already called the feds for us and the state police for your department," Hector said. "Is the little girl safe?"

"Gnarly is guarding her in the home theater." Bogie squinted to peer into the dark corner of the theater where Gnarly had led her. "Gnarly? Sari? Where are you?"

They were both gone.

"Archie is upstairs trying to talk Leah down," he reported.

"Don't you worry, mate," Hector told him. "We've got your back." In his ear, Bogie heard Hector rallying the guards outside to move in.

❋   ❋   ❋

"It's dark, Gnarly," Sari whimpered. "I can't see anything."

In the dark corner of the home theater, she could feel, but not see, the dark tunnel that Gnarly had urged her to crawl into on her hands and knees. It seemed like a game of follow the leader.

She had not seen Gnarly jump up to push the button that popped open the hatch door built into the wall beneath the movie screen. Grasping the hem of her skirt in his mouth, he had pulled her into the tunnel behind him. Clinging to the dog's tail as her lifeline, Sari crawled behind him until they reached the end of the tunnel, at which she felt a flight of stairs. Using his nose, Gnarly nudged her up the stairs.

"What's up there?" she asked with a whine.

As if to show the way, Gnarly trotted up the stairs to what seemed to be a dead end.

She followed. The sound of birds singing and the lake water seeped down to her ears. With a push on the roof above her, the trap door opened to reveal a multi-colored floral scene around them.

"Cool!" she squealed.

Gnarly leapt out of the secret passageway.

Outside in Robin Spencer's rose garden, Hector Langford was squinting through his binoculars into the living room while praying, as he always did when he found himself in a tough situation.

When he had signed on as security manager at the five-star Spencer Inn, he had assumed the toughest situation he would run into would be a sticky fingered housekeeper. He had needed a break after retiring from a career in covert operations.

No one warned him that anything is possible when you go to work at an inn owned by a world famous mystery writer. When Robin Spencer died, her son, who turned out to be the personification of her literary detective, Mickey Forsythe, stepped things up a notch.

How did I ever get into this? Oh, Lord, let that little girl be okay. The answer to his prayer came in the form of a bark.

"Is that Gnarly?" one of the officers nearby asked a security guard hiding a few paces away.

The glasses still in front of his eyes, Hector turned in the direction of the bark in time to spot a magnified dog snout racing straight for his face. Before he could prepare himself, Hector Langford was flat on his back in the rose garden with a hundred pounds of fur on his chest and a squealing child wrapped around his leg.

US Marshal Randi Finnegan was bleeding. One whole side of her shirt and pants was covered in blood where Leah had shot her. Leah held a gun to her head, with a second gun tucked into the waistband of her slacks.

Archie's blue Ruger was on the floor between them where Leah had ordered her to toss it.

Archie refrained from covering her mouth in horror while watching Leah shove the wounded woman, her friend and confidante of a decade, down the stairs into the living room. "It doesn't have to be like this, Leah. It's clear that you killed Ray Bonito in self-defense and to protect Sari. You covered up his murder because you were afraid that once his people found out who you were and what you had done—"

"That's not what I'm afraid of them finding out," Leah said. "It's what happened afterwards."

"You took over running his operation," Archie said.

"I can't believe it." Randi struggled against Leah's hold with her arm around her throat. "You mean you were running a major crime syndicate while in the program?"

Leah laughed. "Who would have ever guessed that some-one who was being protected from the mob would be running the mob?"

"I'm going to be so fired for this," Randi said.

"Or dead," Leah replied.

Spying movement in the shadows beyond the deck, Archie eased over toward the fireplace on the other side of the living room. "Leah, it doesn't have to be like this."

"Yes, it does," Leah said. "You don't get it, do you? I have been running a major identity theft operation, illegal arms deals, swapping drugs for weapons and then selling them to the cartels—all of it and I loved it," she hissed. "All that power. All those men doing what I said, when I said. Someone gives me grief, and with one text, they're dead. Someone gets in the way, just the tap of a few fingertips on the keypad, and the way is clear. It's exhilarating…and addictive." She waved her gun at Archie. "Really—seriously—I never planned for it to be that way. I didn't go to see Ray to kill him. But it happened. And I thought that I would pretend to be him, using the phone, sending texts, for only a few days until I figured out what I was going to do. But then, I couldn't give all that up. Don't you understand?"

"No," Archie said.

"Admit it," Leah taunted her. "Wouldn't you like to be Mac Faraday—have all his power—have people cow-towing to you—for only one day?"

✳   ✳   ✳

"Ariel," David said while trying to ease away from the group of officers, "you have to believe us. Alan is not here. We don't have him, Ariel, and we have no authority to bring him to you."

As he was talking, David eased up toward her. "You have every reason to be scared. That's why they have the witness protection program, so that people who are brave, like Alan, can help to put people like Tommy Cruze away without getting hurt."

Slowly drawing his gun, Mac eased around behind the hostages and slipped out of the range of Ariel's peripheral vision.

They could all see that the terrified woman was indeed an amateur. It was with little difficulty that David had managed to draw her attention away from the rest of the officers. Taking them hostage was not planned. It was a desperate act of survival.

When David took a step toward her, Ariel held her ground. He reached out his hand to her. "Ariel, you don't want to do this. You're not a killer like Cruze. Everyone will see that everything you did, and everything that Alan took the credit for, was for self-defense." He reached for her. "Hand me the gun."

Mac saw Tonya's Taser resting on top in her open hand bag.

Indecisive, Ariel was breathing hard.

David inched in closer. "We'll talk to the prosecutor. The feds will protect you."

As he reached for the gun, she pulled back. "No!" Her resolved returned and she thrust the gun up and at David. "They'll kill us both. We—"

Mac dove for her from behind. With one arm, he thrust her hand up into the air. The bullet flew wild to hit the ceiling. With his other arm, Mac planted the Taser against her neck and hit the trigger to send a jolt of electric shock through her body.

With a single scream, Ariel Richardson collapsed into Mac's arms.

✳   ✳   ✳

"Why did you kill Ray Bonito?" Archie asked Leah. "When he recognized you, why didn't you tell Randi and get relocated?"

Leah laughed. "Do you have any idea how many people Mario worked for and with? No matter where they put me, no matter how they had me live, one of Mario's people was going to locate me. I thought Ray—he knew my father. He said he had a lot of respect for my family, which was why he wasn't going to rat me out to Mario's people, as long as I did as he said. Do you know what he wanted me to do?"

Randi replied in a weak voice. "I can imagine." Her clothes were soaked with blood. Losing consciousness, she staggered to stay on her feet.

Lying on the floor in the dining room, with his gun aimed at Leah from over the lower wall, Bogie was in position. He got her into his sights.

Without warning, Leah whirled around to aim her gun at him.

"Oh," Archie called out as she collided with the end table. Both it and the lamp fell over onto the floor.

The sudden movement in the other direction caught Leah off guard. Pulling the trigger at the same time, she turned toward Archie, who had dropped to the floor behind the end table. Her shot went wild and took out a picture of a Spanish bull fighter that Archie always hated.

When Leah ping-ponged to find her target, she lost her hold on Randi, who slumped to the floor.

Seeing Leah firing in Archie's direction, Bogie grabbed the precious second to fire his gun, but he didn't have enough time to readjust his aim. The shot ended up taking out the grandfather clock. It wasn't the first time the grandfather clock had been shot out. Before he could take another shot, Leah had spotted him and had him in her sights.

Archie was back up on her knees and firing. The little pearl-handled revolver that she had concealed in her ankle holster was more for appearances, but in the hands of an experienced shooter like she had become, it was good enough.

The bullet tore into Leah's side, traveled upward and shot out through her upper chest. During its flight through her body, it tore through her heart. She was dead before she hit the ground.

"Randi!" Archie was by the marshal's side.

"Target is dead," Bogie reported into his ear bud to Hector at the same time that the guards came bursting in from all directions—taking out doors, windows, sheers, and curtains in the process.

Chapter Twenty-Two

"Randi is going to be okay," Archie reported to Mac on the cell phone from the waiting room at the hospital. "The bullet went through and through without hitting any vital organs. She should be out in a few days. How are things there?"

"Complicated." In the squad room, Mac could see David being questioned by the chief of the local state police barracks. "Ariel Richardson, aka Harper Cruze, was the one who had hired the assassins posing as FBI."

"Self-defense," Archie said, "If she hadn't killed him, he would have killed her."

"Yeah, well, she isn't exactly Miss Goody-Two-Shoes," Mac said. "Dr. Reynolds, the man you saw killed, wasn't having an affair with her. She and Alan Richardson set him up so that Cruze wouldn't know who she was really fooling around with."

"Those couple of…" Archie didn't want to say the word.

"That's what they are, all right." Mac rubbed his tired eyes. "You can bet they'll get immunity and protection. Alan

Richardson has been collecting information for years to use as a get-out-of-jail-free card for this very purpose."

"They'll get theirs," she replied. "If not here, then they will in the next world."

"Hey!" The cheerful note in Mac's tone came out as forced. "I haven't told David about Finnegan being shot yet. Bogie told him about the standoff and shooting, but I asked that he let me tell him about Finnegan. So if she asks, tell her that he'll be coming by to see her later. How's Sari in all this?"

"She and Gnarly are inseparable. Hector took them to the Spencer Inn." She sighed. "Another deputy from the US Marshals Office is on the way to take care of her. Sari's still in the program. So the feds will be relocating her. The agent I talked to said there may be a couple, who so happen to be in the program, looking to adopt. They're going to look through their records to find a good permanent home for her. That poor little girl. Both of her parents are murderers."

"If we can get her to talk," Mac said, "we can find out exactly what happened at the Dockside Café."

Released by the two state police officers, David started to cross over to join Mac.

"I have an idea about that," Archie said.

When Mac hung up, David said, "The media is going to have a field day. A police department took hostage by a distraught woman trying to spring her husband." He patted Mac on the shoulder. "You did good. I'm glad you didn't shoot her."

"I don't go around shooting everyone." Mac slipped the phone into its case on his belt.

"It only seems like it lately," David said.

Mac cleared his throat. "Meanwhile, at Spencer Manor, a witness in the witness protection program has been running a crime syndicate right under the government's noses. You do know that Finnegan is going to be the scapegoat in all this."

"I imagine so." He lowered himself into a chair in the reception area. "This certainly doesn't look good for her." Reminded of Randi, David took his cell phone out of the case on his belt. "The way the feds operate, there's going to have to be a fall guy, and since she was Leah's handler—"

"David…"

Seeing no messages, David looked up from his phone. "What?" He took a deep breath. "What other bad news do you have for me? Go ahead, make my day complete."

"Leah shot Finnegan." When David jumped to his feet, Mac placed his hands on his shoulders. "She's okay. The bullet went through and through. She's at the hospital now and Archie is with her."

At a loss for words, David glanced around. He clasped his gun and equipment belt as if he were looking for something. In reality, he was unsure of what he needed to do. His men needed him there to lead them, but he yearned to go be with Randi Finnegan, who only the week before annoyed him to distraction.

"Would you like me to drive you to the hospital?" Mac looked over at the chief detective in charge of the scene who had been standing in ear shot to overhear their conversation.

"I got your information," the detective said. "We'll be in touch with additional questions."

Free to leave, Mac ushered David out the door.

"Why do you think Nora Crump is lying about Gordon planting the poison?" David asked on the way to the hospital in Oakland, the next town over. Sitting in the front passenger seat of his cruiser, instead of the driver's seat, he felt out of place.

David hated the silence that filled the air in moments like this. It seemed to suck up the oxygen in the nursing home when he tried to visit his mother. Everyone was afraid to talk as if their words could burst it. He asked questions to break the silence. "Because Richardson says they got into a fight over the bodyguard taking the cream from their table?"

"Exactly," Mac said. "I remember what the Crumps were saying to each other when they were leaving. We overheard part of their fight through the agent's wire. Gordon was asking her what she wanted him to do. She said she wanted him to be a man for once. She was upset because he let the bodyguard take the cream from their table. Why if it was meant for Cruze?"

"The fight could have been staged to give them an excuse to leave the scene," David said. "But think about it. How would Gordon Crump have known Tommy Cruze was in Deep Creek Lake?"

"According to Alan Richardson," Mac answered, "Cruze decided to come out at the last minute after Archie killed two of his men. The desk clerk says the Crumps had made their reservations over a week ago and checked in the same day Cruze arrived in town. Another question. How did Gordon Crump know Cruze was going to be at the Dockside Café?"

"If Nora is lying, then Leah killed Tommy Cruze," David said. "She had to recognize Tommy Cruze, who was demanding to meet with Bonito, who no one knew was dead. Cruze was probably starting to figure it out, and picked the Dockside Café for a reason. When Cruze walked in, Leah freaked and poisoned him."

"Two problems with that." Mac ticked off on his fingers. "One, Richardson admitted in his confession that he suggested the Dockside Café. Two, he also states that the poisoned cream came from the Crumps' table. Nora says her husband planted it for Cruze, which brings us back to how did Crump know Cruze was in Deep Creek Lake and going to be at the

Dockside Café? Nora Crump isn't telling us the truth and I hate it when witnesses lie."

David sat back in his seat. "We're right back to square one."

Mac held up a finger. "We still have one witness left to question."

With a warm hug, Archie greeted David in front of the hospital's reception desk. "Randi's going to be okay," she assured him. "She's resting now." She led him over to the waiting area to sit down.

"How did this happen?" David asked her.

"She sneaked up on Leah while she was sending a text and read it over her shoulder," Archie said while taking her cell phone from her purse. "I guess I wasn't the only one suspicious of her." She handed the phone to David. "I had made a clone of her phone. She was sending out a message to the rest of Bonito—her—people to scatter and lay low."

David looked up at Mac. "After the ambush last night. When Randi got home, Leah must have learned about how it played out and realized that the phone she had been forwarding her texts through had been discovered."

"She risked one last message to tell her people to lay low until after she was relocated," Mac said.

"She had become addicted to the power," Archie said. "She probably could have gone on to her new identity with no one ever being the wiser if she hadn't risked sending out this last message with hope of continuing to run the mob after being relocated."

"Leah killed Ray Bonito and took over his operation," Mac said. "But was she behind the poisoning at the café, and Gordon Crump's and Mary Catherine Skeltner's murders?"

"I really can't think about this anymore." David stood up. "I need to see Finnegan."

Archie's glance at Mac told him that he was obsessing again. He was so focused on catching the culprit in the latest series of murder to strike Spencer, Maryland, that he had forgotten that their friend had almost been killed. Leaving Mac alone with his thoughts, Archie escorted David down the hallway to where Randi Finnegan was asleep.

Funny. I never really pictured Randi Finnegan as David's type. Finding the apprehension he felt at the thought of David becoming involved with the US Marshal unnerving, Mac paced the waiting room until he found himself staring out the window at the park across the street without really seeing it.

In the brief time that they had known each other, David had always been involved with beautiful, leggy, curvaceous women who were eager to please the handsome, slender young man with deep blue eyes. He had no problem attracting women. It was those that he chose to go beyond a one night stand who either got him into trouble or ended up breaking his heart—sometimes both.

With her abrasive manner and plain looks, Randi Finnegan was nothing like any of David's past conquests. Recalling his latest love, Yvonne Harding, a leggy, blonde beauty queen who had broken his heart by moving to New York for a network anchor news show, Mac reconsidered his position. *A change in pattern may do David some good.*

"Why would Mary Catherine Skeltner's murder be connected to this?" Archie's voice broke through his thoughts.

Mac whirled around and grabbed his gun before realizing it was Archie who had come up behind him.

"I guess we're both jumpy," she said.

"We have reason to be." Mac took her into his arms to give her a hug. "I'm sorry I wasn't there to help you."

214

"You can't be everywhere at once," she sighed against his chest. "Besides, I had Bogie, Hector, and six armed men who basically tore apart the house while barging in. We've got some redecorating to do … again."

After they sat down, she repeated her question about Mary Catherine Skeltner.

"In both murders, the suspect was wearing a hoodie and riding a silver bike," Mac said. "Nora Crump claims that the killer said the hit on her husband was for Tommy Cruze. That's what makes it appear as if all three murders are connected."

"But," Archie argued, "Mary Catherine Skeltner was tossed down a flight of stairs."

"Bashed in her head and snapped her neck," Mac said with a nod of his head, "to make it look like an accident."

"Hired killer," Archie said. "The hit on Gordon Crump certainly sounds like a hired gun. Maybe both Nora Crump and Russell Skeltner hired the same assassin to take out their spouses. He could have worked for Tommy Cruze."

"But who is this black hooded, bike-riding killer?"

"That's the question of the day," Archie said.

Chapter Twenty-Three

They all cringed when Sari, after licking a tongue full of strawberry ice cream from the cone, held it out for Gnarly to do the same. Surprisingly, even though the German shepherd could have taken the whole two scoops from the top of the cone, he behaved gentlemanly and only took his share to allow the little girl to take her lick before offering him the next.

And so on and so on the two best friends ate their treat on the sofa in the reception area of the police station while the grown-ups conspired in Bogie's office.

The federal marshal assigned to take custody of and be in charge of Sari until she was placed with a new home watched the dog sharing the cone with the little girl with complete amusement. Sari and the grandmotherly agent had hit it off like old friends from the start after the woman had showed up at the Spencer Inn with a bag of toys and goodies.

Archie came out of the office and crossed the area to sit in Tonya's desk chair across from the little girl.

"Sari," Archie began, "are you enjoying your ice cream?"

Sari nodded her head while taking her next lick before holding out the cone to Gnarly for his turn. "Gnarly likes it, too."

"I see that." Archie glanced over her shoulder at where Mac was watching from inside the doorway of the office. He gestured for her to continue with the questioning as they had discussed. "Sari, did you tell Gnarly about all that excitement at the café the other day?"

Sari's eyes met hers.

"You know, Gnarly works for the police. Maybe if you told him what you saw, he could help to catch the people who hurt those people."

"Mommy did something bad," Sari said.

Startled by her directness, Archie said, "Did your mother ever discuss the bad things she did?"

"I listened," Sari said. "She told me that Daddy did really bad things. But I think she did, too. She kept a lot of secrets. Sometimes she would forget I was there and I'd find them out." She cocked her head at Archie. "Did Mommy kill anyone? My Daddy killed people. Did she kill people, too?"

With tears in her eyes, Archie nodded her head. "But you do know that killing people is wrong, don't you?"

"That's what Gnarly says."

"Gnarly told you that?" Archie asked with a smile that didn't quite come off.

"Gnarly's really smart about stuff like that." Sari patted his head while gazing into his eyes. "He led me out of the house through that secret room when Mommy went crazy. He's my best friend."

Behind her, Archie heard Mac mutter, "Secret room? What secret room?"

"Secret passage out of the manor," Bogie whispered. "Robin had it installed when Archie moved in."

"I think Gnarly wants you to tell him what you saw that morning at your mommy's cafe," Archie was saying, "the morning that those people died."

Sari eyed Archie over the top of her ice cream cone. She then held it over for Gnarly to take his lick. "I saw you out the window eating a croissant that Mr. Faraday bought for you," she told the German shepherd.

She took her lick. "Then Mr. Skeltner came up to Mr. Faraday and made fun of him before coming in and ordering an espresso like he does every morning." She lowered her voice to a harsh whisper. "I don't like Mr. Skeltner. Do you, Gnarly?"

Gnarly lifted his paw and bowed his head as if in agreement before taking his lick.

"He never looks at people when he talks to them," she said while he took a lick from the strawberry ice cream. "My Daddy would never look at people either. I find that when someone doesn't look at you, you can't trust them. Mommy used to look at me. Then, she stopped. That was when she became like Daddy—all secretive and stuff. What do you think, Gnarly?"

Gnarly rose to a sitting position. His head now towered over Sari. She sat up so that their eyes could meet.

"That's what I think, too," Sari said with a nod of her head.

"What else happened, Sari?" Archie asked.

The little girl continued talking to Gnarly. "Mommy was making Mr. Skeltner his espresso and he went into the dining room and was looking out the window at the lake and doing his stretching exercises, like he does every morning. He puts his hands over his head and bends over and touches his toes. A lady runner came in and stood there and looked at him. Mom didn't see her because she was making the espresso. Mr. Skeltner then took a bunch of creams from out of his fanny pouch and put them on a table. Then he dumped the creams that were in the bowl into his pouch, and put his creams in the bowl and put it on the table."

Gnarly cocked his head at her.

"Yeah," Sari said. "Weird. Why did he take our creams when he had his own?" She shrugged. "So then, Mom was done with the espresso. So she gave it to Mr. Skeltner. Then, the lady runner's husband came in and Mr. Skeltner left. After she was done with Mr. Skeltner, Mom took them to their table and the lady wanted to sit at the table where Mr. Skeltner left his creams."

Gnarly let out a yap.

"The lady runner wanted the creams that Mr. Skeltner had left," Sari said. "I know because she got real mad when those bunch of men came in and the one took them. Her and the funny smelling man didn't have their coffee yet because the man said Mom's coffee wasn't fresh enough because it was twenty minutes old. But the men took Mom's coffee even though it was old, and the one took Mr. Skeltner's cream. That was when the lady runner got real mad at her husband and called him a wuss—what's a wuss?"

Gnarly barked his answer.

"Oh," Sari responded like she understood him. "You're not a wuss, are you?" With that, she presented Gnarly with the remainder of the ice cream cone.

Mac turned to David, Bogie, and Special Agents Delaney and Bennett. "Not only did Skeltner have his wife killed, but he also tried to kill Gordon Crump, and ended up killing Tommy Cruze and his bodyguard by accident. Gordon Crump took double cream in his coffee. He would have been killed instantly if he hadn't insisted on Leah making a fresh pot. When Skeltner failed to kill him the first time, he completed the job the second time."

"And Gordon's wife pointed the finger at the mob," David said, "to divert suspicion from Skeltner."

Garrett County Prosecutor Ben Fleming swung the golf club to send the ball sailing across the grass to land with three bounces on the green. A pleased smile crossed his face before he turned to Mac and David. "How old is this witness?"

David bowed his head to look down at his feet. "Six years old."

"And she only talks to Gnarly." Ben chuckled. "Plus, she's in the federal witness protection program."

"Her mother is dead after shooting a federal agent," Mac agreed, "The US Marshals are placing her with another couple who are in the program who have been wanting to adopt a child. Once she's sent to live with them, there's no way the feds will risk bringing her back to testify at trial."

"So she's worthless." Ben dropped his club in the golf bag. "Maybe she made up the stuff about Skeltner planting the poison to protect her mother."

"Who happened to be secretly running a big crime operation," David said.

Mac said, "Russell Skeltner is a killer."

"Is that what your gut is telling you, Mac?" The prosecutor slung the strap of his golf bag over his shoulder.

"My gut has never let me down yet."

"We can't get a search warrant for Skeltner's house for traces of the strychnine based on your gut." They walked as a group across the golf course in the direction of Ben's golf ball. "And don't even think of trying to put Gnarly on the stand to testify to what she told him," he joked. "That's hearsay."

Disgusted, but not surprised, Mac and David failed to connect to the humor.

"Listen." Ben stopped to place his golf-gloved hand on his hip. "I believe you, too. Something in my gut always said Skeltner was a snake. But, he's good buddies with Bill Clark, a town councilman. Try to implicate him in this murder with what you have now, and you," he pointed at David, "will be shooting your career in the foot, even if you are best buds with Mac here. Have you got anything?"

"A bicycle," David said. "A silver bike matching the description of the one the witnesses saw at the Skeltner place was found at the Santa Fe Grill and Cantina after Crump's murder. A couple said they saw the shooter ride up on it before the murder. No fingerprints were found on it. Forensics is looking to see if they can find anything else."

"Have you questioned Skeltner about the Crump murder?" Ben asked.

David and Mac glanced at each other.

"I don't want to question him until I have something more solid," Mac said.

"And I don't want to go looking for a search warrant until you have something more solid, either."

"How about DNA?" Mac asked. "Is that solid?"

Pausing, Fleming turned to Mac. "That is very solid. Tell me more."

"A contact lens was found in Mary Catherine Skeltner's bedroom," David said. "She did not wear contact lenses. Neither does Russell Skeltner. The victim had hair under her fingernails. Forensics collected a woman's DNA from both the lens and hair. We need a suspect to match it with."

"Then get one," Fleming said.

"We're working on it." Mac scratched the back of his head. "We need to find a connection between Russell Skeltner and the Crumps."

"Bogie and Archie are digging into their backgrounds right now," David said. "They couldn't find anything between

Russell and Gordon Crump, so we have them looking for a connection between Russell Skeltner and Nora Crump."

"Are you thinking they were having an affair and decided to do away with their spouses?" Fleming asked.

"Isn't that a classic motive?" Mac grinned.

"So far, we've had no luck proving they've even met," David said with a frown.

"Keep digging. If Skeltner is a killer, I want him out of Spencer." The prosecutor's expression softened when he turned to Mac. "How's Archie?"

"She's fine," Mac said, "especially since Cruze is dead. All of the fed's sources are saying the contract died with him. Now that they seem to have wiped out Bonito's men and their virtual leader, Archie's in the clear. It looks like she can leave the program."

Fleming smiled. "Good news for you both."

"Yes, it is." Mac glanced over at David, who shot a smirk in his direction.

Chapter Twenty-Four

"Well, that went about how I expected," David said when they returned to the Spencer police station and went upstairs to his office with cans of soft drinks.

"Admit it," Mac said, "I was right about Skeltner. He had his wife killed—"

"Too bad you're his alibi." With a chuckle, David plopped down onto the sofa.

"I wish people would stop telling me that." Raking his fingers through his hair, he started pacing the length of the office.

"It's the truth." Smiling at Mac's predicament, David took off his shoes and propped his feet up on the coffee table.

"Do you know what really infuriates me about being his alibi?"

"Skeltner used you and you're taking it personally."

"Not me alone. Anyone who happened to be at the café, Leah and Sari, anyone who happened to be there was his alibi." The snap of Mac's fingers startled David to grab his attention. Mac pointed a finger at him. "The same time his wife was being murdered, Skeltner was planting the cream meant to kill Gordon Crump. Don't you see it? They killed each other's spouses. Nora Crump was the guy on the bike."

"Witnesses said it was a man—a teenager."

"In black sweats with the hood up speeding by on a bike. These witnesses are elderly. Without a clear look, they could have assumed it was a teenaged boy. Nora is very slender and isn't very well endowed. In the right clothes and speeding by, she could be mistaken for a teenaged boy."

David sighed. "Now it's Nora Crump who killed Mary Catherine Skeltner? Wasn't she at the café, too? Sari said she came in and was waiting for her mom to seat her when Skeltner planted the poison."

"She could have made it in time. The terrain on Lakeshore Drive is flat. Nora is athletic enough to have done it." Mac plopped down on the coffee table directly in front of David which forced him to take his feet off the table. "The B and B is three miles from the café. The ME can't be precise down to the minute. She could be a few minutes off."

Mac recalled the moment she first saw Nora Crump running across the parking lot. Her husband was lagging far behind her. As she came down the hill, she stumbled off the curb and almost landed on her face. She couldn't see the curb clearly because she had lost a lens. She wore an athletic suit, and he had thought that she was breathless from running. "She was breathless because she was in a hurry. In order for their plan to work, timing had to be precise. She had to speed three miles on the bike to get to the B and B to kill Mary Catherine Skeltner while Russell Skeltner was establishing an alibi. If she committed the murder too close to when he left, then the argument could be made that he killed his wife before leaving. But, she also had to make sure she got back to the hotel and got her husband to make it to the café in time to get the same table where Skeltner had planted the poison so that no innocent victims would die."

"Which is exactly what happened," David said.

"It was all over the news that it was Tommy Cruze who was murdered," Mac said more to himself. "So they used it to their advantage. That night, Skeltner finished the job while Nora pointed the finger at a mob hit. That whole story about Gordon Crump borrowing money from Cruze is a lie."

When David looked doubtful, Mac asked, "Why else did Nora Crump send you in the opposite direction when you asked her where the shooter went? They had no idea we were going to be on the scene."

"She claims she was in shock and confused," David reminded him. "A jury will find it hard not to believe her."

"You and I both know that's not true." Mac shook his finger at him. "The lady runner."

"What?"

"Out of the mouths of babes," Mac said with a grin. "Sari hit on the connection between Skeltner and Nora Crump. She called Nora 'the lady runner'. I'm willing to bet money that it's what brought them together. They're both runners. Skeltner's neighbor says he's always traveling to run in marathons. Do you realize how many people participate in those things?"

"I do and I have," David said. "It's all a great theory, but we have no proof." He ticked off on his fingers. "Sari says Russell Skeltner is a regular customer. Leah had said he'd been coming in every day for well over six months—same time, right when she opens—to order an espresso."

"He used his regular routine," Mac replied. "Killers do that all the time. They watch a victim, learn their routine and then take advantage of it. Only in this case, it's the killer who has the routine and made use of it to establish his alibi. If he had strayed from it in any way, then that would make us suspicious."

"But you are suspicious," David noted, "with no proof whatsoever that Skeltner and Nora Crump even know each other."

"The neighbor saw the bike," Mac said. "The tread from the bike at the Santa Fee Grill matched the tread marks they found at the Skeltner house."

Mac's cell phone signaled on his hip with Clint Eastwood's dare. "Go ahead. Make my day."

David grinned. "Figures."

Checking the caller ID, Mac told David that it was forensics while answering the phone.

David got up off the sofa and went over to gaze out the window at the lake. It was a windy day. Waves were rocking the boats and jet skis.

Watching him while he listened to the report from the forensics office, Mac saw a look of sadness cross David's face and wondered how he was going to take the news of his and Archie's engagement.

Forcing an upbeat note into his tone, Mac said, "That was forensics." He slipped his cell phone back into its case clipped onto his belt.

"So you said." David turned from the window. "What have they got?"

"DNA from the seat on the bike, which matches the DNA from the contact lens and hair," Mac said. "The DNA on the bike seat is sweat and even some vaginal discharge. Enough for them to collect and run a profile. Whoever rode that bike was a woman." He added, "All from the same woman."

"But was there a match from the data base?"

"No, but if we could get Nora Crump's DNA they could run a comparison."

"Problem is," David said, "we don't have enough to get a warrant for her DNA. Did you hear Ben out there on the course? Have you been listening to me? Without enough evidence to prove any connection between Nora Crump and Mary Catherine Skeltner, we've got squat. Since she was at the café close to the time of the murder, it is going to be hard to prove that she was anywhere near that B and B."

Mac shook his phone at him. "Unless Archie can break into her medical files to see if the prescription from the lens matches Nora's prescription."

"Motive? Since we can't even prove they've met—"

"Medical bills had run the Skeltner's finances into the ground," Mac said. "Now that she's dead, Mary Catherine Skeltner's life insurance will be able to pay off those bills, plus they have mortgage insurance that paid off the house when she got sick. Skeltner's wife's death got him out of debt and free and clear to keep the B and B—a prime piece of real estate."

"So he has a motive," David said. "Everything you have is circumstantial."

A whoop from downstairs drew their attention. A second later, David's intercom buzzed and Bogie announced, "We found something."

His arms folded across his broad chest, Bogie stood tall behind his chair in his office. Sitting at his desk, Archie was before both his computer monitor and her laptop.

"You can run, but you can't hide," Archie said when David and Mac came in.

"Did you find their connection?" David asked.

"Athletes," Bogie said.

"Told you," Mac said to David.

"Specifically, triathlon athletes," Archie clarified.

"Traditional background checks turned up nothing," Bogie said. "Residential addresses. Places where they may have worked together. Clubs, social media sites. Nothing."

"Nora Crump is a physical education teacher in a public middle school," she said. "Russell Skeltner is an online counselor for an investment company. Skeltner originally came from Milwaukee, Wisconsin. Nora has always lived in the Hershey, Pennsylvania, area." She sat forward and leaned her elbows on the desk. "Now their spouses were another story."

"There was a connection between them?" Mac asked.

"Not exactly the way you might think," she said. "Mary Catherine Skeltner came down with cancer a few years ago. She almost died and has since been strung out on drugs."

"According to her doctor, she got hooked on them," Bogie said. "She would have been fine if she had weaned herself off of them once she became cancer free, but she didn't."

"She became a burden to her husband, who ended up taking over everything," Archie said. "Now we come to Gordon Crump and his wife, Nora. Crump's father was a millionaire with a chain of bath and fixture stores in and around the Lancaster, Pennsylvania, area. He was very successful. Some would say he was a big fish in a small pond. Nora actually married an heir. But, when his father died, Gordon ran the family business into the ground. He had a history of bad investments. He lacked the charisma of his father—"

"Not to mention the hygiene," Mac recalled his bad breath and body odor during their brief meeting.

"So we have two people whose spouses become burdens on them," David said. "But both of them are from different locations and worlds."

"*Strangers on a Train*," Archie said with a smile. "Right out of Alfred Hitchcock."

"Triathlon," Mac said. "They were both triathlon athletes. They went to the same event—"

"Those events draw amateur athletes from all over the world," David said. "They all share one thing in common, which creates a feeling of camaraderie."

"Have you ever done a triathlon?" Mac asked.

David nodded. "I did two or three a year back when I was on active duty with the marines. There are amateur athletes who actually follow the circuit going from one event to another. After the event, the local restaurants would be crowded with participants—eating, drinking—hooking up if you're lucky." He let out a breath. "Yeah, I can see where they would hook up at one of these things."

"Then Nora and Russell meet at a triathlon and discover that they share something more than firm, taunt, muscles," Mac said, "Spouses who were dragging them down. They fall in love and decide to kill each other's spouse so that they can be together."

"Which happened last September first." Archie brought up the Internet site for the athletic event on Bogie's computer. "Twelfth annual City of Lenoir triathlon in North Carolina. When I found on both of their Facebook pages that they listed hobbies as triathlons, I started hunting for a common event that they were both registered for and attended."

"Are they friends on Facebook?" David asked.

"No," Bogie said with a growl. "These two are good."

Archie continued, "We have both Russell Skeltner and Nora Crump booked at the same hotel, in separate rooms, where the triathlon was registered."

"Russell Skeltner booked a private flight out of Morgantown's airport to fly him down," Bogie said. "We found no plane reservations for Nora."

"It would have been an eight hour drive," Archie said. "She could have decided to drive instead."

"Russell had booked the plane for a return trip," Bogie said, "but at the last minute he cancelled. When I asked the pilot about it, he said Skeltner told him he got a ride back with a friend."

"That's where they met," Mac said.

"Have you found any evidence of them connecting afterwards?" David asked. "Phone calls? Emails?"

Archie shook her head. "They have to be communicating with throw-away phones."

"Triathlon athletes," Mac said. "It would have been a cinch for Nora to ride that bike three miles to the Skeltner's B and B, kill Mary Catherine Skeltner—an ill, weak woman—and then race back to be there when Russell Skeltner planted the cream at their table. Then, that night, Russell Skeltner rode the same bike to the restaurant and then slipped away and ran back to the B and B along the dark jogging trail. No car to trace."

"Nora Crump has had two of my men on her ever since Gordon was killed," David said. "She and Skeltner have not gone near each other. The only way we can prove they planned this is to get a confession from one of them—"

"Or to get Nora's DNA to connect her to the bike, lens, and hair," Mac said. "Charge her for Mary Catherine's murder and she'll be sure to flip on Skeltner for a deal. We'll have them both."

"Still," David said, "I hate to be the wet blanket, but we need something to connect her to Mary Catherine Skeltner to warrant a subpoena for her DNA."

Slowly, a grin crossed Mac's face. "Give me your cell phone." He held out his hand to David.

"My phone?"

"Your phone."

"Why don't you use yours?" David took his phone off his belt.

"Because your phone has Special Agent Delaney's number programmed into it." Mac hit the button on the phone and pressed it to his ear.

"What are you thinking?" Archie asked him.

Mac held up a finger to silence her. "Agent Delaney… Mac Faraday here… I was wondering… could we borrow a couple of your undercover agents to help close up your poisoning case?"

Chapter Twenty-Five

"I'm sorry, Mrs. Crump," David explained to Gordon Crump's widow, "but once you leave Deep Creep Lake, we can't guarantee your safety."

"I can't stay here indefinitely." She looked around the police station at the various officers working in the squad room. The two officers who had been with her since the shooting at the Southwestern grill were busying themselves at their desks while she signed the paperwork that David had called her into the station to complete. "I want to take my husband's body home, bury him, and put this awful week behind me."

"I understand, Mrs. Crump," David said.

"Please don't call me that," she said with a note of disgust. "Nora."

She frowned. "I've always hated that name."

"Maybe you should have kept your maiden name when you married your husband," David suggested.

"My father-in-law and Gordon wouldn't hear of it," she said with a sharp tone. "When will he get shipped back home?"

"The ME's office will be contacting you about those details." David shook his head. "Are you sure you don't want me to contact the Pennsylvania State Police to arrange for protection until we close the case on your husband's murder? For all we know, you're a target, too. After all, you were at the café."

Her mouth hanging open slightly, she gazed at him. "If I was a target, wouldn't that gunman have shot me at the Grill?"

"He must not have seen you," David said, "since you weren't next to your husband when the gunman shot him. The parking lot was dark—"

"No," she said. "I was close enough to my husband that if the gunman wanted to kill me too, he would have. The business arrangement that my husband had with Tommy Cruze was between the two of them." She sighed. "I only wish I could have known more about it to help the FBI in their investigation."

"But you were confused." It was David's turn to shake his head. "Remember, you told me that he was driving away in a dark SUV, but he wasn't. Witnesses in the parking lot saw the gunman run in the opposite direction and through the back door into the restaurant to dump the gun and sweatshirt in the men's room. He very well may not have seen you. He could be looking for you now."

She backed up a step. "Bull! I was there. They know that I'm an innocent victim in this whole thing and know nothing. The mob isn't going to come after me."

"Mrs. Crump…" David reached out to her.

"Don't call me that!"

"Nora, it's my duty to protect you." He grasped her elbow.

"Get away from me." She jerked out of his grasp.

"If the mob is looking for retaliation for Tommy Cruze's murder, they may not stop with your husband. They are very big on sending messages. They may want to kill you too for whatever deal it was that went sour." He picked up the phone.

"I have friends. Marshal Finnegan is with the federal witness protection program. We can get you into the program. They'll relocate you, give you a new identity. Find you a job. Of course, you'll never be able to see any of your friends and family from your past ever again, but at least you'll be safe—"

"Go to hell!" She hurried out of the police station.

One of the officers assigned to protect her looked over at David. "Shouldn't we go with her?"

With a grin on his face, David shook his head while waiting for the answer on the other end of his cell phone. "She's on her way."

Nora Crump took the long way around the lake to drive past the Skeltner Cove Bed & Breakfast. She slowed when she saw a red convertible in the driveway and a buxom blonde brushing her hand across Russell Skeltner's cheek where the two were standing close to each other on the porch.

Nora was so stunned that she crossed the center line and almost hit a pick-up truck going the other way. "Damn it!" she cursed while wrestling for control of the steering wheel. Once she was back in her lane, she pressed her foot to the gas pedal. She couldn't get out of Deep Creek Lake fast enough.

Back at her hotel, she galloped up the stairs to her room and through the door to find herself face to face with the barrels of two guns.

"Mrs. Crump," the largest of the three men who had made themselves at home in her room said. "Nice to finally meet you." He didn't move from where his enormous body filled the chair in the corner of the room. The bulk, she could see, was not fat, but muscle. He reminded her of a grizzly bear.

"Who are you?" she gasped out while clutching her purse to her chest against which her heart was beating.

"Oscar Feldman," he said. "I'm running things here in this area now, since you and your husband eliminated Tommy Cruze from our corporate ladder."

"I didn't kill Tommy Cruze."

"That's not what my people tell me."

"Your people are wrong," she said in a desperate tone.

"Are you telling me that I have dummies working for me?" Oscar dared her to give the wrong answer.

The two gunmen moved in closer.

Clutching her chest, she stepped backwards to find her back against the wall. "This is all a big misunderstanding. That poisoned cream was already on the table when Gordon and I went into the café and were seated there. One of Mr. Cruze's people took the cream from our table. That was how Mr. Cruze was poisoned. It wasn't our fault. It was the bodyguard who took our cream." She brightened up.

The big man furrowed his brow and slowly shook his head. "But our informant in the police department told us that you told them that it was your husband who planted the poison to take out our boss."

"With all due respect," she said "it was the bodyguard's fault that Mr. Cruze was killed. If he hadn't taken that cream, then my husband would have put it in his coffee and he'd be dead…which he is anyway."

"Oh," the large man said. "I don't understand. Why would your husband plant the poison cream and then drink it?"

"My husband didn't plant it."

"But you told the police that he did."

"I was lying!"

"Oh, you were lying?" He chuckled at his men, who chuckled as well. "I get it now. You were trying to kill your husband, but Tommy Cruze got whacked by mistake."

"Exactly," she laughed nervously. "It was all a big mistake."

"And I guess our killing your husband, who was actually your intended victim, was a mistake."

"You killed my husband?" Nora gasped.

"Hey," he said, "We did you a favor since you were planning to kill him in the first place." His smile fell. "Too bad we don't believe in mistakes in our business."

"Huh?" she asked with a heavy breath.

"You killed one of our own," he said. "Now, granted, it worked out great for me. I mean, I got a promotion because of it. But, for me to not act on your murder of Tommy Cruze would be like saying that it's okay to go around killing our people. I have to make you pay for it. You were lucky that my man missed you the other night." He rubbed his finger across his thick lips while looking her up and down. "Lucky for me, too. Now that I see you, I can see that killing you would have been a big waste of such feminine beauty. Better that you should work off your debt."

"You didn't kill my husband," she cried out.

"Oh, yes, we did," Oscar said. "Bert here pulled the trigger himself. Didn't you, Bert?"

One of the gunmen nodded his head. "Two nights ago at the Santa Fe Grill and Cantina. I waited forty minutes for you and your husband to come out of the restaurant before taking him out."

"Enough talk." Oscar stood up. "You're a little bit older than we like our girls, but I have some business associates who like their women firm and athletic—"

When one of the gunmen moved in, Nora whacked him in the face with her purse and ran screaming from the room. While digging through her handbag for her cell phone, she fell down the stairs. The contents spilled out. Spying Oscar Feldman and his two men at the top of the stairs, she grabbed only her keys and cell phone and ran through the lobby and out into the parking lot.

In the dining room, Mac and Archie watched her punching buttons on her cell phone and pressing it to her ear before looking at the screen. She repeated the ritual over again before reaching the car.

"No signal?" Mac asked Archie.

Across from him, Archie looked down at the signal blocker she held in her hand. "None within a half mile radius."

"Damn it!" the clerk gazing with disgust at his cell phone called out from behind the reception desk.

"See?" she said. "Told you these things work."

"My girl and her toys." Mac smiled at her.

Out in the parking lot, Nora hurled her phone inside the car and sped off.

"She's on the move." Mac got up and took Archie's hand. "This is going to be fun."

※　　※　　※

Without any concern about blocking anyone in, Nora tore her broken-down sedan into the driveway at the Skeltner Cove Bed & Breakfast. After slamming the car door shut, she ran across the driveway, up the steps to the porch, and threw open the door to find Russell Skeltner on the sofa with the buxom blonde.

The beauty gasped. "You told me that you weren't open for business."

"I'm not." Russell jumped up to his feet. "Excuse me, but the sign outside says we're closed."

"Well, if she's not a guest, then who is she?" Nora pointed at the blonde who was buttoning her shirt.

Russell gazed at her with wide eyes. "Excuse me, lady, but have you been drinking?"

"Should I call the police?" the woman on the sofa called out.

"No!" Russell yelled back over his shoulder before turning back to Nora. "You need to leave. Now!"

"Do you have any idea what I've gone through in the last hour?" Nora cried out in desperation.

"Considering that you're a stranger," Russell said, "no."

"She looks like she needs help to me," the blonde said.

"She's deranged," he said.

Out the front window, Nora saw a long black sedan slow down. It came to a halt. The rear window lowered to reveal Oscar Feldman.

Nora screamed. "Russell, how can you abandon me after all I did for you? I killed your wife for you!"

"She did what?" the blonde yelled.

"She's crazy!" he said.

Nora pointed out the window. "Those men are trying to kidnap me and force me into prostitution!"

"What men?" he asked.

She looked out the window to see David climbing out of his police cruiser. The sedan was nowhere in sight.

"You have completely lost your mind!" Russell said. "What men are you talking about?"

"The mobsters that killed Gordon."

"Mobsters didn't kill Gordon," Russell said. "I did."

"Really?" David replied as he stepped into the room from the foyer. "I guess you two didn't hear me knock over your argument. I came out because your neighbor across the road called to complain about the yelling. I happened to be in the neighborhood."

"You can't use what I said in court," Russell said. "There's an expectation of privacy in my own home."

"Unless," Mac said as he stepped in, "someone who happens to be in the room chooses to testify to what she heard."

Russell's eyes narrowed on Nora. "You know now that you got played." When her gaze fell to the floor, he grinned.

"Sorry, your trick didn't work. No one here is going to testify to anything that was said."

The woman on the sofa cleared her throat. "That's the problem with being a blonde. They forget about us so quickly."

Russell whirled around to see that the beauty he had picked up after a round of golf with the town councilman now held up a shield identifying herself as an agent with the FBI.

"I need protection," Nora said. "The mob is trying to kill me."

"Sorry, Mrs. Crump." David whipped out his hand cuffs. "But you can't get protection unless you've got something to offer."

"Don't call me Mrs. Crump." She pointed her finger at Russell Skeltner, who struggled against the police chief handcuffing him. "I'll testify against him. It was all his idea. He seduced me into killing his wife while he was out for his morning run, and in exchange he said he would leave the poison at our table at the café to kill Gordon. Then, six months from now, we would meet at a triathlon in Boston and no one would know." Her voice rose while Mac handcuffed her. "He killed my husband!"

"She killed my wife," Russell said. "She couldn't wait to get rid of her so that she could move here and live on the lake. She's a classic gold digger." He offered to David, "I'll testify against her. Give me immunity and I'll tell you everything."

"He's the killer!"

On their way out the door, David turned back to Mac. "I think you broke up the lovebirds."

"I know I broke up the lovebirds."

Epilogue

"I must say, this was the most plush assignment I've ever been given," said US Marshal Fran Cook, the grandmotherly agent tasked with taking care of Sari.

The couple the US Marshal's office had in mind for adopting Sari was quick to say yes. While arrangements were being made for them to fly out to Deep Creek Lake to pick up their new daughter, Sari and the agent were staying in a penthouse suite at the Spencer Inn under the watchful eye of a Spencer police officer, partnered with a member of Spencer Inn's security …and Gnarly, who was with his new best friend constantly.

Within three days of the death of her mother, the arrangements had been made for Sari to be picked up by her new parents in the lobby of the Spencer Inn. She and Gnarly played on the Oriental rug in front of the fireplace in the lobby.

A mixture of anticipation and anxiety filled the air while the marshal, David, Archie, and Mac drank coffee in the sitting area on either side of them. Anticipation of Sari meeting her new parents, who were taking on the responsibility of raising the little girl whose parents had turned out to be killers, and anxiety about how she would take the news that Gnarly was not going with her.

In a matter of days, Sari had begun to open up. She had become less hesitant about speaking to Archie, and was almost as open to talking to Fran. With Gnarly—she talked to him almost non-stop. It was as if she had stored up a lifetime of information to share with him.

It went without saying that she expected him to go to her new home.

They all feared how she would react when she was forced to leave her beloved best friend behind. Worst case was that it would set her back completely and she would never speak again.

"Here they are." Fran rose to her feet.

Archie, Mac, and David followed suit.

Seeming to sense what was up, Gnarly rolled over from where Sari was giving him a belly rub and sat up.

All eyes turned to the young couple being escorted through the door by a man in a suit. He had dark hair and a thick mustache.

Amazing how you can pick a government agent out of a crowd, Mac thought with a smile.

Fran stepped forward to shake hands with her colleague while the couple, who appeared to be in their thirties, eyed Sari. Excitement seemed to ooze from their pores.

Seeing how they had to refrain from running up to grab the little girl who they would be taking home with them into their arms, Mac and Archie exchanged smiles.

Fran made the introductions. "Sari, I'd like for you to meet the Castles. They have invited you to come live with them."

The wife moved in to kneel in front of the little girl. "Hello, Sari, my name is Lucy. I have heard so much about you."

Sari gazed at her.

"Is this Gnarly?" Lucy offered her hand to the German shepherd to sniff. "I've heard a lot of about you, too, Gnarly. I heard that you have been taking very good care of Sari. Andy and I are so grateful to you for being such a brave dog."

After Gnarly offered Lucy a lick on the cheek, Sari determined that she was okay. "Gnarly is really smart. He's a genius."

"So we heard." Andy had knelt down next to his wife. Seeing that the way to Sari was through Gnarly, he petted the German shepherd with both hands.

"I think you're going to like living with us, Sari," Lucy said. "We live on a farm, and you're going to have a pony all your own to ride. Do you like riding?"

"I've never ridden a pony," she said.

"It's lots of fun," Lucy said. "I'll teach you."

"Do you hear that, Gnarly?" Sari said in a high pitched squeal. "We're going to learn how to ride a pony."

The moment had come. Everyone exchanged glances while waiting for someone to break the news to the little girl.

"Sari," Lucy said in a gentle voice, "Gnarly can't come."

Her eyes filled with tears, Sari wrapped both arms around the German shepherd. "Why not?"

"Because he wants to live with Miss Archie and Mister Mac. They're his family the same way you're going to become part of our family."

Sari buried her face in Gnarly's mane.

"But," Lucy said, "Gnarly told us how much he loves you and wants to make sure someone continues to watch over you the way he has. So we all talked about it. Since he can't come to watch over you himself, he's going to hand his job off to someone who can do it."

"Who?" Sari sobbed.

Lucy turned around to direct the girl's gaze to the agent who had escorted them in. While introductions were being made, he had gone outside and returned with a bundle of fur in his arms.

Sari's eyes grew big.

"He's all yours," Andy said.

The agent barely knelt in time for Sari to grab the German shepherd puppy into her arms and squeeze him into a tight hug.

"He doesn't have a name yet," Lucy said. "So you need to come up with a name for him."

"I know exactly what I'm going to name him."

Archie's eyes were moist when she turned to Mac. They all knew what name she was going to pick.

"Toto," Sari announced.

With a quick good-bye to Gnarly, Sari and her new family hurried out of the lobby to go begin their new lives at a location that the US Marshal's office would not divulge to anyone.

"What a fickle little girl," Archie said once they were gone. "After all Gnarly had done for her. Oh!" She stomped one of her feet. "Can you believe it?"

"She's a little girl." Mac knelt next to Gnarly, who had lay down on the sofa with a sad look in his eyes. "Girls are like that, Gnarly. One minute you're the center of their universe. Then someone younger and cuter comes along and you're suddenly old news."

"Gnarly!" Sari's squeal made heads turn in the lobby as she came running at top speed from the front door. "I forgot—"

Gnarly sat up.

Sari threw both arms around him to take him into a tight hug. "I'll never forget you, Gnarly." She kissed him on the snout. He returned the kiss with a lick to her mouth. "I love you, Gnarly."

After another quick hug and kiss on Gnarly's snout, Sari waved good-bye to everyone before running back out the doors where the two federal agents and her new parents were waiting with her new puppy.

"Well, I'm glad to see that ended well," David said while checking his cell phone. "Means less paperwork on my part."

"Want to join us for lunch?" Mac offered. "My treat."

David declined. "I've got to go to the hospital to see Finnegan."

"You've been going to see her every day," Archie noted with a naughty grin. "Is it serious?"

David responded with a wordless smirk.

"I'm glad," she said.

"When are you two planning to tell me your news?" David asked.

Archie glanced up to Mac to respond.

"During the lunch that you just turned down," Mac said. "How long have you known?"

"I suspected a few days ago," he replied. "I'm glad for you. You two belong together. And you don't have to worry about me—"

"I'm not worried about you," Mac said.

"We want you to take the cottage," Archie said.

"I don't want to live in the cottage," David said. "Look, I have a home. I simply have to man up to live—"

"Not if you have bad feelings about it," she said. "I'm living in the manor. The cottage is empty."

"I don't want to live in the cottage," David said.

"Because you feel like its charity," Mac said.

"Charity has nothing to do with it."

"Then what is it?" Mac asked.

"I hate pink."

Clutching her pink sweater, Archie gasped.

After a stunned silence, Mac laughed.

"I refuse to live in a house with pink walls," David said.

"They're not pink," Archie said, "they're rose."

"I don't care what you call them," David said. "They're girlie and I'm not living in a girlie house."

"Then we'll redecorate," Mac said in a tone louder than he meant it to be.

More than a couple of hotel guests turned to see what the fuss was about. Gnarly was watching the squabbling with a puzzled look in his eyes. Archie and David eyed each other like a pair of fuming siblings.

"Archie," Mac said, "since you've moved into the manor, and David is moving into the guest cottage, he should be able to redecorate it in a manner befitting a manly police chief, don't you think?"

"I love those rose accent walls," Archie said. "I selected the color myself. It's a custom mix."

"Archie, we're getting married," Mac said. "You've already moved into the manor. Let David make himself at home in the cottage."

"Yeah," David said with a wicked grin. "You can paint the whole master suite any shade of pink you want now—no matter how much it costs."

A wide grin filled Archie's face while Mac felt the blood drain from his. "Now wait a minute," he objected.

David wasn't waiting around to hear him finish. His work was done. With a slap on Mac's arm and a quick hug and kiss for Archie, he went out of the lobby to leave Mac to negotiate wall colors in the master suite.

After four days of drifting in and out of a drug-induced coma, Randi Finnegan was finally able to sit up and look at solid food, such as it was at the hospital. Staring at the tray of dried up macaroni and cheese, she felt like throwing up. She didn't know if it was the drugs or the confirmation of what she knew was coming.

What kind of marshal spends two years handling a witness in the program who's secretly running a major crime operation? Then, before that, a major crime boss managed to locate another one of her charges and almost kill her. Forget that it was someone else who sold the information. Ginger Altman was dead. Dead scapegoats aren't as affective as live ones.

"Don't you like mac and cheese?" David was leaning in the doorway with a small bouquet of flowers. He had brought her some each day. She called them pity flowers.

"I hate mac and cheese." She shoved the tray away.

"Remind me never to take you to the Macaroni Grill." He handed her the flowers and leaned over to kiss her on the cheek. "You look better, Finnegan."

"Than what? Road kill?"

"Feisty, too." He sat on the edge of her bed facing her. "That's a good sign."

"You don't have to keep coming in to see me." She placed the flowers on the bedside table.

"Yes, I do."

"I don't like pity."

"I don't pity you," he said.

"Well, you should."

"Why?" he asked.

"I got fired."

"You were put on indefinite leave."

"They're waiting for me to get better before they fire me."

"I know," David said. "I didn't know you were smart enough to figure that out."

"Do I look stupid to you?"

"Do you really want me to answer that?"

She grabbed the flowers from out of the vase and hit him with them. Laughing, he blocked the blow before grabbing her. As she struggled, he placed his mouth over hers. She stopped wrestling. When he pulled back, she grabbed him to kiss him again.

"I never liked that job anyway," she said.

It had been a red-letter day for Gnarly. Not only did he get his aromatherapy, nails trimmed, and teeth brushed, but Misty also gave him an extra deep body massage and a crisp red bandana.

With his head hanging out the window, the wind blowing through his fluffy fur, the taste of mint in his mouth with his extra white teeth, Gnarly relished the crisp lake breeze as Archie cruised along Spencer Lane to turn onto Spencer Point.

When she rolled through the stone pillars marking the entrance of Spencer Manor, she and Gnarly went on alert.

A fleet of vehicles filled the circular drive in front of the cedar and stone porch. Some were old. Some were new. Some were pickup trucks. There was a white van. Most of the plates were from West Virginia, Pennsylvania, and two from Ohio.

"What?" She unclasped her seat belt. "Did Mac suddenly decide to turn sociable?"

When she opened the door, Gnarly leapt out and trotted up to the porch where Mac came out to meet them.

"Well, Gnarly, are you all relaxed now that you got your massage?" he rubbed the top of Gnarly's head and back of his ears.

"What's with all the cars?" She stepped into his arms. "You decided to give a party and not invite me."

Mac clasped his chest. "I would never do that."

"Who do these cars belong to?"

Mac gestured for her to step inside. "Come inside and find out."

Casting him a suspicious look, Archie opened the door.

"Surprise!" The volume from over sixty voices almost knocked her over.

Archie did not know what to focus on. A mob swarmed around to quickly envelope her. She recognized many of the faces and voices from her past. On a banner hanging above the dining room table were the words: "We Love You, Kendra!" Under the banner, she saw the chef from the Spencer Inn and four servers that Mac had hired for the family reunion.

"Stand back! Stand back!" Archie recognized a hulking man who had taken a position by her side as her oldest brother. "Let Mom get to her!"

She had six brothers and quickly spotted each one among the members of the mob.

The sea parted and a tall, slender woman, who hadn't seemed to age a day in the years since Archie had ten minutes to say good-bye, stepped forward to take her only daughter into a hug. "I always knew that one day I would get to see my baby girl again."

Through the tears in her eyes, Archie was able to make out Mac ushering Gnarly away from the table and out onto the deck.

After greeting everyone and meeting new members of her family, Archie hurried out onto the dock to where Mac was admiring the start of the sunset. "You are really something else."

"Who? Me?" he feigned innocence.

"I never told you anything about my family. How did you find all of them?"

"I'm a great detective," Mac said. "If I had known you had six big brothers—who are all very protective of their little sister—I may have had second thoughts about doing it.

You should have seen the interrogation I've been getting all afternoon."

She felt the tears coming to her eyes again. "How can I ever thank you for bringing me back to my family?" She wrapped her arms around him and wiped her tears on his chest.

"Well," he said, "we could set a date."

"You can't be serious," she said. "We both know you were only asking me to marry you because you were scared you were going to lose me."

"You did say yes." He pulled away and looked down into her face.

"Because I do want to marry you," she said. "But I'm not holding you to that proposal that you asked in the heat of the moment."

"I'm not in the heat of the moment now." Mac lifted her face to look into her eyes. He wiped the tears from her cheeks. "Archie Monday—or Kendra Douglas—whoever you are—will you be my wife?"

She answered him with a kiss.

"Hey, what's that rubber duck doing in the punch!" one of Archie's brothers yelled. The question was followed by a loud crash, which was then followed by squeals of childish laughter when Archie's nieces and nephews pursued the way-ward dog.

When Mac turned to go help, Archie pulled him back. "Let someone else kill Gnarly for once."

"I like the way you think, my lady." He wrapped his arms around her to kiss her in the sunset.

The End

About the Author

LAUREN CARR

Lauren Carr fell in love with mysteries when her mother read Perry Mason to her at bedtime. The first installment in the Joshua Thornton mysteries, *A Small Case of Murder* was a finalist for the Independent Publisher Book Award.

Lauren is also the author of the Mac Faraday Mysteries, which takes place in Deep Creek Lake, Maryland. *It's Murder, My Son*, *Old Loves Die Hard, and Shades of Murder,* have all been getting rave reviews from readers and reviewers. *Blast from the Past* is the fourth installment in the Mac Faraday Mystery series.

Released September 1012, *Dead on Ice* introduces a new series entitled Lovers in Crime, which features prosecutor Joshua Thornton with homicide detective Cameron Gates. The second book in this series, *Real Murder* will be released Spring 2013.

The owner of Acorn Book Services, Lauren is also a publishing manager, consultant, editor, cover and layout designer, and marketing agent for independent authors. This spring, two books written by independent authors will be released through the management of Acorn Book Services.

Lauren is a popular speaker who has made appearances at schools, youth groups, and on author panels at conventions. She also passes on what she has learned in her years of writing and publishing by conducting workshops and teaching in community education classes.

She lives with her husband, son, and two dogs on a mountain in Harpers Ferry, WV.

Visit Lauren's websites and blog at:
E-Mail: writerlaurencarr@comcast.net
Website: http://acornbookservices.com/
          http://mysterylady.net/
Blog: Literary Wealth:
          http://literarywealth.wordpress.com/

LAUREN CARR MYSTERIES!

THE MAC FARADAY MYSTERIES

The story takes hold immediately and the reader quickly identifies with Mac. The plot is well done without being overplotted. There are just enough twists and turns to keep the reader guessing. The climatic confrontation with the killer is good and the wrap up leaves you laughing and feeling good. The writing style is easy and draws the reader in effortlessly. I am looking forward to the next installment! **Reviewer: Ariel Heart, Mystery and My Musings Review**

What started out as the worst day of Mac Faraday's life, would end up being a completely new beginning. After a messy divorce hearing, the last person that Mac wanted to see is another lawyer. Yet, this lawyer looked very unlawyer-like, wearing the expression of a child about to reveal a guarded secret. This secret would reveal Mac as heir to undreamed of fortunes and lead him to Spencer, Maryland, the birthplace of America's Queen of Mystery, with her millions and an investigation that unfolds like one of her famous mystery novels.

It's Murder, My Son is Author Lauren Carr's third mystery novel. Carr's first novel A Small Case of Murder was named finalist for the Independent Publisher Book Awards. She resides in Harpers Ferry, West Virginia, where she lives with her husband and son on a mountaintop. "I love a good mystery," said Author Lauren Carr. "Growing up in a small community an argument at the corner store can become a murder by dinner. Making the story a reality on paper is a real thrill."

Behind the gated community in Spencer, Maryland, multi-millionaire Katrina Singleton learns that life in an exclusive community is not all good. She thought her good looks and charm made her untouchable; but, for reasons unknown, a strange man calling himself "Pay Back" begins terrorizing her and her home. When Katrina was found strangled in her lake house, all evidence points to her terrorist, who is nowhere to be found. Three months later the file on Katrina's murder was still open with only vague speculations from the local police department.

In walks Mac Faraday, sole heir to his unknown birth mother's home and fortune. Little does he know as he drives his new Dodge Viper up to Spencer Manor that he is driving into a closed gate community that is hiding more suspicious deaths than his DC workload as a homicide detective. With the help of his late mother's journals and two newfound companions, this recently retired cop puts all his detective skills to work to pick up where the local police have left off to following clues to Katrina's killer.

The fast-paced complex plot brings surprising twists into a storyline that leads Mac and his friends into grave danger. Readers are drawn into Mac's past, meet his children, and experience the troubling relationships of his former in-laws. New fans will surely look forward to the next installment in this great new series. **Reviewer: Edie Dykeman, Bellaonline Mystery Books Editor**

Old Loves Die Hard… and in the worst places.

Retired homicide detective Mac Faraday, heir of the late mystery writer Robin Spencer, is settling nicely into his new life at Spencer Manor when his ex-wife Christine shows up— and she wants him back! Before Mac can send her packing, Christine and her estranged lover are murdered in Mac's private penthouse suite at the Spencer Inn, the five-star resort built by his ancestors.

The investigation leads to the discovery of cases files for some of Mac's murder cases in the room of the man responsible for destroying his marriage. Why would his ex-wife's lover come to Spencer to dig into Mac's old cases?

With the help of his new friends on Deep Creek Lake, Mac must use all of his detective skills to clear his name and the Spencer Inn's reputation, before its five-stars—and more bodies—start dropping!

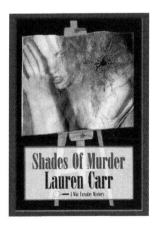

Lauren Carr could give Agatha Christie a run for her money! This hypnotic page-turner is a whirlwind of romance, murder, and espionage. Lots of creativity went into the unforeseen twists, and culminated in a climactic ending that tied the multi-faceted story into a nice little package. I also appreciated the special attention paid to the animal characters, which were every bit as developed as their human counterparts. This was an absolutely delightful read that is sure to be a hit with mystery readers. I look forward to reading her other books, as I am now a fan!

Reviewer: Charlene Mabie-Gamble, Literary R&R

In *Shades of Murder*, Mac Faraday is once again the heir to an unbelievable fortune. This time the benefactor is a stolen art collector. But this isn't just any stolen work-of-art—it's a masterpiece with a murder attached to it.

Ilysa Ramsay was in the midst of taking the art world by storm. Hours after unveiling her latest masterpiece—she is found dead in her Deep Creek Lake studio—and her painting is nowhere to be found. Almost a decade later, the long lost Ilysa Ramsay masterpiece has found its way into Mac Faraday's hands and he can't resist the urge to delve into the case.

In Pittsburgh, Pennsylvania, former JAG lawyer Joshua Thornton agrees to do a favor for the last person he would ever expect to do a favor—a convicted serial killer. The Favor: Solve the one murder wrongly attributed to him.

In *Shades of Murder*, author Lauren Carr tackles the task of penning two mysteries with two detectives in two different settings and bringing them together to find one killer. "What can I say?" Carr says. "I love mysteries and mystery writing. Two cases are twice the fun."

In her fifth mystery, Lauren Car brings back her first literary detective while introducing a new one. In Shades of Murder, Joshua Thornton teams up with Cameron Gates, a spunky detective who has reason to believe the young woman listed as the victim of a serial killer was murdered by a copycat. Together, Joshua and Cameron set out to light a flame under the cold case only to find that someone behind the scenes wants the case to remain cold, and is willing to kill to keep it that way.

DEAD ON ICE

LAUREN CARR'S LATEST MYSTERY SERIES

Lead investigator in the case was Cameron Gates, whose love interest is Joshua Thornton, a prosecuting attorney; the pairing of these two adds just the right romantic interest to "Dead on Ice: A Lovers In Crime Mystery," the first in a new series featuring them. I can't wait for the next book! Five stars, and recommended for all those who enjoy romantic suspense, as well as for fans of Lauren Carr. **Reviewer: Laurel-Rain Snow**

Dead on Ice is the first installment of Lauren Carr's new series (Lovers in Crime). It features Hancock County Prosecuting Attorney Joshua Thornton and his new love, Pennsylvania State Police homicide detective Cameron Gates.

In this Lovers in Crime Mystery, spunky Pennsylvania State Homicide Detective Cameron Gates is tasked with solving the murder of Cherry Pickens, a legendary star of pornographic films, when her body turns up in an abandoned freezer. The case has a personal connection to Cameron's lover, Joshua Thornton, because the freezer was found in his cousin's basement. It doesn't take long for their investigation to reveal that the risqué star's roots were buried in their rural Ohio Valley community, something that Cherry had kept off her show business bio. She should have kept her hometown off her road map, too—because when this starlet came running home from the mob, it proved to be a fatal homecoming.

In her new series, Lauren Car teams up her first literary detective with a new and exciting partner. Homicide Detective Cameron Gates has a spunky personality that's a perfect complement to Joshua Thornton's logical and responsible nature.

"Readers of my first series kept asking when I would bring back Joshua Thornton," Carr explained. "However, they are going to find that single father Joshua Thornton is not in the same place since we left him in A Reunion to Die For. His children are grown. He's more independent, and he's ready for some romance and adventure. That's where Cameron Gates comes in."

With that, Joshua Thornton and Cameron Gates strike out to explore the mysteries of both murder and love!

Coming Spring 2013!

REAL MURDER

A LOVERS IN CRIME MYSTERY